P9-CDD-771
3 5674 056...

A LADY *of*

RESOURCES

A steampunk adventure novel

Magnificent Devices Book Five

Shelley Adina

Chase Branch Library
17731 W. Seven Mile Rd.
Detroit, MI 48235

Moonshell
Books

Copyright © 2013 by Shelley Adina Bates.

All rights reserved. No part of this publication may be reproduced, distributed or transmitted in any form or by any means, including photocopying, recording, or other electronic or mechanical methods, without the prior written permission of the publisher, except in the case of brief quotations embodied in critical reviews and certain other noncommercial uses permitted by copyright law. For permission requests, write to the publisher at the address below.

Moonshell Books, Inc.
www.moonshellbooks.com

This is a work of fiction. Names, characters, places, and incidents are a product of the author's imagination. Locales and public names are sometimes used for atmospheric purposes. Any resemblance to actual people, living or dead, or to businesses, companies, events, institutions, or locales is completely coincidental.

Book Layout ©2013 BookDesignTemplates.com
Art by Claudia McKinney at phatpuppyart.com
Images from Shutterstock.com and the author's collection, used under license
Design by Kalen O'Donnell
Author font by Anthony Piraino at OneButtonMouse.com

A Lady of Resources / Shelley Adina -- 1st ed.
ISBN 978-1-518826-95-5

For Elly and Nancy, with gratitude

Praise for the bestselling Magnificent Devices series

"This is the first in a series of well-reviewed books set in the steampunk world. For those who like the melding of Victorian culture with the fantastic fantasy of reality-bending science fiction, this one will be right up their alley."
–READERS' REALM,
ON *LADY OF DEVICES*

"Another immensely fun book in an immensely fun series with some excellent anti-sexist messages, a wonderful main character (one of my favourites in the genre) and a great sense of Victorian style and language that's both fun and beautiful to read."
–FANGS FOR THE FANTASY,
ON *MAGNIFICENT DEVICES*

"Adina manages to lure us into the steampunk era with joy and excitement."
–NOVEL CHATTER

1

Munich, the Prussian Empire
June 1894

"Of all the infernal instruments man ever made, the corset is the worst." Lizzie de Maupassant struggled with the hooks on the front of the glossy brocade undergarment, which one had to wear in order to make everything that went on top of it hang properly. "Look at this, Maggie. It bends where it oughtn't and pokes everywhere else." She smashed the placket together, which only made the hooks she'd managed already pop apart.

"Argh!" Lizzie flung the wretched thing across the Lady's room, where it landed on the windowsill like an exhausted accordion.

"Fits of temper won't solve anything." Her twin's tone held no criticism, only reason. "Come on. Let me have a go."

Maggie rescued the poor corset, bought new for the grand occasion of the graduation of Lady Claire Trevelyan, the girls' guardian, from the University of Bavaria, and passed it about Lizzie's chemise- and petticoat-clad form.

"I don't miss the old lace-ups," Lizzie said, feeling calmer as Maggie's clever fingers made short work of the row of hooks, "but I'll say this for them—they were more forgiving of a mort's curves than these new ones. Even if it were made specially for me."

"Don't say *mort*."

"Ent nobody here but us. We don't have to be so careful about our *diction and deportment*—" She mimicked the squeaky tones of Mademoiselle Dupree, the mistress of their class by that name. "—when we're on our own."

"The Lady says that's the test of a true lady—that she does the right thing even when nobody's looking."

"Aye, more's the pity," Lizzie sighed. "We might pass our exams, but we'll never remember everything she probably knew by the time she was ten."

The door opened and the Lady herself breezed in. "All who knew? Goodness, Lizzie, we're to be in the ballroom in two hours and you're not even dressed, to say nothing of your hair."

Maggie patted the corset and released her. "Won't be a tick, Lady." The corset now lay obediently where it ought, hugging Lizzie's waist into a satisfyingly narrow width, and flaring out over hips and bust, which possessed dimensions not quite so satisfying. The Lady said to give it time, that she herself had been eighteen before resigning herself to a sylph-like silhouette rather than the majestic curves fashion now favored. But if one didn't have an idea of one's silhouette by now, then the odds weren't very good, were they?

"Darlings, now that you're sixteen, you really must call me by my given name."

The twins, having only the vaguest idea of their birth date, had chosen the first day of spring when they had to make it official, such details being necessary when they had arrived in Munich and begun their formal educations at the Lycée des Jeunes Filles. By this reckoning, they had turned sixteen three months ago, and upon their own graduation from the fifth form at the end of June, would be considered young ladies, permitted to call an unmarried woman by her first name.

Young ladies now ... out in society two years from now. A whole other problem. Lizzie shoved it from her mind and gave the Lady a hug, marveling once again that she was nearly as tall as the young woman to whom she and Maggie owed their very lives.

"But you know why we call you that in private," she said. "And it's got nothing to do with age, innit?"

The Lady hugged her back. "Not one bit. I suppose that if you were to stop altogether, I'd quite go to pieces and fear you didn't love me anymore."

Maggie laughed at this impossibility. "If it hadn't

been for you, we wouldn't be here. Wouldn't have lived in the cottage and learned our letters and numbers."

"Wouldn't have gone to the Texican Territories or the Canadas," Lizzie added. "Or come here."

"Or been shot at, blown up, or starved nearly to death," the Lady said ruefully. "I'm afraid my skills as a guardian have been tested rather sorely."

"Nothing wrong with guarding our own selves," Lizzie said stoutly. "And you, even, sometimes."

Claire laughed at the reminder. "Too true. There has been many a time when I've been thankful we were all fighting on the same side. The affair of the Kaiser's nephew, for instance."

Maggie crinkled up her nose. "Frog-face, you mean."

"Precisely. I don't think his dignity has recovered from that fish-pond yet."

"If he wouldn't propose to ladies who can't stand him, such things wouldn't happen," Lizzie said.

"Ever my practical girl." Warm fingers touched her cheek, and Lizzie felt a surge of love mixed with exasperation—a familiar feeling, and one she had struggled with since the very inauspicious moment of their first meeting.

She adored the Lady, and had for most of the six years they had known each other, but tangled in with the love was the uncomfortable knowledge that she could never be like her guardian—so calm, so competent, so sure of what to say and do in any circumstance, from breaking a mad scientist out of Bedlam to curtseying to the Empress.

Oh, dear. The wretched bloody curtsey.

A LADY OF RESOURCES

"Lady, do I really have to go?" came out of her mouth before she could stop it—something that seemed to happen with distressing regularity these days.

But instead of a crisp "Of course," which was all such a babyish whinge deserved, the Lady took Lizzie's gown from the wardrobe. It was her first real, grownup gown, the palest shade of moss-green silk, with glorious puffed sleeves and a neckline trimmed with lace as fine as a spider web that dipped just low enough to show her collarbones and no lower. Considering there wasn't much below that to show off, it was just as well.

The cool silk slid over her head, and when she emerged and the Lady began to fasten the hooks behind, Lizzie thought perhaps she had decided not to dignify her whining with a reply.

But no. "Of course you do not need to go, if you don't wish it," Claire said quietly. "You are sixteen, and able to make up your own mind about such things. But I should like you and Maggie to be there. I should like to know that you are proud of me, and that when you write to Tigg and Jake and Willie, you will be able to give a good account."

What a selfish wretch she was! Lizzie turned into the Lady's arms as her cheeks heated with shame. "Of course I'll come, Lady," she said into her neck. "I wouldn't miss it for anything. I'm just afraid I'll do something stupid, is all, and embarrass you."

"Nothing you could do is any worse than I could do—or have done—myself," Claire said on a sigh. "Just ask Julia Wellesley—I beg her pardon, Lady Mount-Batting. Come. Let's practice the curtsey one more time

SHELLEY ADINA

so it's fresh in your mind, and then Lady Dunsmuir has
lent us her maid to do our hair. We must give her time
to produce perfection."

Lord and Lady Dunsmuir had arrived the night before and were the honored guests of the Landgraf von
Zeppelin, as the engineer of the Zeppelin airship and the
director of the worldwide "empire of the air" was known
throughout the Kingdom of Prussia. But to Maggie and
Lizzie, he had become Uncle Ferdinand, the man who
smelled of pipe tobacco and bay rum, who kept peppermints in the pockets of even his business suits, and
who had changed all of their lives so astonishingly five
years before.

MacMillan came in as quickly as if she'd been listening at the door, and proceeded to brush, braid, coil, and
generally subdue Lizzie's dark-honey mane so thor-
oughly that she hardly recognized herself in the cheval
glass afterward. The French braid in a coronet about
her head was awfully pretty, though. And beneath her
wispy fringe, her green eyes sparkled with nerves and
anticipation.

"The same for you, miss?" MacMillan asked Maggie.

They'd never dressed or done their hair alike—
because before they'd met the Lady, they'd never had
anything better than what they could filch from the
rag-picker's pile, where finding a matched set of anything was impossible. But MacMillan's fingers were
skilled, and Maggie's gaze so admiring, that Lizzie said,
"Do, Mags. You'll look lovely, to be sure. We shall be
as pretty as the princesses themselves."

And she was.

When MacMillan was done, Maggie turned back and forth before the glass, her nut-brown hair far more used to order than Lizzie's was, her hazel eyes set off by the pale amber—"the color of a fine muscatel," Uncle Ferdinand had said—of her gown. It was fortunate that the Prussians didn't believe that young girls should wear white until they were engaged, like they did in England. Lizzie appreciated a bit of color, and while the Lady tended to go about in navy skirts and blouses with sleeves she could roll up, her eye for color and what lines suited a figure best was keen.

"And for you, milady?" MacMillan asked as Claire took her place at the dressing-table. "I've seen a new look many of the ladies are wearing since that Fragonard gentleman had his exhibition."

"Oh?" Claire's eyebrow rose. "Have you seen the exhibition yourself?"

"I have, milady. That one called *Anticipation* caused quite a stir, with that young lady lazing about with hardly a silk curtain to cover herself."

Claire smothered a smile. "But her hair, MacMillan. I thought it particularly striking at the time, and wondered if you had seen it."

"Seen it and marked it for her ladyship. But I wouldn't mind trying it out on you, if you don't mind."

"Have at it," Claire said, settling back in the chair. "I just hope it doesn't fall down when I curtsey to the Empress. If she finds time to attend."

"No coiffure of mine will fall down under any circumstances, milady, empress or no." MacMillan took down Claire's simple chignon and brushed out her thick auburn waves. "It will look as though you had tossed it up and wrapped it about with a bandeau, but under it will be as much engineering as young Miss Elizabeth's corset."

"MacMillan, you are a treasure."

"Thank you, milady. Her ladyship thinks so."

Motionless under MacMillan's authority, Claire caught Lizzie's eye in the glass. "Does it feel strange to think that our time here is coming to an end? It does to me."

"But it isn't at an end for you, Lady," Maggie put in. It was clear she was trying not to move very much, for fear of mussing herself up. Lizzie was tempted to reach over and give her braid a tug, but discarded that idea almost immediately. The wrath of MacMillan over her damaged handiwork was not worth the risk. Maggie went on, "You're to join Uncle Ferdinand's firm. Or have you changed your mind again?"

Claire rolled her eyes at herself. "I change my mind as often as my shoes—and with less success. But we were not talking about me. You girls have some decisions to make once the term ends in two weeks."

"It's not fair that you graduate so soon and we have all our exams yet to go," Lizzie moaned. "It should all be the same."

"You may certainly take it up with the Regents on the State education board."

Lizzie felt rather proud that her five years in the *lycée* had enabled her to control the urge to stick out her tongue at the Lady. But she came close, all the same.

"How are we supposed to decide something as serious as this?" Maggie asked from the upholstered chair, where she had gingerly seated herself, back straight, feet flat on the floor, hands folded in her lap.

"Too many choices," Lizzie agreed. Heedless of wrinkles, she folded herself onto the end of the bed and leaned on one of the turned posts with the pineapple on top. She ticked them off on her fingers. "Finishing school in Geneva ... two more years of sixth form here ... or sign the exit papers, graduate, and go back to London."

"We're going back to London for the summer, anyway, same as always," Maggie pointed out.

"Well, yes, but in September? What happens then?"

"I should think it would be quite straightforward, miss," MacMillan said. "What do you want to make of yourself?"

"That is the question," Lizzie sighed. "I suppose I want to be a fine lady, but that doesn't mean I'll get to be."

Claire straightened, then winced as MacMillan inadvertently ran a hairpin into her scalp. "I do beg your pardon, milady."

"It's quite all right, MacMillan. I should not have moved so suddenly. Lizzie, what do you mean? Why should you not be a lady and move in the finest Wit circles in any country, as you do here?"

How could she explain this without either offending everyone in the room or sounding like a fool? "Lady, you know as well as I do that it's different here. Here, everyone's accepted, as long as you've got a brain. I suppose that's why you've decided to stay, innit?"

Claire's expression softened. "I must admit it's rather refreshing, considering the way I grew up."

"But that's just it. You grew up a lady, with a posh family, no matter what you chose later." Lizzie swung her legs over the foot of the bed and wrapped an arm around the post, as if anchoring herself in a stormy sea. "Can you really believe that a mort who started out an alley mouse—who still is, never mind all the elocution lessons and walking about wi' books on me 'ead—" She let her accent deteriorate on purpose. "—is going to be accepted in the drawing rooms of London?"

"Every drawing room that accepts me will accept you, Lizzie."

And that was the part that she found so hard to believe. The part that was so frustrating. "Lady, I think you'll find that isn't as true as you think it is."

Now it was MacMillan's turn to catch her eye in the mirror while she carefully threaded a pearl-studded bandeau through the coils and waves of the Lady's hair. "I think you'll find that with Lady Dunsmuir as your sponsor for your come-out, there will be no trouble with any drawing room in Mayfair, should you want to set foot in them."

"What?" Claire straightened again and twisted around to look at MacMillan directly. "What did you say?"

"Milady, you must sit still while I secure this comb. You don't want to come unraveled in front of the nobility."

"I rather feel I have come unraveled now. What did you mean, MacMillan?"

Ooh, look at the Lady's face. Lizzie couldn't tell if she was astonished or angry. But she couldn't be angry. Not at this. Lady Dunsmuir was forever springing surprises of a most delightful nature on them, but they usually came in the mail or in an unexpected visit, not by way of her lady's maid.

"I'll say no more now, but you'll want to know that her ladyship is going to find a way to speak to you about it. At least this way you'll be able to give it some thought."

"Sponsoring a come-out." Claire wilted back into the chair, right way round again. "This *will* require some thought—especially since it never entered my head."

Lizzie thought back to the time the Lady had explained what *coming out* was. She'd been educated on the subject quite a lot since then, but her original ideas had not been so far off the mark. "She really does intend to put us in a window with fancy paper round our feet?"

Claire smiled. "At least you will have the correct posture, and your feet will be together in a ladylike manner. Lizzie, I do not know how you manage to slouch like that when I saw Maggie hook your corset myself."

"It's a gift."

"I don't know if I want a come-out," Maggie said, her voice quiet in that way it had when she needed to speak but didn't want to give offense. "It doesn't seem real for the likes of me and Liz."

"You and Liz are as worthy of society's attention as any girls in London or Europe," the Lady informed her crisply. It was not the first time she had said so, and not the first time Lizzie had not believed her. "In any case, it is still two years off. The more pressing decision is what you will choose to do with yourselves in the interval."

This was why the Lady was so good in the laboratory. She refused to be distracted by nonessentials.

"What about finishing school?" Lizzie surprised even herself at the words that came out of her mouth. The Lady and Maggie looked dumbfounded as they both spoke at once.

"In Switzerland?"

"Aren't you coming back to London with me?"

"Of course I am." How could she make Maggie understand what she could hardly put in words herself? "For the summer, to see Lewis and everyone at Carrick House, and to go up to Scotland with the Dunsmuirs for shooting season. But in September … Mags, if her ladyship is to see us presented, oughtn't we to do what we can to—to give her a good bargain? With finishing school, we'd be a little closer to being ladies, at least."

"But—but I thought we'd go home," Maggie said, her eyes huge, her voice a disconsolate whisper. "Or at the very least, stay here and do the sixth-form classes so we can stay with the Lady. You can't go to finishing school, Liz. Why, we were laughing at the idea only the other night."

So they had been. Claire seemed to be having difficulty marshaling her words together, so Lizzie took advantage of it. "But that was before we knew what Lady Dunsmuir was up to. This changes everything, Mags."

"It does not." The Lady finally had her tongue under

control. It was a lucky thing MacMillan had finished her work, because Claire leaped to her feet. "Lizzie, I am utterly astonished at you. Finishing school? You?"

She wasn't slouching now. "What's wrong with me going to finishing school? See, Lady, this is exactly what I mean. You don't think I'm good enough to be finished, never mind presented, do you? *Do you?*"

Two spots of color appeared in the Lady's cheeks, and too late, Lizzie wondered if perhaps she ought to have kept her real opinion to herself.

"I cannot believe you just said those words to me, Elizabeth," the Lady whispered. "Not to *me.*" Her cheeks blotched even more, and to Lizzie's horror, tears welled in her eyes and fell, dripping past her chin and into the lace that edged her *décolletage.*

"I—I—" She looked to Maggie for help, and found none. She had hurt the Lady horribly—the one person in the world to whom she owed everything, the one person who had never shown her anything but respect and consideration and love.

Oh, drat her uncontrollable mouth, that let words fly like birds out of a cage so that she could never call them back!

"Lady, I didn't mean it," she mumbled miserably, unable to look into those gray eyes any more. Outside the window, a pair of swans beat the air, on their way to the lake that was the main feature of the enormous park in front of the Landgraf's palace.

Lizzie heard the door close quietly, and when she dragged her damp gaze back into the room, the Lady was gone.

2

The University of Bavaria's ballroom, Lizzie was quite
convinced, could hold three of the Lady's airship,
Athena, with room to spare. Its white walls were curly
with ornate Empire plasterwork and gold leaf, and its
ceiling held murals and paintings from the previous century, including portraits of previous emperors and em-
presses whose names and reigns she and Maggie had
had to learn by memory during their second year. On a
stage at the front bedecked with potted palms and flow-
ering trees sat the Regents and the university's president, along with Count von Zeppelin, its pre-eminent
patron.

Maggie elbowed her in the side. "They've called her
name. Look, there she is!"

Because they were the guests of Uncle Ferdinand, and sitting with Lord and Lady Dunsmuir, along with the officers of their airship, *Lady Lucy*, their party had been seated in the first section behind the men and women graduating today. Lizzie was not as conscious of this privilege as she was that Tigg, who served aboard *Lady Lucy*, was with them again after an absence of nearly a year.

"What's the silver sash she's wearing?" Tigg whispered as Lady Claire walked down the center aisle and mounted the stage. Her face glowed, all evidence of the blotching that Lizzie had caused erased in the glory of achieving her dream at last.

At least, Lizzie hoped that was the case. If she had been up there, she'd have been turning cartwheels for joy or some other undignified display, but the Lady merely smiled and accepted the rolled-up diploma tied with a scarlet ribbon from the university's president. Then she held out her right hand, and the Dean of Engineering stepped forward to slide the engineer's slender iron ring upon the little finger. The Dean of Women standing beside him embraced her—an unprecedented proceeding thus far—and Claire's smile widened as she crossed the stage and descended the steps to her own seat.

"It means she's graduated from the School of Engineering," Maggie whispered back. "Along with the ring. The doctors have a yellow one, and the humanities lot get green or rose, depending on their field. The Lady explained it to me."

"What's humanities?" Tigg said, puzzled.

"Books, music, art, that sort of thing."

"Why don't they just call it books, music, and art?"

"Because it's humans what do it, and not dancing monkeys," Lizzie hissed. "Quiet, you two, or they'll boot us out."

How good it felt to have Tigg with them again! Though goodness knew he didn't look a bit like the eight-year-old ragamuffin who had found her and Maggie on the Billingsgate river stairs, cold, starving, and with frightening gaps in their memories. Weepin' Willie might have been rendered mute before Snouts had found him in the river, but at least he mostly knew how he'd got there. She and Maggie had not been so lucky. But never mind. Lizzie had been all too happy to forget the past and concentrate on surviving in the present, never dreaming that her future would be so changed by setting upon and robbing a young lady driving a steam landau where she should not have been.

No, Tigg was not that little boy any more, though she suspected his natural protectiveness had not faded with time and acquaintance. At eighteen, he wore a lieutenant's bars with pride on the collar of his khaki airman's uniform, which contrasted rather nicely with his coffee-colored skin and melting brown eyes.

But one should not notice the eyes of a young man one considered a brother, no matter how much affection and even admiration one found in them.

And then it was time for the final procession, to the accompaniment of the full orchestra. With the crush of the crowd, it took some time for their party to locate Lady Claire over near the terrace, where the long afternoon rays of the sun turned everything golden. One long black academic gown and the flat board on the head looked very like another, until you saw the auburn hair and the flash of Nile green silk underneath.

There was to be a ball immediately following the refreshments, and Lizzie's stomach clenched under the restraint of the corset. Three years of dancing lessons had not prepared her for the prospect of dancing with an actual man. No, she would not think of that now. Now was the Lady's moment, and Lizzie hung back as the Dunsmuirs embraced Claire in a flurry of kisses and silk.

"Claire, we are very proud of you." His lordship kissed her upon the cheek. "Congratulations upon realizing your life's dream."

"Thank you, John." Claire swept ten-year-old Willie up in a hug, much to his delighted embarrassment, and gave him a smacking kiss. "It is the realization of one dream and the birth of another," she said gaily. Maggie hugged her, and then Lizzie stepped up to do the same. Was it her imagination, or was the hug perfunctory and slightly less warm than hugs ought to be? Or was it her guilty conscience making mountains out of mole hills?

Claire took a breath, as though she were going to say something privately to her, but she saw something over Lizzie's shoulder that caused her to gently set Lizzie aside. "Captain Hollys," she said, the color rising in her cheeks. "So you have given your officers and crew a day's holiday as well?"

"John and Davina are not the only ones who are happy to see you realize your dream," he said in a tone that Lizzie was quite sure was not meant to be heard by anyone but Claire. The kiss he gave her was so proper that even Queen Victoria might have looked on in approval—but Claire's color deepened even more.

When she turned to hug Tigg, who had been standing a respectful distance behind his superior officer, it looked to Lizzie as though she took the opportunity to hide her face against his uniform collar. "Oh, my dear, I am so glad to see you," she exclaimed, looking his tall form up and down. "How you have grown! I was so disappointed your duties kept you from dinner last night."

"Someone had to command *Lady Lucy*," Tigg said, trying to stifle his pride in being given that responsibility, and failing utterly. "But I was sorry not to see you. You're an honest-to-goodness engineer now?"

Claire waggled her little finger, on which the ring glinted. "Honest to goodness and for true."

Captain Hollys said, "Lieutenant Terwilliger will be writing the engineering entrance exams himself in the fall. Mr. Yau has been coaching him."

Claire clasped her hands beneath her chin in delight. "Tigg! Why did you say nothing of this in your letters?"

Because he did not want you to know if he failed. Lizzie kept her mouth firmly closed. It was for Tigg to say, if he chose to.

"I wanted to surprise you," Tigg said, and Lizzie allowed as how that might have been part of it. "But algebra is a mysterious language and it's lucky that Mr. Yau is a patient man. I almost didn't get through the book."

"Nonsense." The captain clapped him on the back.

"A mind as fine as yours could do nothing but wrestle x and y to the ground and subdue them."

"As you say, sir." Poor Tigg. He was trying so hard to be grown-up and dignified in front of the Dunsmuirs and his captain. It was all Lizzie could do not to stick her fingers in his ribs and tickle the daylights out of him. But one did not tickle the lieutenants of one's acquaintance. They might tickle back—only luckily, in this corset, she'd never feel it.

The ballroom was cleared and then the first-year class, who had been seconded to wait upon the seniors, carried in the refreshments, laying them out on long tables along one side of the room that had been covered in snowy linen with silver vases full of flowers from the horticulture department's gardens.

"Quite the spread," Maggie said out of the side of her mouth some time later, having enjoyed slices of beef and ham, to say nothing of the familiar mountains of Bavarian sausages and at least a dozen different kinds of salad. Now she and Lizzie savored a strawberry ice, allowing the sweet chill to melt upon their tongues. "Uncle Ferdinand likes a good feed, so to guarantee it, he sponsored the dinner."

"How do you know these things?" Lizzie would have licked the delicate china dish if she had not been quite certain that the Lady would have seen it from across the room and descended upon her like Rosie the chicken upon a beetle. Instead, she rose gracefully and brought a second helping back for both herself and Maggie.

"He told me the other night, when we were acting out a play with the grandchildren."

"You'll miss that, back in England."

"I can always act them out with you. Though you'll have to play the boys' parts, unless we can get Lewis and some of the others to join us."

Lizzie was silent. She didn't want to think about Maggie and Lewis and the others, eating Mrs. Morven's wonderful suppers and having loads of fun while she was walking about with a book on her head in Switzerland. So to distract both herself and her sister, she said, "Who's that gentleman there, leaning on the pillar? The one with the odd spectacles, and the waistcoat nearly as fancy as my corset."

"Lizzie, you mustn't mention undergarments in public."

"Yes, Lady," she mocked. "He's looked at us three times since we sat down."

"How would you know, you goose? Those spectacles are dark, and they have driving magnifiers to boot. Anyway, a gentleman is allowed to look at anyone. It's when he wants to speak to a lady that he must be introduced."

It was plain that she, Lizzie, was the only one who needed to go to finishing school. Maggie remembered every word that came out of the Lady's mouth. "Yes, but he's *old.*" Forty at least, with graying temples and a faintly military moustache.

"Maybe he thinks you talk too much and he's wishing someone would come along to set you in your place."

"Oho, Miss Priss. Listen to you. I suppose you're impervious to the looks of gentlemen."

"I am not. But I'm too young to dance. Not that

anyone would ask me. We're not officially out, you know. We're merely here in the Lady's party."

"What if Tigg asked you? Or Lord Dunsmuir?"

Maggie sniffed. "Tigg is different. He's my brother— or as good as. And his lordship would not waste his dances on me—not when Lady Dunsmuir loves it so much. But I would dance with Willie. Lady D. tells me he has been taking lessons, poor darling. I can imagine how I would have felt about that when I was ten."

Lady Dunsmuir would like as not be in a library or boardroom somewhere, meeting with the mysterious personages who ran countries behind the scenes, but Lizzie did not say so.

Lizzie finished the second strawberry ice, and when she looked again, the gentleman was gone. How odd. Not odd that he was in the company, or that he had been gazing at her and Maggie, but odd that she had noticed him at all. Her experience with gentlemen was flavored heavily by her years on the streets of London, where one trusted at one's own risk and one's mind categorized people as *safe* or *not safe* at a glance. That instinct had become a little rusty of late with so little material to work with. Between the count's palace and the *lycée*, there were not many people she could say were not safe, unless you counted random aeronauts who became lost in the palace corridors after one too many glasses of beer in the mess hall.

Lizzie shook her head at herself and smiled as Tigg joined them. "Is the grub usually this good at a university?" he asked. "If it is, I might abandon ship and come study here."

"It's not the university, it's Bavaria in general," Maggie told him. "They like to eat and drink, and the count is no exception." She explained about his sponsorship, and then said, "Do you happen to know if the Lady has spoken to the Dunsmuirs about her plans?"

Tigg looked a little surprised. "You live in the same rooms, don't you? I'd think you would know before anyone else."

Lizzie shook her head. "I don't think she knows herself. But things might come clearer in London." Over the heads of the crowd was one that stood a little taller, neatly brushed and held with the pride that came with both breeding and responsibility. "Did you see Captain Hollys kiss her?"

"It was only on the cheek." Tigg straightened a little, as if the mere mention of his name might make that gentleman look his way with a measuring eye. "But he makes no secret of his admiration of the Lady."

"She makes quite a secret of her admiration for him," Lizzie said. "I can't tell which she likes better. When she's with Mr. Malvern, I'm sure it's him. But you should have seen her blush when the captain spoke to her."

"Maybe she can't decide, either." Maggie beckoned them both a little closer with a crook of her finger. "Mr. Malvern's proposed, you know. I saw the letter he wrote, after we left Charlottetown that first time."

"He never," Tigg said. "She didn't let on at all. I was with them in the laboratory at Christmas and it was just like always."

"He's waiting to speak again until she's graduated."

Lizzie's tone held the authority of someone who knew absolutely nothing about the subject. But it made sense, didn't it? "But what I don't understand is how a girl can be married and engineer airships. Who's going to wash Mr. Malvern's socks if she's in the Antipodes testing a flying something-or-other?"

"Servants, silly," Maggie said. "They'll live in Carrick House with all of us, and Mrs. Morven, just like we've talked about a hundred times."

"She won't be engineering airships from London if she's employed by the Zeppelin Airship Works," Tigg said. "That plan doesn't make a bit of sense. Enough chatter, you two. We oughtn't to talk about the Lady behind her back."

"Then you go and ask her to dance, and while you're at it, find out what we want to know." Lizzie stuck out her tongue at him, just a little, so no one but he would see.

"I will."

"You don't know how to dance."

"I do, Miss Impudence. All the officers do, in case the Dunsmuirs have extra ladies among their guests."

"You, dance? Oh, how Snouts would laugh at that." She was egging him on, needling him for no reason in the world other than to see how he'd take it.

What she didn't expect was for him to seize her round the waist and whirl her out onto the floor just as the orchestra swung into a rousing polka. Tigg's gloved hand was firm on her back and he moved with flawless rhythm to the music. It was hard not to dance well with him as a partner, and once she got over her astonishment, she found it was fun.

"All right, all right, I take it back," she said breath-lessly as the polka ended and a waltz began. "We should go join Maggie. I shouldn't be out here at all, you know. She was quite right—neither of us are out yet."

"This is a graduation party, not a society ball, you gumpus."

She stepped on his polished shoe on purpose, just to remind him that she didn't permit name-calling, even by her oldest friends. "You can explain that to Lady Dunsmuir when you're dancing with her, so she won't come and read us a lecture."

"Good idea." With that, he danced her over to where Lord and Lady Dunsmuir circled the floor, smil-ing into each other's eyes like a pair of moony spooners. "Pardon me, your lordship, may I claim her ladyship in exchange for this minx?"

Lady Dunsmuir laughed, the diamonds in her tiara and at her throat sparkling in the soft electrick lights. "You'll be getting the best of that bargain, John. Go on. Show Lizzie what she has to look forward to."

In the space of a single measure of music, the earl whirled her away and Tigg and her ladyship disap-peared from view in the current of elegantly dressed couples. His lordship was still smiling as he glanced down at her. "All right?"

"Yes, sir. We practice three times a week at the *ly-cée*, you know."

The smile grew broader. "You make it sound rather like calisthenics, Lizzie. You had best get used to it as the most efficient way to converse privately with a member of the opposite sex."

"I'll remember that." A brocade waistcoat caught her eye, and irrepressible curiosity made her say, "Your lordship, do you know that man there? The one by the punch bowl, with the dark spectacles and the waistcoat with peacocks on it?"

"Shocking bad taste on both counts. But only to be expected."

"So you do know him."

"Yes, by reputation. That is Charles Seacombe, a man with his fingers in several pies both here and in England. He reminds me rather forcibly of a certain shipping magnate in the Americas whose name will not pass my lips. Seacombe's largest concern, I believe, is based in Paris—something to do with electricks—but he has homes in several places. Why do you ask?"

"Oh, no reason. I thought he looked familiar, that's all."

"I should think not. Men like the Count von Zeppelin do not need to associate with men like Seacombe in order to be successful, though there are several who will tell you I am wrong."

"They are foolish, then."

The smile lit his eyes once again, but not because she had flattered him. They knew each other too well for that. "And when did you become interested in what my wife so vulgarly calls the movers and shakers of the world, my dear?"

"Oh, I'm not. He just looked out of place, that's all. I expect he's here for one of the graduates. Perhaps his son has got his diploma and will join him in the business."

"He does have a son, if I recall. Or perhaps I'm thinking of the Rothschild boy. Never mind." He gave her a stern look as the music ended and he led her from the floor. "You do not need to concern yourself with the sons of anyone at all for at least two more years, and after that I believe my wife has a plan."

"So I hear. And I would love to hear more."

"That is a sphere in which my clumsy boots are emphatically not welcome, so I shall say no more." He bowed to her with enviable grace, and Lizzie did her best to curtsey without falling over onto Maggie, who joined them just then.

"Well?" Maggie said as the earl moved away. "Did you find anything out?"

"Not a single useful thing except what we already knew—that his lordship is a lovely man and Davina is a lucky woman. Come on, Mags. I'm dying for another strawberry ice. Last one to the table is a nit-picking mudlark."

3

It would have been easy, in the glittering and celebratory crowd, to avoid the Lady and wait for another day to resolve the unsettled spirit between them. But Lizzie, sadly, did not possess the gift of finding the easy way to do anything. She didn't think she could bear having the Lady look at her again with the memory of the tears that she had caused between them. If she was to enjoy this revel, she had to do it with a clean conscience, even if it meant calling upon her old scouting skills to do it.

"Liz, you're making too much of this." Maggie attempted to gather up her gown's miniscule train, of which she was inordinately proud, to follow her sister. "What d'you want to go bringing it up for in the middle of a ball?"

"Because it's spoiling it for me."

"It might spoil it for the Lady, you trailing her around the room looking desperate. Tonight's a night for congratulations, not apologies."

But Lizzie ignored her, for there was the Lady over at a table with Davina and Captain Hollys. Getting to her in the crush proved more than a little difficult, though, between brushing up against people talking, dodging first-year students carrying trays, and avoiding being swatted by the skirts of ladies whirling past in the waltz. By the time she reached the table, Claire and Captain Hollys had drifted out the French doors into the garden.

Lizzie changed course and dodged down a short hallway that led to the music rooms.

"Liz, you're never going to follow them," Maggie said, her voice low. "What if Captain Hollys wants to steal a kiss?"

"And risk the Lady zapping him with her little lightning pistol? He'll be glad to see us, at least, if we have to pick him up off the ground."

Claire and the girls had amused themselves during the Christmas break designing and fabricating a device that a lady could carry in her pocketbook or muff to provide more discreet protection than that of the lightning rifle. The latter still resided in Claire's room, but since they'd moved into Carrick House and become respectable, the demand for its services had lessened.

Still, one never knew—and as the Lady said, a little

practice in how to take a power cell apart and put it back together again never went amiss.

If only they could make such useful things in Lizzie's physics class! But no. For their term project—on which she was already nearly a week behind—Professor Sturm required that they focus on the basics, which meant an assignment to either harness or defy the power of gravity in some way. If she didn't come up with something in the next fourteen days, she would fail the course, and then what would happen to finishing school?

The French doors of a piano studio decanted them on the far side of the lawn, just in time to see the captain hand the Lady down the flagged steps to the gazing pool. Maggie gripped Lizzie's elbow so hard that her dancing slippers nearly went out from under her in the grass. "Liz. You can't go down there."

"Why ever not? It's only the captain, and he'll excuse me."

"Liz, stop!"

Gaping at the vehemence of her hissed whisper, Lizzie sank down next to her on a bench screened by a huge mound of French lavender. The scent, as familiar as linens and sachets, washed over them in a wave as the movement of their skirts disturbed it, and Lizzie's nose twitched.

"Fine, but if they don't start back up here in the next five minutes, I'm going down."

"Isn't it a lovely night?" they heard Claire say as she gazed over the pool to where the stars were just beginning to prick out on the horizon. "I just wish my mother and brother had been here to share it. And Sir Richard Jermyn, of course. But dear Nicholas has the chicken pox and my mother could not leave him."

"Of course not," the captain agreed, his voice carrying to Lizzie and Maggie in an agreeable bass tone that carried both sympathy and comfort. "You will be able to go to them now, however."

"I shall wait until after the girls graduate from the *lycée*," she said. "By then he will have recovered and my mother will be better able to receive visitors. I'm afraid she finds Maggie and Lizzie rather ... trying."

The girls glanced at one another, and Maggie made a rueful moue of the mouth. It was only too true. Lizzie had never been able to fathom how such a beautiful woman could have produced a daughter like the Lady. Not, she amended, that the Lady was not pretty. The light of intelligence lay upon her brow, and her mouth curved up in humor much of the time, creating the best kind of beauty. But Lady Flora's beauty went skin deep, and she expected everyone else's to, as well, in the service of catching a husband. It was exhausting, having to care so much about one's looks—no wonder Claire's visits to Gwynn Place were limited to the summer holidays, and only in the company of as many of the inhabitants of Carrick House as possible.

How Lady Flora would rejoice that Claire looked so well in her Nile-green ball gown, and had ventured into a garden in the company of a baronet!

"The girls are a credit to you," Captain Hollys said, and Maggie and Lizzie exchanged an altogether different glance—one filled with pleasure, visible in the glow spilling from the doors behind them. "You can be proud of all you have done for them."

"They have done all the work for themselves since we arrived here," Claire told him. "Though something Lizzie said this afternoon disturbs me."

Lizzie straightened, and Maggie laid a gloved hand upon her arm. Was the Lady about to tell him all her sins? Was that really fair, when she hadn't had a chance to explain?

"She has got it into her head to go to finishing school, and I cannot in all conscience agree to it."

"Why not? If she wants to, it seems harmless. Many young ladies do, I understand."

"Yes, but they are not Lizzie. With a mind like hers, she would be utterly wasted learning to cut cucumber sandwiches and reciting the rules of precedence. When she told me she wanted to go because of some mistaken idea of her suitability as a debutante in two years, I wanted to weep. In fact, I believe I did."

Lizzie pressed a hand to her mouth. That was what the Lady had meant, and she'd got it all backward. She should have known that Claire would never think she wasn't good enough. In fact, the opposite was true. The Lady thought she was too good—that she had set her sights on a goal too low for her true abilities.

Captain Hollys moved closer. "I should hate to think that anything would make you weep, dear."

Claire breathed a laugh. "Oh, it has happened a time or two. I love the girls with all my heart, but such emotion only makes that organ easier to bruise, it seems."

"And is your heart filled only with maternal impulses?" he asked softly. "Is there no room in it for emotions of a sturdier sort? That would not bruise it, but rather, heal it and prepare it for a lifetime?"

Claire fell silent, and Maggie's hand tightened even more on Lizzie's arm. Oh goodness, he was going to propose, right here in the garden. How exciting—and romantic—and horrible! "We have to rescue her," she breathed in Maggie's ear. "Right now, before he says it."

"If you go down there, I will never forgive you," Maggie whispered back. "We must go back to the ball now, before they realize we're here."

Too late. The captain had taken the Lady's hands in both of his.

"Claire, my feelings for you have not changed in the five years we have known one another. I have waited faithfully for you to complete your education, and have celebrated your success with all the joy a man can feel."

"I did not ask you to wait," the Lady said in a tone so low the Mopsies could barely hear her.

"I know, but it was my honor and purpose to do so. Claire, will you end my waiting now, and make me the happiest man on earth by consenting to be my wife?"

Breathlessly, the girls waited for her answer with as much attention as Captain Hollys did. Because she would not only be answering for herself—one word would change their own lives at the same time it did hers.

"Ian … I must know … do you plan to continue as

captain of *Lady Lucy*?"

"That would depend on your answer," he said with a smile they could hear in his voice. "If we marry, I should turn over the helm to Mr. Yau without a backward glance, and return to my estates with you."

"Then ... the career that I have prepared for—that Count von Zeppelin has prepared for me—what would become of it?"

"There is nothing to prevent you having an engineering salon connected with our home, as many inventors do. Great things have come out of private laboratories, as our friend Andrew Malvern has proven many times over. And speaking of that worthy individual, does he have any influence on the direction of these questions?"

"No—no, not at all. At least, not in the way you imagine. He has hinted at a jointly operated laboratory, but only if for some reason I could not fulfill the terms of Count von Zeppelin's offer."

"I see."

"Ian, I do not think you do. I hope you will understand ... How can I accept the count's hospitality and kindness these four years, and then back out of my promise to join him at Zeppelin Airship Works? How will he then realize the benefit of the education he has made possible?"

"The count is a man of the world. Do you not feel that your becoming a baroness would assuage his disappointment in some small degree?"

"I cannot see the connection."

"No, perhaps not. Your mind is as clear as your

heart is considerate, and it is one of the reasons I love you. No, dear, please do not look away. I love you, and I should like to know if you love me, too."

"Ian ... dear Ian ... of course I do, in—in my way."

"What way?"

She looked up at him, her face in his shadow as he moved a little closer. Lizzie didn't dare move to see better, in case the Lady glanced over his shoulder in her agitation and spotted them, frozen behind the lavender.

"In the way of close friends and companions at arms. In the way that two people who have weathered the next best thing to a war love one another. As family. As someone whose loss would leave a hole in my heart that cannot be repaired."

He was silent in his turn, for the space of a breath. "And what of the other kind of love? The love a woman has for a man?"

"That, too, a little. But Ian ... I can still care about you without our becoming engaged. The one does not necessarily preclude the other. I am only twenty-three and there are so many things I want to do with my life I can hardly count them all."

"And I am nearly thirty, with responsibilities to my family and my name that are beginning to weigh more heavily than ever before."

"She's going to turn him down," Maggie breathed. "Oh, Lady, how can you do this to the captain?"

Maggie had a gift for seeing things that people were going to do before they actually did them. Claire called it perception and empathy, but Lizzie simply thought it was because Maggie paid attention. She drew in a huge breath of relief—

—and the scent of lavender went up her nose—

—and she sneezed.

৩৽৽

Lizzie wasn't sure who hustled whom through the open doors of the ballroom, but when the two trumpets sounded to announce the arrival of Her August Majesty, the Empress of Prussia, the entire company and grounds, right down to the goldfish in the gazing pool, were electrified to attention at the royal presence.

Claire's grip on the Mopsies' hands was cold as they squeezed through the doors and into the crowd. "I don't know who I am happier to see—you and Maggie, or the empress. Come. We must find Tigg and the others."

For once, Lizzie felt she could have been right, if Maggie had only let her. When Claire released their hands in order to squeeze through the crush, she lost no time in bringing this fact to her sister's attention. "See? She didn't want him to propose. If you'd just let me go down there, she wouldn't have had to go through it."

"He won't be satisfied with not getting an answer," Maggie said. "You know the captain."

And then Claire spotted Tigg and there was no more time to talk, because the trumpets sounded again on either side of the door. Lizzie craned her neck to get a glimpse of the empress, whom she had never seen close up. At a distance, yes, in parades and processions and such, but a faraway glimpse of glossy dark hair and a lot of diamonds didn't count. The empress would be congratulating a select number of graduates in person this evening, and Lizzie had bet Maggie a hundred schillings that their Lady would be one of them.

She didn't actually have a hundred schillings, but if she lost, Maggie would forgive the debt.

A slender figure dressed in—in a split skirt and an aviator's jacket and goggles dashed into the room.

"Who is that?" Maggie wondered out loud. "Did one of the aeronauts lose her way again?"

But then the crowd began to sink into the deepest of curtseys, like a wave that spread outward, washing them to the floor with it and losing its energy at the walls.

The president of the university approached the young woman—for she couldn't be very much older than Lady Dunsmuir—and bowed himself nearly in half. "Your August Majesty," he said clearly into his knees. "Welcome to our graduation celebrations."

"Oh, do get up, Friedrich." As he straightened, Lizzie heard a whisper like a wave on the beach below Gwynn Place, as the entire company rose from the floor. "I'm so sorry I'm late. I took up the velocithopter and the wretched thing caught an unexpected draft. That's the last time I'll go without a rocket rucksack, I'll tell you."

"Velocithopter?" the Lady repeated in astonishment as a chuckle ran through the crowd. "If I'd known one could wear the next best thing to raiding rig to this ball, I'd have done it."

"Is His August Majesty to honor us with his presence?" the president inquired.

"No, sadly, it's only me you have to put up with," Her August Majesty said. "But I am looking forward to meeting your new crop of brilliant minds. Shall we begin?"

After that, the lengthy program that Lizzie had no doubt the president intended to inflict upon his guests had perforce to be abandoned.

As they made their way through the crowd to Tigg and the Dunsmuirs' party, Claire smiled at the girls over her shoulder. "You see now why Prussia is neck and neck with England for progress. There is a good reason the empress was the first civilian to travel in the CET-100 model airship when it was launched. She was so impatient to see our automaton intelligence in action that she ordered it to lift even before the First Admiral of the Navy could get aboard."

Which had caused headlines around the world, and which had subsequently caused the stock in the Zeppelin Airship Works to hit an all-time high, making Claire a rich woman. And, of course, Lizzie and Maggie and Snouts and the others back in London, in whose names the Lady had been prudent enough to buy stock as well.

Lizzie, whose head for mathematics had improved since the old days of counting spades on playing cards, had found herself the proud owner of a healthy little competency. How that would help her at finishing school, she wasn't sure, but at least it would help pay to get her there herself, if the Lady was not willing.

A young man in livery appeared at Claire's elbow. "Milady, if you would be so good as to come with me?"

Claire froze, and Lizzie saw Davina hide a smile. The rascal, she already knew! Of course she did. She'd probably had a personal audience already and hob-nobbed with the empress over a cup of tea, talking over the list of those to be honored.

Wordlessly, Claire followed the young man to the front of the ballroom and up onto the stage once more, where a small cluster of graduates in evening clothes shuffled nervously. Five young men and three young women, all persons of accomplishment, all completely ignored by Lizzie and Maggie, who waited breathlessly to see what would happen.

And then the empress held out a hand to Claire, who sank into a curtsey in front of her. She raised her gently, but her voice rang out, resonant and clear, as if she'd been making speeches to crowds since she was born.

"I am pleased to introduce to you all Lady Claire Trevelyan, from London, England, whose achievements in the field of engineering have earned her a special place in the history of this, the Prussian Empire. For it is her invention—jointly with Miss Alice Chalmers of the Texican Territory—of the automaton intelligence system that has revolutionized the airship industry in this country, and put it ahead of its competitors."

A LADY OF RESOURCES

Maggie and Lizzie held hands, breathless with delight, and Tigg's face glowed with pride.

The empress directed her next words to Claire. "I was present to christen the CET-100 ship that bears your initials, and words cannot express how proud I was that a woman was responsible for such a breakthrough."

"Two women, ma'am," Claire said. "It was my friend Alice Chalmers who invented the automaton's intelligence engine. I wish she could have been here to share this moment."

Instead of being taken aback by being corrected in mid-speech, the empress's infectious smile broke out. "So do I. I think we would have had a lot to talk about, don't you?" She cleared her throat and turned to a footman bearing something on a purple cushion. "I understand you were able to waive your senior project requirement and claim the intelligence engine in its place. But this is from me. Lady Claire, I am pleased to present the Medal of Honor for service to the Empire—known to most as the Iron Wings—oh, no, please don't kneel again. I'm sure to poke you trying to get it pinned on."

Claire straightened as the empress pinned something on a bit of royal-blue ribbon to the breast of her gown, and Lizzie clasped Maggie's hand more tightly. "Oh, Maggie, she's crying."

For it was true. Though she bravely tried to hold her lips steady, tears overflowed the Lady's eyes and rolled down her cheeks as the assembled company of dignitaries and students applauded.

"Come on, Mags. I've got a hanky in my pocket." Lizzie pushed through the barrier of two stout matrons, slid around a crowd of chattering third-year students, and emerged at the front of the crowd just as Claire descended the steps. She dashed over to her and offered her hanky in the nick of time.

"Oh, Lizzie," the Lady whispered, mopping her face, "please tell me I did not blotch."

"No, Lady, you looked wonderful. We were all so proud. I just wish Snouts and Jake and our Alice could have been here to see it."

"I do, too." Claire sniffled and huffed the ghost of a laugh. "There is apparently some kind of bursary attached to the receiving of this medal." She touched it, gazing down at the iron eagle's wings with the crown between them. "Wherever she is, I'm sure Alice will be glad of it, for I intend to give her the entire amount."

By now Maggie had joined them, and Claire hugged them both, all three heedless of the wrinkles pressed into their silken skirts by love.

Love.

What answer was Claire going to give Captain Hollys, who was among the happy group even now bearing down on them?

There was no chance to find out, and Lizzie had a feeling that the Lady was just as glad to leave it that way.

4

Term project. The words were like a death knell in Lizzie's mind—the sound you heard just before your professor of physics announced your failure of his class.

She sat, disconsolate, at the workbench in the *lycée*'s physics laboratory, supposedly working on her project, but in reality merely pushing gears and springs around on the polished surface like an oracle searching for meaning in mechanical entrails.

She didn't even have the comfort of Maggie as a laboratory partner, because they'd been split up during their first year as a means of strengthening their characters as individuals—a stupid theory that neither of them could understand, since they did their preps together in their apartments with the Lady anyway.

"I'm dying to see your project on Friday, Elizabeth," purred Sophie "Bug Eyes" Bruckheim as she passed Lizzie's bench. "I'm sure it will be a wonder on the level of your sycophantic friend's intelligence system."

"Nothing could be," Lizzie returned in flawless German, cool as you please. "Including your poor papa's navigation assembly. I hear the count turned it down and it had to go to the Americas to find a buyer."

Sophie glared daggers at her, and Lizzie had a feeling her brief victory would probably net her a splash of tea on her uniform at lunch or some other petty revenge.

Ah well. Sophie's reign as queen of the fifth form was nearly over, and with any luck, she wouldn't choose finishing school afterward.

Lizzie pushed away from the bench. This was getting her nowhere. She obtained permission from the professor to go down to the supply cellar, which would mean a climb of eighty stairs down and eighty back up again, but perhaps the extra oxygen to her brain would produce an idea for a project. The best idea she could come up with now was to fling herself on the Lady's mercy and beg an idea from her—a plan she'd so far managed to resist out of sheer stubbornness.

If Alice and Claire could apply their minds to groundbreaking inventions, then she could, too. And she didn't even have to break ground. She'd be happy with a mere furrow. A tunnel. Anything.

In the cellar, she signed the log-book and paced

along the shelves and barrels of materials and equipment. Gears, ironworks, and mechanical bits and bobs shared space with bottles of chemicals, lengths of rope, and the boxes of punch-cards used by the difference engines to run the university. Farther and farther back she went, with the feeling that she was going back in time to older and older components of long-ago breakthroughs. Finally she hit a wall.

Literally. She was in an old part of the cellar, which contained things of so small a value that they sat on metal shelves that dripped with cobwebs and dust. This would net her nothing. She turned, and her uniform skirt brushed a lower shelf. Something rolled off it and bounced.

Without touching the ground.

It arced over her head, to within a few inches of the ten-foot ceiling.

She lifted her moonglobe and watched the fragment of ... whatever it was ... bounce again and again, until it lost momentum and rolled under the shelving unit, as if it were ashamed of its performance.

Lizzie knelt down and fished about under the shelf, withdrawing the fragment at last, her skirt and white shirtwaist covered in dust and dirt that had been collecting there for a lifetime. "Where did you come from?"

It looked like a rock. Or a shard of iron, the size of her palm.

She bent over and dropped it.

Again, it hit a point about four inches above the ground, resisted the landing, and bounced up, whacking her on the chin. "Ow!" She grabbed it, then cradled her face, touching the tender spot to make sure the skin was not broken.

A rock that bounced. That resisted gravity. In a way.

Was there any more?

She spent an hour searching through boxes and barrels, growing increasingly dirty and frustrated, but apparently there was no more. Well, goodness, this wouldn't do. She could not simply present a rock to her professor, bounce it between floor and ceiling, and take credit for a great discovery, could she? Sophie would cover her mouth and snicker that horrid, whimpering laugh Lizzie detested, and she'd be made a fool of again.

No, she must look into this. Surely such an interesting element would have a history of its usefulness in some dusty book somewhere? Or perhaps the Lady would know?

But when the Lady examined it after tea that afternoon, watching with some fascination as it resisted hitting the floor with each bounce, she had no more to offer than Lizzie herself.

"It is fascinating, though, Lizzie. I suggest the university library, and if you can, speak with Herr Himbeer, the science librarian. I'm sure he's been here since the Crusades, and if he can't give you an answer, at least he can give you a book."

During her study period the next day, Lizzie requested and received an hour's pass from school, and leaped aboard a passing cable car as it slowed outside the *lycée*'s gates. The university was only ten minutes' walk, but Lizzie liked to ride the cars. The mystery of the mechanisms below the streets of Munich fascinated her, their cogs and gears pulling the cars about on cables like an enormous, hidden brass spider web—if spider webs could be said to operate like well-oiled clocks.

She leaped down near the imposing building that housed the library, designed to look like an enormous Greek temple. The temple of knowledge, she supposed. In her pocket, the rock bumped against her leg as she climbed the broad staircase and asked directions to the science section.

The Lady may have been poking gentle fun at him, but Herr Himbeer did look as though he might have existed for a couple of centuries at least. His blue eyes, however, were alive with intelligence, and rested upon her with curiosity as she was shown into his cluttered office. She dropped a polite curtsey. It would never do to have it get back to the Lady that her ward had been discourteous to someone belonging to the kingdom she had just conquered.

"Guten abend," she greeted him politely. "My name is Lizzie de Maupassant, and I am the ward of Lady Claire Trevelyan. She suggested that you might be able to help me identify something."

The sea of wrinkles split into a smile, and his white beard twitched above the horn buttons of his loden-green boiled wool jacket. "Ah. Lady Claire. A fine mind. You are most welcome, my dear. Sit down. How may I help you?"

She pulled the rock from her pocket and tossed it

on his desk, where it did not hit, but bounced until its momentum lessened enough to make it drop.

"I should like to identify this mineral, if indeed that is what it is."

He picked up the rock from the pile of yellowed papers on which it had landed, and sat back in his wooden chair. "Goodness. Did I leave some of this behind?"

"I beg your pardon, sir? I found it in the materials cellar at the Lycée des Jeunes Filles. Away at the back, under a shelf."

"I imagine you did. I taught there many years ago, before I took up my first post here." He tossed it in the air himself, and watched it repeat its performance. "This mineral is called repenthium. Perfectly useless stuff, I'm afraid, at one time mined in the Ural Mountains to the east. Years ago the manufactories used it as a kind of accident prevention, smelting it into the fenders and bumpers of the steam buses when they ran here, so they would repel one another if they got too close. But since the cable system was put in, they've had no use for it. Accidents rarely happen now."

Well, goodness. How disappointing. "Is it a metal, or a rock, sir?"

"A metal, of sorts. I can give you a number of treatises penned by men who tried to make it useful, but really, its properties give more amusement than concrete benefit. Can you imagine any machine in which it would be useful?"

Lizzie thought quickly of something over which gravity exercised complete control. "An airship? It might prevent a crash."

"Airships do not crash."

"A long, slow, glide and a soft landing. Yes, I know. But I have been in a ship that crashed, and a substance like this coating the hull would have made it much softer."

"Perhaps, once you'd got done bouncing up and down. Which would be rather trying, do you not agree?"

Lizzie pictured what might have happened if the *Stalwart Lass* had bounced on its hard landing in the Idaho Territory. "Hm. I suppose you're right. It would be. Well then, what about applying it to a landau or a velocithopter?"

"There you run into the same difficulty. The substance does resist gravity at nearly any velocity. That much is true. But it is uncontrollable. Undependable. And in this day and age, one cannot hang about waiting for the bouncing effect to slow enough to get on with one's business. In fact, in the open air, it does not stop at all unless some means of slowing the bounce is introduced."

How very annoying that she should find something so interesting, and yet so useless at the same time. Just her luck. Well, she must be honest, at least. "My term project is due on Friday, sir, and I haven't a single idea in my head. What do you suppose I could do with this so that I don't fail the term?"

Herr Himbeer regarded her with some sympathy. "Better you should build a miniature velocithopter or solve some physics equation using the difference engine than mess about with an element with such a poor reputation." He handed it to her, careful not to toss it across the desktop. "The best you could do is use it for a paperweight, or entertain your friends with it. Or melt off a bit and wear it round your neck to remind yourself that sometimes the elements found in nature are just not made for humanity to put to work. A valuable lesson, sometimes, I think."

Lizzie thanked him, pocketed the repenthium, and escaped before he got up enough steam to launch into a philosophy lecture. She made it back to the *lycée* just in time to join the river of students ebbing and flowing up the staircases to their next class. She was just rounding the landing, heading up to the French classroom, when she met Bug Eyes coming down the stairs.

"Get out of the way, Maupassant," Sophie drawled, and somehow her satchel of heavy books swung out, knocking Lizzie across the landing and into the wall.

But she did not hit it.

Instead, she distinctly felt her heels leave the ground as the repenthium in her pocket, which had been closest to the wall, resisted the force of impact. She staggered a little and fetched up against the marble balustrade, the breath going out of her in astonishment.

"Honestly, Maupassant, have a little more beer with your lunch!" floated up the stairwell below her, and the giggles of her classmates echoed like a fluttering chorus of derision.

She took the rock out of her pocket and stared at it. Maybe it wouldn't do an airship or a steambus any good. But wouldn't it be interesting to have a little of this about one's person. In a belt, say, or—or—

Her hand crept across her ribs, where she might have bruises now if it hadn't been for the rock and her corset. Under the fabric of her blouse, the bones of the corset, which weren't actually made of whalebone anymore, but steel, ran in ten orderly channels about her person. She'd made the corset herself, in Home Arts. All the girls were required to sew and learn fine work, like Brussels lace to trim their blouses, or crochet to enliven an apron.

She'd put the bones in herself. But what would happen if she replaced them with bones made of ... repenthium?

5

"Lizzie—no, you mustn't," the Lady said, laughter trembling on her lips. "You cannot wear the antigravity corset to your graduation ceremony—it simply won't do."

Lizzie smoothed her hands over the new corset, which she'd finished mere hours before having to demonstrate it for her physics final. The twins' white fifth-form graduation robes hung upon the wardrobe door, waiting to go on over their school uniforms. Unlike the Lady's more glamorous graduation, no empress was likely to brighten the auditorium at the *lycée*, nor was there to be a ball. But that did not lessen their jubilation any—the Dunsmuirs were putting on a fête in honor of all three of the graduates ... and who would want to stand about in the school gymnasium with a lot of awkward boys from the neighboring Lycée des Jeunes Hommes when the Dunsmuirs were throwing a party?

"Why not? I'm rather proud of it," she said, and just for fun, threw herself to the floor.

Her hair swung over her shoulders and brushed the carpet, but her body itself did not touch it. Instead, she bounced back up again, and flung a hand out to catch herself against the dresser. The corset wanted to keep on bouncing, but she'd got the hang of it in the few days since she'd made it, and had learned to control at least some of the movement.

"Lizzie!" The Lady laughed out loud, unable to keep it in any longer. "If you trip over your skirt and take a tumble on the way up to the stage, I can't answer for the consequences. There will be no walls or chests of drawers to stop you, and then what will you do? Spend the afternoon dusting the ceiling with your petticoat?"

She had a point.

"Oh, very well." Lizzie unhooked the corset—in deep green brocade, and trimmed with lace—and tossed it on the bed, where it found only a little resistance. After a couple of tiny bounces, it settled on the soft duvet with a sigh. "But I am proud of it, Lady. No one in my physics class had anything like it. Everybody's gravity experiments seemed to involve miniature airships or flying machines. Mine was the only wearable thing—and once I'd figured out how to melt it down and make the bones, the fact that I'd actually made something relatively useful out of repenthium pushed my grade up by one."

Which was the only reason she'd managed to pass the class, but the Lady was too sensitive to the feelings of others to bring that up.

"Come along, Liz," Maggie said impatiently, having been dressed for half an hour. "Get your togs on— we've got a graduation to go to."

Lizzie could barely contain herself in her seat in the auditorium as the headmistress called one name after another. What a lucky thing they'd chosen a surname that began so close to the beginning of the alphabet!

"Elizabeth de Maupassant, eighteenth in her class, with firsts in German, French, and mathematics."

There, now, that wasn't such a bad show, was it, for a girl who had begun life as a street sparrow?

The Lady beamed with pride as, up on the stage, Lizzie bobbed a curtsey to the headmistress and took the rolled-up diploma. She and Maggie had given the Lady a rough go of it sometimes, but to see the tears of happiness in her eyes now, you'd never know it.

"Margaret de Maupassant, twelfth in her class, with firsts in Home Management, English, and chemistry."

Lizzie clapped as Maggie followed her onto the stage, waiting for her so that they descended the steps together, holding hands that were slightly clammy from nerves. When they returned to their seats, they could see the Lady sitting next to Davina Dunsmuir and Willie in the audience, clapping madly.

"I'm so proud of you," she mouthed to them. "Well done!"

Maggie slid her program out from under her skirt and looked at what was coming next. Awards and a prayer and then they'd be *free!* Lizzie unrolled her diploma and gazed at it with a sense of satisfaction she'd never experienced before. It wasn't much different than getting a report card, really, so why did she have this quiet glow that went deeper than merely the happy fact of passing into another form?

"We done it, ent we, Liz?" Maggie whispered in the vernacular of their childhood. "All our own selves, we proved we could. Imagine us with firsts in anything!"

And maybe that was the key. Yes, between Lady Claire and Count von Zeppelin, they'd had opportunities that even Snouts and Tigg had not had. But they had taken those opportunities and applied all the brain power they possessed to catch up on five years of schooling that all the other students had undergone and they had not. Summer school. Tutors. Extra classes. It had been a grind at times, but they'd stuck to it, determined not to let the Lady down.

And now, she held the result of all her past efforts in her own hand. Even as she held the future.

She came out of her reverie as Maggie straightened beside her. "What do you suppose our chances are of getting an award?" she whispered.

"Yours are better than mine," Lizzie whispered back. "I'm eighteenth, remember?" Out of a class of forty, that wasn't too shabby, in her opinion. But it didn't exactly put her in the running for awards.

Predictably, Sophie Bug Eyes carried off the sports trophy, but she was beaten out by Katrina Grünwald for the all-around academic award. Katrina was the most studious girl in all the school, so this was no surprise to anyone. Then, to Maggie's astonishment, she was called up to receive a ten-guinea bursary from one of the Prussian lace-makers' guilds, for her success in Home Management. "Fancy that," she breathed, opening the little lace purse to examine the gold coins as if she'd never seen a guinea before.

"You've earned every one," Lizzie whispered proudly.

The headmistress leaned into the amplification horn. "Our last award has been funded only very recently, and is awarded to the student who has overcome great barriers in the pursuit of her education, and has come further than any student in her five years at this institution through application and sheer determination."

"Katrina," Lizzie whispered to Maggie. "She's an orphan, remember, and has to work for her tuition every summer."

"The award is a very generous—a *very* generous—five hundred guineas, provided by a captain of industry known throughout the Empire, Mr. Charles Seacombe."

Lizzie hardly registered the man's name, so bowled over was she by the magnitude of the bursary. Five hundred guineas! That would buy a house. Or fund two years of finishing school with money left over for clothes, books, and skiing trips to Chamonix at Christmas. Goodness! But what was she even thinking about it for? It was Katrina's name the headmistress was opening her mouth to call.

"I am very proud to announce that this bursary is awarded to Elizabeth de Maupassant."

For a moment, all Lizzie could think was, *oh, poor Katrina, it's gone to someone else.*

Then Maggie's elbow landed hard in her ribs. "Go on! That's you!"

"What?"

"It's you, *stupenagel!* Go on!"

She? She had won it? But that was impossible.

Maggie took her arm and hauled her up out of her seat, and gave her a push in the small of her back out into the aisle for good measure.

Lizzie never remembered getting to the stage. The only thing she could recall later were the gold embroidered lions on the waistcoat of the man handing her the bank draft for five hundred guineas. The man who had seemed to stare at her at the ball two weeks ago, and whom she had forgotten completely since.

"Congratulations, my dear," he said as she took the envelope with fingers that felt numb. "You have worked hard and deserve such recognition. Your mother would be proud."

He must have her mixed up with someone else. She didn't have a mother—never had—unless he meant the Lady.

"I don't think—" she began, but then the applause swelled and the gentleman stepped back and there she was in the center of the stage, a bank of flowers massed at her feet, accepting an award she didn't deserve from a man she didn't know.

಄

After that, of course, the only polite thing for Lady Dunsmuir to do was to invite Mr. Seacombe to the graduation party aboard *Lady Lucy.*

"Which, of course, is a fine way to insinuate himself among people moving at our level of society," his lordship said rather grumpily at the small dinner *en famille* that preceded the festivities.

"On what do you base your opinion, John?" the Lady inquired. "I must say, his singling Lizzie out for such an honor goes a long way to putting him in *my* good books."

"But you tend to expect the best in people, and as a result you most often find it. I cannot say why I do not like him." The earl frowned down at his *pflaumekuchen,* a country dessert of which he was particularly fond. "His business dealings are on the up and up, but there always seems to be a whiff of the predatory about them. He moves in good circles, but he is not completely accepted by the best. In short, I can find nothing to criticize about the man ... but nothing for which I can like him, either."

"I find five hundred reasons to like him," Lizzie said, daring to speak up. "I won't judge the man unless I discover that his bank draft is no good."

At last the earl smiled. "Quite right, Lizzie. And anyway, after this evening, it is unlikely you will see him again, isn't it?"

"True. I still think he got the wrong girl," she said.

"Why should you think that?" Her ladyship's eyes sparkled with pride. "You deserve this award—everything the headmistress said of you was true."

"Maybe, but he said the oddest thing to me on stage. He said my mother would be proud."

"Perhaps he meant the Lady," Maggie said, having already heard Lizzie's thoughts on the subject and agreeing with them.

"I hope not," the Lady said, and laughed. "We are only seven years apart in age—biology would preclude such a supposition, if nothing else."

"Perhaps he was speaking in generalities," Lady Dunsmuir said in a comforting tone. "One can generally suppose that a young lady has a mother, cannot one? And that she might be proud of such accomplishments in her daughter?"

"It seems to me he would say, *your parents would be proud,* then." Lizzie did not want to argue with Davina, whom she adored almost as much as the Lady, but at the same time, her logical mind had been offended by the comment.

But then, it was offended by many things. The need to wear a corset, for one, and the fact that a Blood Prime Minister had been voted into Parliament, and that the Black Forest was called black when trees were quite obviously green. The remarks of a stranger should not demand so much of her attention, when so many other odd things abounded in the world.

And then the first of their guests were announced, and they hastily abandoned the table and went into the grand salon, which had been cleared for dancing.

By the time they returned to the small dining room, it would have been cleared and reset with refreshments for the dancers, along with a selection of the cakes and *petits fours* that Lizzie had seen being unloaded from the baker's steam-dray earlier.

For the first time, she and Maggie were to be part of the receiving line. The Lady had coached them in what to do. "Simply listen for their names as they're announced by the Chief Steward, greet them, and curtsey to everyone."

"Are you going to curtsey to everyone?" Lizzie had wanted to know. Wouldn't it be easier to curtsey when the Lady did? Otherwise her legs were going to feel as they did after a gymnastics class, worn out with all the bending.

"I shall if the person outranks me," the Lady said.

"But everyone outranks us," Maggie reminded her sister.

Lady Dunsmuir would have to do the least curtseying of all, unless the empress turned up, or one of the royal dukes. And none of them had been invited.

Ah well. She and Maggie knew better than anyone that the world was not fair. It was only on occasions like this that you felt a little extra grateful that it had gone your way at all.

The receiving line seemed to last ages, but it couldn't have been more than an hour. By the time the guests seemed to have all arrived, Lizzie's and Maggie's curtseys had been reduced to mere bobs, and titles and faces had begun to blur. Even Mr. Seacombe hardly registered, though he shook her hand heartily and said nice things that went in one ear and out the other.

And then at last they were free. The orchestra struck up a lively waltz and the earl led Lady Claire out onto the floor. To Lizzie's surprise, Mr. Yau bowed before her and took her hand, and Captain Hollys partnered Maggie as if they were proper young debutantes already.

Oh, what a good thing she had not come as close to failing dance class as she had physics! With only three couples on the floor, every misstep would be seen by the entire company. But Mr. Yau did not allow a misstep—and besides, she'd had enough practice at dodging and running that dancing was easy in comparison. In fact, it was, as the Lady had explained to her in her first year, a little like geometry patterns, one after the other, around and around the room. You just had to memorize the order they came in, and Bob's your uncle.

When the opening waltz ended, the earl made a little speech of congratulations to the new graduates, and the orchestra struck up again.

The guests flooded onto the floor, and Lizzie found herself being handed off to the earl, and then Captain Hollys claimed the Lady, and he must have forgotten she was to be next after that, because Tigg appeared for the schottische and bowed like a proper gentleman before taking her hand.

"I'm supposed to be dancing with the captain," she said, and then wished she could unsay it. Tigg would think she didn't want to dance with him.

"The captain's distracted." Tigg grinned and whirled her around when the steps of the schottische didn't strictly call for it. "I waited for my moment, you see."

"He proposed the other night, you know," Lizzie confided as they skipped shoulder to shoulder down the length of the room. "She hasn't answered yet. I hope he doesn't press her."

"The Lady is always being proposed to. I shouldn't worry about it. If anyone can handle herself, it's she."

"What about you, Tigg?"

"Have I proposed to her?" Another whirl. "Are you mad?"

Boys, honestly. "I meant, have you met any girls on your travels about the world?"

"Oh, lots," he said in an airy tone that made her wonder if there was a girl waiting for him at every landing field on two continents. "But none that I like so well as you and Mags. We're a flock, remember?"

Yes, like brothers and sisters. But that wasn't what she wanted to know—and she was beginning to think that wasn't what she wanted to be, either. "So no one special, then?"

"Why? Should you care if there was?"

"Of course I should. But you're awfully young to be thinking of it, if there is."

He squeezed her and laughed. "You're the one who brought it up, so clearly you're the one who's thinking of it, and you're even younger than me."

"No one is going to propose to me, Tigg."

Another squeeze, that somehow felt different this

time. "Don't be so sure. You're a wealthy woman now, I hear."

"I wouldn't want a man who even thought of money."

"We all have to live on something." The music moved into the slow part, and he took both her hands, holding them crossed as the skaters did on the frozen Isar in the winter.

"I didn't mean it that way. I meant, if a man courted me because of what I had rather than what I am ... that would be awful."

"It's a shame your five hundred guineas are already the talk of the town."

Lizzie's eyebrows went up. "They are?"

"Aye. I bet you sixpence that someone asks if he can court you before the end of the evening."

"You would lose, Tom Terwilliger. I'm not out yet. The Lady would never permit it—and the earl would toss him off the ship for being forward."

"Doesn't mean a man wouldn't try, on the sly, like. You're a fine lady now, Liz. Too fine for the likes of some, but that wouldn't prevent them trying."

Something in his tone made her look up into his face, and she pulled him out of the current of dancers to a mahogany table with an arrangement of flowers on it that partially shielded them from view.

"What do you mean, Tigg?" She didn't want to be fine, if it meant her friends no longer felt they could be friends with her. "I'm not too fine. I'm the same as ever—just with more knowledge in me noggin."

His long lashes fell and he looked away. "Don't talk

like that. You've got on a silk gown and you have more money now than I'll see in ten years of a lieutenant's wages. You could have your pick of any of these gentlemen's sons, if you wanted."

"But I don't want them."

"You say that now, but when you're eighteen, you'll look at things differently, I promise you. With finishing school and some money, you'll forget your old friends, and where you came from."

What had got into him? And why would he not look at her with his usual frank, honest manner? "Not likely, and you know it."

"Do I? How do I know?" Now he was looking at her, his dark brown gaze examining her—expecting her to look some way or say something—and not finding what he wanted.

That gaze unbalanced her to the point that she fell back on bravado. "Because I can still pick a pocket with the best of them—and if you tell the Lady I said that, I'll pin you for a liar."

"After five years of French lessons and lace-making and deportment, you can no more pick a pocket than I can. Besides, why would you want to?"

Lizzie's temper, which seemed to boil up out of nowhere these days, began to sizzle deep inside her. So Tigg thought she'd got above herself, did he? Well, she'd just prove she hadn't. She hadn't forgotten where she came from, even if Mr. High-and-Mighty Lieutenant had.

"You bet sixpence that someone will ask if he can court me? Fine. I bet one of my gold guineas that I can pick a man's pocket before the end of the evening."

He was looking at her now, right enough. Staring in horror, in fact. Ha! "You would not."

"You started this—and when have you ever known me to back down from a dare?"

"I didn't mean it, Liz. You can't. The Lady would have your hide, to say nothing of his lordship—and mine for putting the thought in your head."

"I'm not afraid of them."

"Then you ruddy well should be. Don't you dare."

Of course, the moment the words were out of his mouth, she had to take that dare. "I shall. And not just any old pocket, either. Anyone can lift a comb or a bit of change. A gold guinea is worth a—" Inspiration struck. "—a pocket watch!"

"No. Absolutely not."

"Watch me."

"Lizzie!"

And before he could reach out to stop her, Lizzie had darted around the table and into the crowd, leaving him alone with the flowers—which had come out of the dirt and into polite society, too, with no one to judge or dare.

6

I wandered gentle as a cloud. She'd had to learn that
in Poetry and Drama. Or was it *lonely as a cloud?*
Never mind, the point was that if she were to find a
watch to pocket, she needed to drift about looking
harmless and pretty, with enough firmness in her step
that it would look as though she were looking for
someone without committing exactly to whom.

Bother Tigg anyway.

Now that her unreliable mouth had got her into
this, she was going to have to go through with it, even
though, as Tigg had so rightly pointed out, the Lady
would have a fit if she got wind of it—might even hus-
tle her back to London without so much as a please or
thank you—and as for finishing school ... well, it

wasn't likely they'd admit a pickpocket among the bevy of young ladies, would they?

Oh, dear. She'd dug herself a moldy grave for true on this one. Once she'd proved her point to Tigg, she'd find a way to slip the gentleman's watch back onto his person as quiet as you please, and then swear Tigg to secrecy for the remainder of his life.

"Miss Elizabeth, if I might have a word?"

Lizzie realized a moment too late that she had drifted right in front of Mr. Seacombe and was face to face with the gold lions on his waistcoat. Settling her expression into vacant politeness and trying not to stare at his spectacles while trying to see his eyes, she said, "Good evening, sir. Please allow me to thank you once again for your generosity, which I am afraid I do not deserve."

"Nonsense. I conferred with your headmistress and of all the possibilities, you were the student who stood out."

"But sir, Katrina—"

"Your concern for others is a credit to you, my dear. Say nothing more about it. I am happy to be in a position to give assistance where I see the need."

Which was not terribly delicate of him, but Lizzie, eyeing the golden lions, was in no position to criticize. Like most gentlemen of her acquaintance, Seacombe kept his watch in its own pocket, with the chain extending across the stomach and hooking through the bottom buttonhole of the waistcoat. Her task, then, was to either find a man who did not wear a chain, or to find an opportunity to pop the fob through the buttonhole and lift the watch silently.

What she required was a distraction.

"Such modesty in a young woman," he went on. "I should like to introduce my son to you, with your permission?"

Goodness. For a moment Lizzie wanted to cast about wildly for the Lady, who ought to be here to manage the situation. But then she stopped the impulse. *I am old enough to be introduced to someone, for goodness sake. Two minutes and I either get a chance at that watch or I don't, but in either case I move on to more congenial company.* Vacant politeness became pleasant expectation.

"Miss Elizabeth de Maupassant, may I present my son, Claude Seacombe. He is in his third year at the Sorbonne, and will be joining me in the business upon his graduation." He laughed. "Though his will not, perhaps, have the fanfare of that of your guardian."

Lizzie smiled and extended her hand to the young man looming over his father's shoulder. Goodness, he was tall. And very handsome, if you liked macassar oil and merry blue eyes and exceedingly white teeth.

And dimples. He smiled at her in return and bowed over her hand as if she were a great lady. Then he straightened and squeezed her fingers, as if she were an utter flirt. "My very great pleasure, Miss de Maupassant. I hope you are enjoying your celebration party?"

"I am, thank you." She removed her hand from his.

He glanced from her to the couples whirling past. "But what's this? You're not dancing. I must rectify this situation at once. May I have the honor?"

"But I'm not yet—"

Whether she was out yet or not, it didn't make a bit of difference, since clearly he'd seen her dancing with Tigg. He swung her onto the dance floor, where she felt a bit like a duck doing the polka with a stork. He was such a weed that she barely came up to his shoulder.

She hadn't had much practice in polite conversation with young men with whom introductions were necessary, either. What did one say in situations like this? "Do you have plans for the summer, sir?" she finally asked, a little breathlessly. His hold rode just on the edge of propriety, close and warm despite the speed of their movements, but not yet offensive.

"Oh yes. The pater is spending the warm months in England, you know, which we do every summer that we're not traveling."

"Oh? You have a home there, too?"

"Yes, a grand old pile he bought from some impoverished lord. His breeding couldn't pay the taxes, so it was going for a song. Papa considered buying the title along with it, but that seemed a bit *nouveau riche*, don't you know."

"Your ... pater ... is a man of restraint as well as sensitivity, then."

Claude laughed. "I don't know about that. You haven't seen him going at it in the gambling salons in Monte Carlo."

"And your mother? Does she travel with you?"

The laughter faded, and Claude steered her into a turn. "My mother is no longer with us in any form.

She died when I was just a puppy."

"I'm sorry. I didn't mean—"

"Don't worry your pretty head. It was a long time ago—I'm twenty-one now, and past the age of needing my mother."

Lizzie wondered how anyone could be past needing a mother, or a father. She and Maggie had had neither for many years. But sometimes, when she woke in the night after a dream of water and navy-blue skirts, she got a tight feeling, like a scab that was trying to grow over a wound.

Even now, deep down, she missed her mother. Missed even the memories of her. Didn't most people have those, at least?

Claude peered into her face. "Did I say something to offend you, Miss de Maupassant?"

"No. No, of course not. I have no memory of my own mother, that's all." Which was a terribly personal thing to admit to a perfect stranger. She pasted on a smile. "So tell me about this pile. Is it terribly grand?"

Another turn, and a whirl out and in. He really was a good dancer—better than Tigg, if it wasn't too disloyal to say so.

"It is—or at least, it will be once the pater pours some cash into it. It's actually a castle—there's a keep and a bailey and a moat that has flowers in it now instead of water, and two big towers on the corners. Her Majesty stayed in one of them once. Hence they call it the Queen's Tower."

"It sounds lovely. Fancy a moat filled with flowers."

"You'll have to come and see it." A flash of those white teeth, and mischief in the merry eyes. "I can get Papa to invite your guardian and the Dunsmuirs. It would be quite the social coup for him."

Lizzie didn't know as much about the finer points of society as she hoped to once she finished school in Geneva, but even she was aware this was a little bit much to divulge to a young lady under their protection.

"Oh, don't give me that look," he said cheerfully. "I'm quite the free spirit, you know. Say what I mean and none of this polite flummery that causes people to misunderstand one another. I'm all about clarity—and good fun, of course. Especially in the company of a pretty young lady."

Lizzie hadn't blushed in so long she'd almost forgotten what it felt like. Heat crept into her cheeks and she kept her eyes down so she wouldn't see him laughing at her. Blushing probably wasn't the done thing among his fashionable friends, either.

"Come, come, Miss de Maupassant. Surely you've heard a man say such things before."

"No," she managed. And in the interests of clarity, she said, "It's my first proper compliment."

He waggled his eyebrows. "Are there improper compliments?"

The cheek of him! "I'm sure you would know more about that than I. The polka is over, sir. I should like a glass of punch, if you don't mind."

"A paragon of proper behavior. Come, let's find the pater. I want to share my bright idea with him."

Fortunately, Seacombe was standing not far away, and while Claude cantered off to get her some punch, she smiled at him and prepared to be her own distraction.

"I see your interest in my spectacles," he said, removing them and handing the double-lensed marvels to her. "My eyes do not seem to react well to the electricks over here on the Continent. They seem to be of a harsher persuasion than those in England. I find the amber lenses helpful."

"I should not want to cause you discomfort." She lifted her gaze to his and—

—tiger eyes—

—a crack in the door—

She dropped the spectacles.

"Careful, now—"

"I'm so sorry, how clumsy—"

He bent, but she beat him to it, handing them up to him as she crouched. And as he straightened and held the lenses up to check them for damage, she straightened, too, her clever fingers working his watch fob through the buttonhole. In less time than her next breath, she lifted the watch from its pocket and stuffed it into the one sewn into the side seam of her gown. Simultaneously, she raised her right hand to tend the curls MacMillan had teased from her Psyche knot, as if they had been disordered in their little *contretemps*.

His gaze followed her hand as he adjusted the spectacles on his nose, and she pulled her left hand from her pocket just in time to accept the glass of punch from Claude.

Breathe. Calm your heart before it beats right out of your chest.

"Pater, I was telling Miss de Maupassant about Colliford Castle. Wouldn't it be a fine plan to invite the Dunsmuirs and Lady Claire for a house party? Perhaps the week my set will be there. We're going to race our boats on the river, you know," he added, turning to Lizzie. "Have you ever rowed?"

The closest she'd ever been to a boat was the coracles they used in the surf below Gwynn Place, and in the old days, the skiff they used to cross the river from the cottage.

"A little. Not big ones, though—that would be lovely." Which was a bald-faced lie. She liked boats and water even less than she liked airships—or rather, than her stomach did.

"A capital plan," Seacombe said heartily. Goodness, did fathers normally agree to have houseguests they'd only just met? Or was he so used to Claude and his "set" racketing about that it was just another lot of place settings to order at dinner?

"I shall speak to your guardian directly, Miss de Maupassant. In the meanwhile, do enjoy your party. Shall I see you over to Lady Claire?"

"No, thank you. I want a word with Captain Hollys." She dropped a curtsey and hurried in the direction of the captain, who was laughing with Mr. Yau as they tucked into the cakes.

Directly past them was the door into the corridor, and she hurried along it until she found the cabin that Lady Dunsmuir was in the habit of giving them when they travelled together. Only when the carved, glossy door closed behind her did she take a long breath and sink onto the lower bunk.

Amber eyes. Tiger eyes.

—a crack—

—and then the smoke and the cold—

Was it a memory? Or a dream?

7

It would not do to let Mr. Seacombe know he had disturbed her so profoundly—and so irrationally—so Lizzie spent the rest of the evening staying out of his line of sight. As one of the three guests of honor, expected to be in everyone's sight, this was no easy feat. They were, after all, in the grand salon of *Lady Lucy*, not in the palace, where she could disappear at will.

After she had been politely dragged over to the graduation cake and made to help cut it, then hand out pieces, the Lady found her hovering near the orchestra, where she was distracting the euphonium player to the point that his face had reddened far in excess of the strength of his wind.

"Lizzie, what is the matter? I have been watching

you these five minutes and cannot fathom what you are doing. Have you eaten too much cake?"

She mumbled something and wished herself at the bottom of the count's lake.

Under the pretext of rearranging the Alençon lace draped across one puffed sleeve, the Lady spoke softly. "Has something disturbed you, dear? Has one of the gentlemen taken some liberty? If so, you have only to tell me and Lord Dunsmuir will put the fear of Hades into him."

"No—yes—oh, Lady, I've done something ever so stupid." Her lip trembled, and the laughing remark hovering on Claire's tongue immediately dissolved into concern.

"What is it, dear?"

"I can't tell you." Claire's only response was the level, expectant gaze that never failed to make you spill your darkest secrets, whether you wanted to or not. "It's Tigg's fault," she finally blurted.

"Shall I go and ask him?"

"No!" Then in a quieter tone, she said, "He said I was forgetting where I came from and—"

"That is hardly fair. Or likely."

"—and to prove I wasn't, I—" Her throat closed and she pulled out the pocket watch just enough for the Lady and no one else to see it.

Claire's gloved fingers gently pressed the watch back where it had come from. "Oh, Lizzie. You didn't." The Lady's voice held no censure, only sorrow. And a tremble that only disappointment could put there.

Lizzie's heart felt as though it was going to crack in two. "I'm going to put it back, honestly I am, as soon as I figure out how to do it."

"Whose is it?"

"Mr. Seacombe's."

"Oh, dear."

Lizzie froze. "Is that bad?"

"No worse than your pickpocketing anyone else among the Dunsmuirs' guests and abusing their hospitality so shamefully."

If the Lady had struck her, she could not have flinched any more acutely, nor found her shoulders and body curving around the injured portion—her own heart.

"Unfortunately, Seacombe senior and junior have already left. I expect we shall have an inquiry from them tomorrow as to the lost item. And when we do, you will deliver it to Mr. Seacombe personally."

"What will I tell him?" Lizzie whispered.

"Perhaps you will not have to tell him anything. If you recall a similar situation at the beginning of our acquaintance, the person concerned was only too glad to see her property again, and not too fussy as to how it came about."

"Yes, Lady." Claire had made Lizzie undo her dishonest work then, and she'd tried so hard over the years since to cure herself of this tendency. But it was clear that such defects of character required constant vigilance—and resistance, if not to temptation, then certainly to being teased by her friends.

"Come, darling. We will make our farewells to the

Dunsmuirs and return to the palace."

"Oh, no, Lady. I don't want to spoil your evening." A glance, a raised eyebrow. "Any more than I have, that is. Please. I'll give them my thanks and slip back to the palace quietly on my own."

"You cannot go unescorted with all these people and coachmen and aeronauts about."

"Then I'll ask Tigg to come with me."

"And get you into more trouble? Never mind. I shall take this opportunity to have a word with him myself."

Whatever that word was, Tigg looked as though his balloon had been well and truly punctured as she kissed the earl and countess good night and thanked them for the party. The Lady intercepted Maggie before she could join them, and then two of the *Lady Lucy*'s crew asked them to dance, so telling her sad story to her sister was put off for an hour, at least.

The two of them descended the gangway and hopped to the ground, Tigg handing her down as if he thought she might break. "So you really did it?" he asked. "You really were such a little fool?"

Lizzie came close to throwing the watch at his head, but instead she merely handed it to him as they paced, arm in arm, across the airfield and onto the broad gravel avenue that ran with perfect rectitude through the park to the palace. "It belongs to Mr. Seacombe. The Lady says I must return it to him tomorrow. Perhaps I'll give it to his son and say I lifted it for a lark. He seems like the sort to appreciate a joke."

Tigg examined the watch, turning it in the palm of his white dress glove. "I think you're the one who's the butt of the joke. Lizzie, this isn't a pocket watch at all."

"What? Of course it is. There's the stem, and there's the chain, and it's even chased with a design. What else do gentlemen keep in their watch pockets but watches?"

"I don't know, but look. It's shaped like a watch, but it doesn't open. There's no catch, and no back or front."

She released his arm and took it herself, but she could gain no more information about the curious gold object than he. "Well, blow me down, as the aeronauts say. Bad enough I must prove myself a fool for a watch, but now it isn't even that. What kind of device is it, do you suppose?"

"A puzzle, for sure."

She slipped it back in her pocket with a sigh. "I'm glad you're with me, anyway, Tigg. I was feeling a little peculiar earlier."

"Too much cake."

"Not as much as you. I saw you go back for a second piece."

"*Hazelnuss* is my favorite. Say, Liz, move out into the center of the avenue. Looks like those chaps behind the elms have been celebrating a little too heartily."

Sure enough, a small group of men were pushing and shoving in the shadows of the trees, and one of them stumbled out onto the gravel, bumping up against a lamp post with a curse. Lizzie lengthened her step, thankful all over again that Tigg was with her. They wouldn't be likely to make impertinent remarks to a young lady accompanied by an officer.

Two more men lurched onto the avenue, reeling along behind them. Tigg quickened his pace, and the curls bounced against her cheeks as she did her best to keep up. But the men increased their pace, too, and suddenly Lizzie realized that they were not drunk at all.

Something snatched at her skirt and she shrieked. "Tigg!"

He whirled and shoved her behind him. One of the men threw a punch, but they could not know that every middy in the Dunsmuirs' service had been trained in the defensive arts by Mr. Yau. Tigg's leg swept out and caught the man behind the knees as he lunged past him, mowing him down as efficiently as the serving knife had cut the cake. The second man leaped into the breach, and Tigg moved in to engage him, but that left the third man. He made as if to go to the aid of his fallen companion, then dodged, whirled, and grabbed Lizzie around the waist, lifting her off her feet.

Fortunately, Lizzie and Maggie had talked Mr. Yau into giving them the same lessons.

The man might have been expecting a gently reared young lady to dissolve in a paroxysm of fear, or at the most, to kick her dainty feet. An elbow to the ribs and a second to his nose made him drop both her and his illusions about her, which gave her just enough time to plant the leather heel of her dancing slipper hard between his legs.

And then the second man saw his advantage just as Tigg realized she had been in danger. The man's fist caught him square on the chin and Tigg went over backward, measuring his length on the gravel.

"You beast!" she shrieked, realizing a moment too late that now all three were advancing upon her. She took to her heels. If she could get off the avenue and into the trees, she could lose them in the dark. After all, it wasn't likely three bully-boys from the *Victualienmarkt* knew this park half as well as she and Maggie did. Her scream would alert the count's watchmen, and they would be taken in a trice.

But they were fast. She wasn't going to make it. She dodged behind a fountain, the watch bumping against her thigh—

The watch. Or the not-watch. Seacombe was going to have to sing for it, because the single advantage she had at the moment was her fine right arm.

Running, looking over her shoulder to aim, she snatched it out of her pocket and flung it as hard as she could at the man slightly ahead of the pack. Except the chain wrapped around her gloved hand and the pin on the top of it came right out.

The watch landed with a clatter on the gravel practically at the men's feet, doing no harm whatsoever.

Lizzie cursed in a manner that the banks of the Thames had not heard in some time, and flung herself sideways to hide behind a marble statue that had no clothes on.

And the night exploded into a thousand pieces.

Her hands over her ears, Lizzie hit the ground face first as the statue was torn from its pedestal and catapulted end over end right overtop her body. Half the water in the fountain rocked out of the basin in a huge wave, and drenched her.

—the cold, the awful water—

—*London Bridge is falling down*—

Screaming, her head ringing, she felt rather than heard a vibration in the ground, and tried to roll over to grab a rock, a branch, anything with which to defend herself. Hands went around her waist and she threw an elbow back, but as it connected she heard, as if from deep underwater, "Liz! Liz! My God, are you dead?"

Her gloves were gone. So were those of the hands that held her. Smooth, caring, coffee-colored hands.

Lizzie burst into tears and turned into Tigg's chest, clutching his jacket in both fists. He pulled her into his lap and held her, rocking back and forth, back and forth, his wet face pressed to hers, as the night came alive with running people, swirling around them like a current.

And then silk skirts descended like a cloud beside them, and Lizzie smelled the Lady's rosewater and cinnamon scent as she wrapped her arms around them both, her voice urgent, nearly hysterical, as she demanded of Tigg whether they were hurt.

But her own name on Tigg's lips was all Lizzie could hear, in tones as broken and full of tears as her own had been. "Oh Lizzie, please don't be hurt. Please, Lizzie-love, please be all right. I swear I will never do anything bad again, if you'll only be all right."

She lifted her head, straining at the tightness of his hold. "You mustn't swear," she gasped, and fainted dead away.

8

Claire Trevelyan had just finished instructing the count's footmen as to the cabins in which their various trunks should be placed aboard *Athena*, when one of them returned from the gangway. "Your pardon, my lady, but there are two gentlemen here inquiring as to whether you are at home."

In social parlance, "at home" meant that one was available to visitors. One could quite conceivably be physically at home, and at the same time not at home to company ... which was the case at this moment. Did these callers not see that the airship was preparing to lift? Or was it the investigators, come back again with one more question?

"Who is it, please?"

"The messieurs Seacombe, my lady. I have told them that you and the young ladies are on the point of lifting, but the elder is insisting."

Oh, dear. There was only one thing that could have brought them here, on a morning where it was clear that, due to the terrible events of the evening before, the count's estate was open only to the magistrate's investigators and not visitors. "I shall see him in the small salon. Would you be so kind as to visit the galley and see if there are biscuits to be had, or possibly tea? *Danke schön.*"

He bowed and she made her way to the small salon, the first of the private rooms one came to upon walking up the gangway. *Athena*, while not as large as *Lady Lucy*, was still large enough for a crew of a dozen. Its cargo hold was enormous, though, which was why it had been used to smuggle weapons through the skies by its previous owner. She had been meaning to have some of the space converted to cabins, or perhaps a grand salon like that of the Dunsmuirs, but she had so far not found the time. Now that her years of study were concluded, perhaps she could turn her mind to such happy domestic pursuits.

Happy ... domestic ...

She had not yet given Captain Hollys an answer, and time was running out.

But first things first.

She waited by one of the port side curving windows as the footman showed in the Seacombe men. The elder crossed the room at once, hesitating only slightly when he saw how she was dressed. Her raiding rig often took people by surprise, but that did not stop her from wearing it, especially in the air on her own ship.

"My dear Lady Claire, I am shocked and dismayed at the events of last night. It seems our early departure from the party was providential. I hope neither you nor the guests of the Dunsmuirs were injured?"

She smiled and gave him her hand, over which he bowed in the European fashion. "No indeed."

"And how is Miss de Maupassant?" the younger inquired, his brow wrinkled in concern. "I heard she was somewhat closer to the blast than many others, and that she was trapped under some bit of masonry?"

"The fountain saved her life," Claire said, indicating the tea the footman brought in, and seating herself at the small table to pour. "I am saddened to report that the bully-boys—those who set upon her and the officer who was escorting her—were not so fortunate. All three were killed."

"Mon Dieu!" Claude's face paled in shock. "Do we know who they were?"

"Or what caused the blast?" his father put in.

Goodness. How innocent he looks. Can he really not be aware of the true circumstances here—that it was his own device that killed these men?

She did not answer his question immediately, nor did she betray the fact that they were both playacting. Instead, she handed them their tea and offered slices of the cake from last night, which was clearly all the footman could scare up in her bare galley. Hopefully the count's steward would soon deliver the traveling stores she had ordered from the market that morning.

"It is fortunate indeed that you left early," she said with a smile as Seacombe selected a piece of cake.

"Yes, it was. I had discovered something missing and hurried home, believing I had left it upon the dressing-table. But when I arrived, it was not there, either."

He was not lying. Claire had been around enough members of street gangs to become aware of the physical tics of someone attempting to conceal the truth. So he was not aware that he had been robbed. The question remained: What had he been doing with a bomb—for clearly, that was what the small gold object was—in his watch pocket?

"What was this object?" she inquired. "Perhaps we ought to make a search of the grounds immediately around *Lady Lucy*—or perhaps aboard her?"

"It was a small device I had intended to show Count von Zeppelin. As a former Navy man, he is keenly interested in weaponry, and one of my subsidiaries is engaged in the manufacture of ordnance for the protection of the Empire."

"A small device, you say?"

Claude leaned forward, his fingers two inches apart. "Yes, about this big. Looks a bit like a pocket watch, but when you pull the pin, you get about five seconds before it explodes."

Claire leaned back in her chair, a hand laid— convincingly, she hoped—at her breast. "Good heavens. Because, you know, small bits of brass were found in the crater, and a pin and chain under the bowl of the fountain. Is it really possible that a device so small could cause such dreadful loss of life?"

Drat the man's spectacles, which concealed his eyes from her!

She must translate the language of his body, then, which had gone as still as that of an animal who has scented danger. "Yes, entirely possible," he said slowly. "Might I be permitted to see these pieces?"

"They are in the magistrate's hands," she said, "but I am sure he would have no objection, if you were going to show the device to the count in any case. But what a dreadful way to find your property has been abused! I am terribly sorry, sir."

"Quite," Claude said. "Only think, Pater. How did the device get from your dressing-table to the Schwanenburg park?"

"I am perfectly certain I slipped it into my watch pocket," his father said. "I can only surmise that it somehow slipped out as we walked across the park— possibly when we accidentally disturbed those swans by the lake—and the miscreants picked it up." He laid his hands upon his knees, and Claire saw how they trembled. "Lady Claire, I must say I am—I am quite shattered at the thought that the mishandling of the device might have brought Miss de Maupassant harm. Can you forgive me for putting your ward in danger, even unawares?"

Claire could hardly help the softening of her heart. "I cannot see that you are to blame if, as you say, the device was taken without your knowledge and mishandled." Which was quite true whether he had dropped it, as he thought, or Lizzie had taken it. It would not change the end result. "Please do not be troubled on our account."

"Easier said than done, I am afraid." He rose. "Claude, I must speak to the magistrates, and we must not keep Lady Claire from her departure any longer." His son unfolded himself from the chair, swiping a second piece of cake as he did so. "Are you preparing for a long voyage, my lady?"

Claire did her best to conceal her relief at their going, and her impatience at yet more questions that required polite answers. "Yes, we are returning to England this afternoon with the Dunsmuirs' party. The magistrates have given us leave to go, but sir, you must certainly tell them of this sample ordnance, as you say. I cannot see that they would hold you culpable." When he nodded, she went on, "Regardless of their findings, Lady Dunsmuir is exceedingly protective of her son's wellbeing, and she is anxious to remove him from the vicinity of danger."

"Ah, a mother's love," said Seacombe. "A force that can move mountains—or at least, airships."

"Pater ..." Claude said, making urgent motions with his eyebrows.

"Ah yes." Seacombe turned back to Claire, who stifled a sigh and arranged her features in an expression of polite interest. "My son here made the acquaintance of Miss de Maupassant last night before these terrible events, and it appears she has made quite the conquest. He wishes me to ask if—once the young lady has made a full recovery from her ordeal—you and she and perhaps the Dunsmuirs might give us the pleasure

of your company for a visit at Castle Colliford? That is
my estate in Warwickshire. I feel I must make reparation of some kind—to give you all more pleasant
thoughts and memories of us than you have had thus
far."

How extraordinary! Lizzie had said nothing of
this—but then, she had hardly been in a condition to
say anything at all except, "Please can we go home?"

"Why—my goodness, sir, I am sure reparation is
not necessary. But how very kind you are."

"And as my son reminds me," he said, recovered
enough to smile, "young people these days do not wait
upon such boring social conventions as length of acquaintance or depth of conviviality to find reasons to
enjoy each other's company."

"Oh, come, Pater, you like a house party as well as
the next man." Clearly intent on lightening the atmosphere, Claude addressed her. "Do come. My crowd
from the Sorbonne are coming on the fifteenth and it
will be no end of fun. The castle's huge and Liz—er,
Miss de Maupassant was keen to see it."

"Was she?"

"Yes indeed. It will be a jolly time. Say, five days?
We'll send a proper invitation to the Dunsmuirs, of
course. Say yes, do!"

Claire couldn't help but laugh at his artless enthusiasm and good intentions. "It will all depend on Miss
de Maupassant's recovery, I'm afraid. Shall I send you
a tube by the end of next week?"

"Jolly good. Here's our address." He scribbled the
letters and numbers on a calling card and handed it to

her. "I do hope you'll come. The gang will be agog to hear of her harrowing adventure."

Claire resisted the urge to remark dryly upon those who turned the unfortunate experiences of others into entertainment for themselves. Indeed, he did not mean it negatively. He saw the recounting of last night as a way to give Lizzie stature in his friends' eyes—which, she supposed, was a function of how he had been brought up. A businessman and a succession of governesses might not be inclined to develop the finer sensibilities of their young charge.

"We will take our leave and wish you a safe flight," Seacombe said, bending again over her hand. "Good-bye, Lady Claire."

"Good-bye, sir. I do hope you and the magistrates find the person responsible for the misadventures of your device."

It was entirely possible that he had intended to share the device with the count, and if Lizzie had not been so foolish, none of this would have happened. What a strange confluence of circumstances that a man willing to risk having a bomb upon his person and a young woman willing to relieve him of it had met on the same night.

෧෧෯

Captain Hollys found Claire in the hold, supervising the loading of the landau, which Tigg insisted on piloting up the ramp. When it became clear the younger man needed the assistance of neither of them to tie it down and make it safe for the air voyage, Claire allowed herself to be guided away from *Athena*. Her hand in the crook of the captain's elbow, the wool of his flight jacket warm under her fingers, they strolled under the trees at the edge of the park.

"We shall have good weather," he remarked. "The skies are clear, with only a few bumps and buffets expected over the Channel."

"Lizzie will be happy to hear it. Her stomach finds flight a sore trial indeed."

"I am glad she is recovering. Tigg gives me faithful reports practically every hour. His devotion to her is touching."

Devotion? Or guilt? For if anyone could be said to have teased Lizzie into her rash behavior, it was he. It was only by chance that he had not been within range of the blast when the bomb had gone off.

She made a sound of agreement, and Captain Hollys came to a stop under a broad oak whose leafy canopy blocked the view of anyone looking down upon them from *Athena*'s viewing ports. "Claire, have you thought any further upon an answer to my question?" he asked without further preamble. "While we discussed it somewhat, I do not feel we reached a definite conclusion."

Because a timely sneeze in the garden had put an end to conclusions of any sort, much to Claire's relief. She did not want to be definite. She wanted things to go on as they were. Which was utterly unreasonable and unfair of her.

"Dear Ian," she said, meeting his gaze with her

own. "Should you really give up the helm of *Lady Lucy* to be married? Would you not rather stay in the sky while I pursue my career with the Zeppelin Airship Works?"

His brow furrowed with confusion. "If I were to do so, we would not see each other at all."

"But we would. Between voyages, and on land leaves, as you and your crew have done since the beginning of our acquaintance."

"But the question of my responsibility to my family and title is then left unanswered. It is high time, Claire, for me to leave one career behind and take up another—the one I was born to—that of a landed gentleman."

She had been born to be a lady, but that did not mean she wanted to leave behind her life. "At least you have *had* a career."

"Does it mean so much to you, then? You would rather give the best years of your life to a company, a business, no matter your fondness for its leader? And what then, Claire? When you are thirty—forty—fifty? What will you have to show for your labors?"

"Airships," she blurted. "Inventions. And Maggie and Lizzie and Tigg and the others, living useful, happy lives that might not have been possible without me."

"But what of the children who could be? Who may never be, if you continue on this course?"

In the branches above their heads, birds twittered and fluttered among the leaves, where nests no doubt were concealed. She had thought of motherhood. More than once, if the truth be told. She had held the babies of others and felt the warm trust of those innocent little bundles.

But to imagine one of those bundles as hers—and within the next two years, as seemed to be his intention? Her imagination simply could not reach that far.

"Must it all boil down to children, Ian? Is that the sum and summation of my purpose in the world? Can I not affect others positively in other ways? I told Lizzie not long ago that I would rather see her living a productive life than an ornamental one. I should be a liar if I did not apply that to myself."

"Being a mother is far from ornamental. And there is no reason why, as I said before, you cannot go from nursery to laboratory in the course of a day. Though I hope you would put our children first."

How small he made the sphere of her influence sound! Perhaps the future would not be too small for her, but the present, the reality, the day to day, certainly would be. "Will you do the same? After a life spent traveling the hemispheres, will you be content to live as a country squire, your days devoted to lambs and crops and stock prices rather than world events and political influence?"

"I welcome it," he said emphatically, releasing her hands. "I am ready for a quiet life. Ready to devote myself to family, friends, and farms."

And because he was ready to end his career, she must be ready to give up the beginning of hers? "Oh, Ian, can you not wait?" she said softly, the words a cry from her heart.

She reached out, but he had already taken one step away, his head bowed as if there were something interesting in the grass. "I have been waiting, as I told you. As you have known for these five years."

"But can you not wait a little longer, until I have had a chance to fly the skies you have flown, to taste influence in the world, to know the respect that you know both as a right of birth and as a result of your own accomplishments?"

At last he turned toward her. "You have had all those things, Claire," he burst out. "Why are you not satisfied?"

I had not suspected this need for recognition in you, this constant desire to be in the spotlight. It is unwomanly. Lord James Selwyn's voice whispered in her memory. She shook her head, as if to dislodge the words from her mind. Did all men think this way, or had she merely been unlucky enough to attract the two who did?

Perhaps Ian was right on the first point. But just because someone had tasted a thimbleful of elixir did not mean she no longer wanted to drain the flagon dry. Why should she not drain it? Why should she be restrained by the random chance of her sex to a quiet life on another's schedule? What example would that set for Lizzie and Maggie? They may as well all go to finishing school at that rate, and become the ornaments that men seemed to want far more than the happy, intelligent women they had.

"I *am* satisfied," she replied quietly, and before he could speak further, she added, "But I see what I have accomplished as a beginning, whereas you see it as an end. And there, I fear, the courses we have charted must diverge, though it pains me deeply to say so."

A few moments of silence ticked by. "So that is your answer, then?" he asked at last.

Oh, she dared not look in his eyes. For if she did, and she saw the love that lay in them, she would wobble and waver and all that she had worked for would be lost in the desire to please him, to know herself safe in his love.

"I am afraid it must be," she whispered. "For now." And when he turned away, biting his lips together so as not to show his emotion, she would not allow him to take that first step. She slipped her hand back into the crook of his elbow and tugged him back to her. "Oh, please do not say I have lost your friendship," she begged. "I could not bear it. No one can fill the place you occupy in my heart, Ian."

"It must be a very small place, if you are not willing to give me room in your life."

But he wished her to make her life small in order to occupy it with him. There were some things, she was beginning to learn, on which a man and a woman could never agree.

"It is not small," she said. "It is unique."

"I will not wait any longer, Claire. I value your friendship also, but if another woman is willing to share my life and my responsibilities, I know my duty. I will not hesitate."

"I understand," she whispered.

He turned, she found herself in the circle of his

arms—and then he kissed her with all the power and passion of which he was capable, as if to remind her of exactly what she was prepared to lose.

Oh, if she did not know it before, she knew it fully now. She closed her eyes and fell into his kiss, enjoying for the last time the richness of what he was willing to give her. Realizing for the first time that she may never have such an opportunity for such a life with such a man again.

It was a wonderful kiss.

And he was a wonderful man.

And then, when he broke the kiss and turned away, she took a long breath ... and let him go.

A LADY OF RESOURCES

9

Snouts and Lewis stood beaming upon the step of 23 Wilton Crescent as Lizzie and Maggie dashed up the path and flew into their hugs. "How's our Mopsies, then?" Lewis said, squeezing Maggie and then releasing her to bow to the Lady. "Though we can't be calling you Mopsies any more, can we? You're fine young ladies now."

"And soon to be finer, thanks ever so." Lizzie hugged Snouts and led the way into the hall, where she dropped her valise on the black and white checkered marble and spun, arms lifted. "It's so good to be home!" She was halfway up the stairs when Snouts's voice stopped her.

"What do you mean, finer?" Snouts picked up the

valise and dropped it on the polished step below her. "There's no footman here to pick up after you, and Lewis has got better things to do."

Lizzie stuck out her tongue at him and raced up the stairs. What a way to spoil her homecoming, with nitting and picking. He wasn't her father—or her elder brother. He was just Snouts, and he couldn't tell her what to do. She had graduated from the fifth form in Munich, and he'd had no education at all apart from what the Lady had given him and what he'd been able to glean from the books in the library and his years at the Morton Glass Works.

"Back in fighting form, I see." Maggie bumped their bedroom door closed with her hip and dropped both valises next to their beds. This had been the Lady's room growing up, but when she had moved into her parents' room overlooking the garden, this one had become their exclusive domain. "You'd never know you'd been blown up by a bomb last night."

"I know it." Lizzie lifted her skirt—hems let down to a respectable ankle length when she had turned sixteen—to inspect one shin. "I have bruises on my legs the size of eggs, and I still can't hear properly in my left ear."

"Oh, is that why you ignored Lewis at the door and I had to carry up your valise?"

"A gentleman would have brought it up for me."

"And our Snouts isn't a gentleman, is that it? Or our Lewis?"

What a thing to say! "Of course they aren't."

"And you're not a lady, so I suggest you leave the

airs and graces to those that are born to them, and treat your friends as they ought to be treated."

Lizzie stared. Since when did Maggie speak to her like this?

"I don't mean to sound like Mademoiselle Dupree, but you hurt Snouts's feelings, too."

Lizzie flushed and turned away. "I nearly died last night. Some might think my feelings ought to be taken into account."

"I think some have. Our Lewis was so glad to see you he nearly burst, and you barely said hello."

"Are you quite finished?"

"Yes. Though I can't speak for everyone else."

"Then have the goodness not to."

Her only answer was the closing of the door, as Maggie left her alone and went down to the others, where Lizzie could hear the excited clamor of conversation and news.

Hmph. Well, she was above feeling sorry for herself. Why not think of something happy?

The letter had been burning a hole in her pocket the whole voyage, but since both she and Maggie were needed as crew along with the four automaton brains still obediently working in *Athena*'s hull, there had been absolutely no chance to read it after the footman had handed it to her.

The paper was thick and creamy—the kind that gentlemen bought, not schoolboys, or even the Lady, whose taste ran to the thinner sheets that the pigeons carried.

My dear Miss de Maupassant,

It is with great relief that I heard from your guardian that you had emerged relatively unscathed from your terrible experience of last night. I hope you will soon return to health, and that society will have the pleasure of meeting its newest ornament.

I hope your guardian has told you of my invitation to Colliford Castle. It is situated in a pretty valley in the Cotswolds not far from the Prince of Wales's summer estate, and is a lovely sight when the rays of the late-afternoon sun turn the stone to gold. I am told that the original keep dates back to Norman times, but most of it was demolished to build the wall of the larger castle in King Charles's day. The two towers are the first thing one sees rising above the oaks of the valley—in fact, I have fashioned a large telescope atop the western one so that I may indulge my bent for astronomy. It is said to be the most powerful in England save for that housed in the Greenwich Observatory.

I am patron of a young scientist, Evan Douglas, who has taken over the interior of the tower for his experiments in the new field of mnemosomniography. He is a connection of my late wife's, and his brilliance has already made him a name in that burgeoning field.

If the delights of science are not an attraction to a young lady of vivacious temperament, there are plenty of social events planned for our summer stay. I will let my son enclose a note giving that account.

A LADY OF RESOURCES

In the meanwhile, Miss de Maupassant, I very much hope that the estimable Lady Claire will permit herself a few days to enjoy a beautiful setting and good company. And, if you will forgive the liberty, I cherish the hope that we can overlook an inauspicious start and begin afresh as friends.

Yours sincerely,
Charles Seacombe

What a kind man! And how perceptive he was, to realize that, while the Lady's focus on changing the world was admirable, it could also be exhausting. A few days devoted to nothing but fun could only be good for them all, especially after the slog of final examinations and the excitement of graduation.

Eagerly, she ripped open the note enclosed, which ran to only one sheet and was covered in a slapdash hand with lots of underlines and flourishes.

Dear Lizzie—

Are you shocked that I have not Miss-ed you? You know you think of me as Claude and I think of you as Lizzie, so let us dispense at once with these tiresome honorifics, shall we?

Do prevail upon Lady Claire and the Dunsmuirs to come to Colliford. I shall be in quite the pet if you do not, and then we shall all descend upon you in London like a pack of harpies and she will regret her hard-heartedness!

Must dash—we're stopping in Paris on the way back to pick up my new skiff for the races, and I'm in the mood for a jolly razzle at the Moulin Rouge. Are you jealous?

Ever your
Claude

Laughing, shaking her head, Lizzie folded the letters one into the other and slipped them into the book she had been reading during the Christmas holidays.

Her friends might not appreciate her as much as they could, but at least there were *some* people in this world—knowledgeable, powerful people—who did. She was not such an immature fool as to believe the occupants of Wilton Crescent discounted her, or even that they did not love her. She had ample proof to the contrary, and perhaps she had been a bit of a snipe to the boys a little while ago. She would set that right and they would all be jolly again.

She smiled at herself.

Claude's slangy way of speaking was rubbing off. It must be the way the young, rich set spoke in Paris—the way the girls would speak in Geneva, at Maison Villeneuve. That was one more reason why she wanted with every fiber of her being to go to this country house party—she would watch Claude's friends and learn and practice the things they did and said. She was a good mimic. Not as good as Maggie, but good enough to pass herself off as one of the Paris set, careless and rich and ever so slightly blasé about the world.

A LADY OF RESOURCES

Oh, yes, she could do this.

All she had to do was convince the Lady.

తంలు

Lady Claire regarded the pile of correspondence upon her desk the next morning with some dismay. "Good heavens. There must be a month's worth of letters and invitations here. Lewis, why did you not forward them to us in Munich?"

"That lot's just come in the last week, Lady," he said. "Once it came out in the papers that the empress had shook yer 'and, it started, and it ent let up yet." As if to put a full stop to the sentence, the hydraulic system gave a whoosh and another tube dropped into the slot in the library wall behind them.

"We shall be inundated. Lizzie, call your sister. We must sort the urgent from the mundane at once."

Lizzie slipped past Lewis with a smile, and he stood aside a little stiffly, as if he had not quite forgiven her despite the pretty apology she had made to him and Snouts last night.

Ah well. His feelings always had been a little touchy, probably from the less kind of the boys perpetually calling him Loser, though no one did that now. He had become a sort of general factotum to the Lady, who introduced him as her secretary upon the occasions that called for it. Snouts no longer held that position, having bigger fish to fry at the Morton Glass Works. She would chivvy him out of his sulks and they would be good friends as they had been before, just you wait.

She fetched Maggie from her unpacking and the two of them pulled up chairs around the great oak desk.

"We must sort these, girls. Invitations shall go to Maggie, letters to me, and Lizzie, you take everything else and sort it by type."

Within the hour, Maggie's pile was much higher than either of the other two. "How popular we are," she said in a wondering tone, waving one that possessed engraving and a red seal.

Lady Claire looked up from a letter that bore a schoolboy's scrawl and the St. Ives family crest. "Maggie, darling, that one is from Buckingham Palace. Do be careful. What does it say?"

"Her Majesty the Queen requests the honor of your company at a garden party." She peered at the date. "This afternoon."

"Good heavens. Really? We must send our regrets—our trunks haven't come and unless Her Majesty wishes the honor of our raiding rigs as well, we have nothing to wear."

"Here's another, Lady." Maggie picked up a similar invitation, with a slightly smaller seal. "His Highness the Prince Consort, in his capacity of patron of the Royal Society of Engineers, requests the honor of your attendance at the investiture of the newest members of the Society. Is that like getting a knighthood?"

Claire laughed. "No indeed. More like a stamp of approval. Who is being invested this year? There should be a list."

Maggie read through the names, then stumbled. "Lady Claire Trevelyan, Carrick House, London. Lady, that's you!"

Claire's face flushed with pleasure. "I did receive notice of it some weeks ago, but thought I would be included next year, at the earliest. How lovely! When is it?"

"The twentieth of July."

"Oh, no, Lady," Lizzie blurted before she thought. "We'll be at Colliford Castle still. Don't you remember? We've been invited for the fifteenth to the twentieth."

Claire took the invitation from Maggie to read it again, and Lizzie had the distinct impression that she was not listening.

"Lady? I said—"

"Yes, I heard you, Lizzie." She clasped the invitation to the embroidered bodice of her blouse in delight. "It is a dream come true, girls. I shall be a member of the Royal Society at long last—and by invitation of Prince Albert, too!" Claire laid the invitation down and smoothed her fingers over the engraving. "There will be other opportunities to visit Colliford Castle this summer, I am sure, but only one to be invested as a member of the Royal Society. Unless you would rather I wait until next year for this honor, so that you may spend a week boating with your new friends?"

Lizzie tried not to wilt under the pleasant inquiry in her tone and the steel gray in her eyes.

It wasn't easy.

"I only meant ... I'm sure they would not be offended if we cut our visit a little short. Four days are almost as good as five."

"You are assuming that we are going to begin with. I have not yet decided."

"When will you decide?" Oh, she could not wait to be eighteen, when she would never need to say those words again.

"After I confer with Davina. I would rather be part of a larger party, and not put Mr. Seacombe to the trouble of preparing his home for only three guests."

"Oh, there will be more than just us," she said eagerly. Here was a point on which she could give positive information. "Claude's friends from the Sorbonne will be coming. I don't know how many there are, but we won't be the only ones there."

"It is immaterial in any case, Lizzie. We are three unmarried women, and the Seacombes are unmarried men. We could not accept such an invitation on our own, school friends notwithstanding."

This had never occurred to Lizzie. "But—but Mr. Seacombe is *ancient!*"

"When it comes to propriety, age does not matter, I am afraid." But she did not look very sad about it. "We must go in the Dunsmuirs' company, or not at all. And really, on such short acquaintance I would prefer not at all." At Lizzie's indignant squeak, she went on, "At least, not until we get to know the family better. Lord Dunsmuir, for one, seemed to be of very mixed opinions on the subject."

"Bother Lord Dunsmuir," Lizzie muttered.

"I heard that. But I have my own misgivings. Does

it not strike you as alarming that Mr. Seacombe concealed a bomb upon his person to wear it to a party?"

"He brought it to show to Count von Zeppelin!"

"I am sure he had complete confidence that it would not go off during the dancing," the Lady said with some irony. "But the fact remains that between the two of you, you are responsible for the deaths of three men."

"Those bully-boys intended to hurt us, Lady." Lizzie could not believe it—she had barely escaped with her life, and she was being blamed for the explosion?

"I realize that. I also realize that the matter is in the hands of the magistrates now, and that it is entirely possible you had more to fear from the bully-boys than from Mr. Seacombe, and I am being unfair to him. Now let us change the subject. What is in your pile?"

"Nothing of interest." And there wasn't. What good did court circulars and notices of art exhibits and subscriptions to scientific periodicals do anyone? Even if she wanted to go to an art exhibit, the Lady probably wouldn't let her.

"It is a lucky thing the chickens are not in the house," Lady Claire said quietly. "One might be tempted to roost upon your lower lip."

Maggie giggled, and to Lizzie's disgust, a smile flickered on her own lips—the lower one included. "It's just not fair," she mumbled.

"I remember many things not being fair when I was sixteen, which was not so long ago. Are you so anxious for this visit, darling, despite what you know?"

There was hope! "Yes, Lady, ever so much." Lizzie leaned forward, pushing the pile of circulars out of the way. "Mr. Seacombe has never been anything but kind and generous to me. I want to make friends with them—with Claude's set. There might be girls there who are going to Geneva, too, and I would have friends when I arrive. Don't you see?"

"I do see," Claire said slowly. "I see that this is a means to an end that you seem set on. It is to be finishing school, then, despite Maggie's and my feelings on the subject?"

"I want to go, Lady."

"A woman is not restricted merely to being an ornament to society, dear one. She can fill a useful place—it is still possible to use one's mind while making the world better for others."

Mr. Seacombe, man of the world that he was, had said he looked forward with pleasure to society's newest ornament. "But being an ornament does not mean being brittle and shallow, with conversation that means less than the tinkle of a music box. A woman can be an ornament to society in good ways— encouraging others, supporting her friends, creating places where people can shine and enjoy themselves."

The Lady addressed herself to little Lord Nicholas's letter once again. "And while she is making life beautiful for others, what is she doing for her own?"

Which was just so completely puzzling that Lizzie was sure the Lady, for once, had missed the point.

Maggie squirmed, as if her corset were not sitting comfortably. Finally, she burst out, "But Lizzie, you don't mean for me to go with you to finishing school, do you? Because I am quite sure I should hate it."

"You must make your own choice, Maggie," the Lady said. She slit open another envelope and began to read. "Be influenced by nothing other than your own heart and mind."

A fine thing to say, when the Lady herself was trying to influence Lizzie away from the choice of *her* heart and mind!

"I want to go back to Munich with you, and complete sixth form," Maggie pleaded. "What should I do without you, Liz? Who will I sit with in the park, and laugh with about Sophie Bug Eyes?"

"Sadly, it seems Sophie is going to Maison Villeneuve, too. If you came with me, we could do those things still."

But Maggie only shook her head, staring blindly at the pile of invitations on the table. Never mind. Lizzie still had the whole summer in which to convince her sister that they needed to make this decision together, and choose a path together, the way they always had.

She would succeed. She and Maggie had never been separated before, and there was no reason to begin now.

10

The letter that had arrived as they were sorting the week's mail turned out to be a note from Lady Dunsmuir inviting their entire household to dinner the next evening, with cards and charades to follow. Lizzie suspected that, before they flew to his estate in Scotland for the summer and stayed for the shooting in August, Lord Dunsmuir wanted to come up to scratch on all the latest hands of Cowboy Poker. And who better to teach him than the boys who had been covertly running the card rooms of London for the last several years?

Besides acting as the Lady's secretary, Lewis had built quite the empire. He even owned the building in which the Gaius Club was housed, though he was careful never to appear in any guise there but messenger boy or general factotum. It would not do to let the up-and-coming Wit gentlemen who played there know that the young man who occasionally cleared their empty glasses or carried messages between floors was a former alley mouse building a comfortable life for himself and one or two of the other boys who had gone in with him on the investment.

Since the Lady's steam landau would only carry four, and Hatley House was not far away, they walked to dinner as the soft summer twilight brought out the electrick lamps on the streets of Belgravia.

"I'm not sure it's quite the done thing to walk," Lizzie murmured to Maggie, making a detour around what were clearly bird droppings under one of the trees in the square. "We should have taken a hansom cab."

"We'd have made quite a parade, with Snouts, Lewis, you and I, the Lady, and the younger ones. Three cabs, at least."

"We didn't have to bring the younger ones. The Lady never brought us when we were that age. Where did Snouts find them?" He was given, occasionally, to bringing street sparrows home, but now and again it had turned out badly. The one girl whose light fingers had been caught in the Lady's jewel-box had been escorted to the local orphanage with enough cash to keep her for a year, and she had not been back.

"Same place as he found us, Liz. Have you forgotten so soon?"

"You sound like Tigg. His ragging on me about forgetting where I came from got me blown up by a pocket watch."

"Your picking Mr. Seacombe's pocket got you blown up by a pocket watch, you goose. Don't blame Tigg for your actions."

"If he hadn't ragged, I wouldn't have done it, would I?"

"It was a choice—and you chose to be contrary. You could have just disagreed and gone away and had dessert."

No. At the time, she could not. That contrary spirit had taken hold of her and it had not even occurred to her to simply disagree and have dessert.

"You'd have done the same, in my place," she said, though that wasn't completely true. Maggie thought first and acted second—the opposite of Lizzie herself. The good thing was, between the two of them, things got done ... just not quite the way one often expected.

The Dunsmuirs welcomed them with hugs and kisses (on her ladyship's part) and firm handshakes (on his lordship's part). Willie barreled into the Lady and flung his arms around her waist in a hug, as if he hadn't just seen her a day or two ago. When he turned to Lizzie, she realized that he had been growing again.

"You're nearly up to my chin, now, Your Weediness," she said, laughing, as he hugged her. "You'll be as tall as your papa before long."

"I hope so." His eyes shone and the dimples in his cheeks came and went as he smiled up at her. "I need to be able to see over the wheel on *Lady Lucy* before papa will let me take the helm."

Lizzie made big surprised eyes at him. "And what

does Captain Hollys say to that?"

"He is not saying very much," Willie confided to her, standing on tiptoe to whisper. "The Lady has declined to be his wife and he is very unhappy."

"*Has* she?" Now her surprise was real. Lady Claire had not said a single word on the subject—which meant that perhaps she was just as unhappy. "Then you must be extra kind to him."

"I am." The boy nodded. "I made him a sextant out of my mathematical compasses and some of the gears out of the mother's helper. He said it cheered him immensely to know that there was hope of a right course in the end. What did he mean, Lizzie? What else would he use a sextant for?"

She laughed—he was turning out to be as literal-minded as she was herself. "You will have to ask him in about ten years, Will-Be-Famous."

"Wilberforce."

"Right. I forgot again. Your Weediness." And she tickled him in the ribs, which made Maggie join in, and they all tumbled laughing into the big receiving room. It had been set up with supper tables and card tables and sofas and chairs, all jumbled together so that one could do whatever one liked whenever one liked to do it.

That was the lovely thing about the Dunsmuirs—they tailored their parties to the needs and enjoyments of their guests. And no one could say that Lady Davina Dunsmuir had no influence in the world, could they? Why, she practically held the western half of the Canadas in her soft palm, and was considered one of the principal advisors to the Queen, though she held no official post in the government. How could the Lady think that such a course was not the right one for a young girl like Lizzie, when she had such a marvelous example right in front of her?

When they had finished a delicious dinner of prawns and roundels of pork with lingonberry sauce sent by special post from Lord Peterborough in Charlottetown, Lady Dunsmuir rose from her seat. Such was the power of that gentle gaze that the room fell silent in expectation.

What news? Lizzie telegraphed to Maggie in a glance.

"I am so glad to have you all with us tonight," Lady Dunsmuir said, gazing over them fondly. The youngest ones gazed back, awestruck at her quiet grace and the way she could control a room with just her eyes. "His lordship and I have some wonderful news, and there is no one we should like to first share it with, than you."

Willie wriggled and finally leaped out of his chair. "Mama, may I tell? May I?"

"I think that would be most appropriate, darling."

Willie faced them, his face red with the importance of the announcement. "I'm going to be a brother!"

The Lady clasped her hands. "Oh, Davina! Can it be true?"

"It is indeed." The countess beamed, her hands clasped in front of her stomach under a gown that Lizzie suddenly realized was cut in the new artistic style, falling from the shoulders instead of from the waist.

"Willie will become a big brother in November, and he is already preparing. Whether it is a girl or a boy, he has already modified a mother's helper to come and fetch me or his lordship whenever there is a sound over a certain pitch from the nursery." She gazed upon her son with love, and tousled his hair. "Is he not the cleverest child?"

"I'm not a child, Mama," he mumbled into her robe. "I'm a *big brother*."

The room erupted in congratulations, Lady Claire embracing her friends again and again, and it was some time before everyone could settle to cards or charades. Lizzie watched her ladyship, taken anew by her earlier thoughts. Here was a woman who could do the things Lizzie herself had said—create an environment where others were at their best—have an influence for good upon them—and yet fill a woman's natural sphere with confidence and joy. What was her secret?

Lizzie was not as skilled a mathematician as some, but even she could see the equation falling into place. Her whole future, it seemed, hung on the Dunsmuirs' joining them for this country house visit. And the Dunsmuirs' doing anything, as everyone in the room knew, hung on Lady Dunsmuir's approval. Therefore, her future depended on getting Davina to agree to come.

And she had not a moment to lose.

Lizzie was a dab hand at looking harmless and decorative while practicing the art of deception and outwitting her opponent. These skills had served her well over the years, and she called them up now. As Lady

Dunsmuir rose gracefully and went in search of a book for Claire in the library, Lizzie slipped out of the small audience watching the charades and followed her.

Of course, what she didn't expect was to find Davina locked in a kiss with his lordship in the history section.

She must have made a sound, because the couple pulled apart and Davina, looking rather flustered, patted her pompadour into place. "Lizzie, darling? Was there something you wanted?"

"I'm sorry, I—no indeed—I mean—" Well, she couldn't very well say *Carry on* and back out of the door now, could she? "Your ladyship, I do beg your pardon. I did want a word, but obviously this isn't a good time, so—"

His lordship laughed. "I'm afraid one has to expect the unexpected in this house. Willie has become quite used to seeing his parents exchanging tokens of affection. We forget it can be disconcerting to others. Is this a conversation to which gentlemen are welcome?"

"Oh, yes indeed, sir. In fact, it affects you directly."

"Does it, now? In that case, do come and sit down."

Lizzie settled into a comfortable upholstered chair opposite the couple on the sofa. Both chair and sofa were clearly for the purpose of whiling away a rainy afternoon with a good book. She took a breath and plunged in, conscious that anyone could walk in on them just as she had done herself. "I would like to ask your help concerning my future."

His lordship looked a little taken aback, and exchanged a glance with his wife that Lizzie could not read. "Is that not the province of Lady Claire, Lizzie? Though that is not to say that we are not deeply interested in the futures of all of you, as friends would be, considering what we have all experienced together."

"It is, and I have spoken with her about it, but she believes that it is your opinion that will prevail."

Lady Dunsmuir leaned forward. "Can you be more specific, Lizzie?"

"As you probably know, Mr. Charles Seacombe has invited the Lady and Maggie and me to his estate in the Cotswolds for a brief visit—only four days. But the Lady says it is not proper for three unmarried females to visit a house occupied by two—or more—unmarried men."

Lady Dunsmuir's lips twitched. "I can see the reason for her concern. It will not do, Lizzie, as I am sure you can see."

Here was the crux of the matter on which all else depended. "But it *would* do, your ladyship, if you and Lord Dunsmuir and Willie were to join us there. He has specifically invited you all as well, has he not?"

"He has," Lady Dunsmuir allowed. "Though I had not given it much thought before now. We hardly know him, and I had planned to decline."

She must not let that happen. "But this is how we might get to know him better."

"Why should we do that?" his lordship asked. "You know my opinion of the man, Lizzie."

She must tread carefully here, and at all costs avoid

the appearance of arguing. "I do, sir, but do you not feel that a few days in his company might change your mind? In any case, my eyes are fixed on a more distant horizon. I have learned that his son, Claude, has invited several of his classmates from the Sorbonne, some of whom have sisters attending Maison Villeneuve in Geneva. I cannot help but feel that making the acquaintance of these girls will allow me to feel more at home there when I begin in the autumn." She allowed her earnest gaze to fall. "I fear I shall be alone, you see. Maggie has almost certainly decided to go back to Munich with the Lady." Her voice broke with real emotion, as if this course had truly been decided. The reality was that she could not face it if that were true.

Lady Dunsmuir extended a hand in distress. "Oh, Lizzie, please do not cry. But how dreadful for you, to be separated by such a distance from your sister!"

Lizzie gulped down her tears, bravely lifting her head. "I shall bear it if I must, because I would not deprive her of her education for the world."

"And what of your education?" his lordship asked. "I cannot believe that there will be experiments in physics and engineering in Geneva."

No, there would not, thank goodness. "I have been observing your wife's example for many years, your lordship, and have concluded that I would be happiest following it."

"*My* example?" Lady Dunsmuir said in surprise.

"You have a gift, my lady, for making others feel welcome and comfortable in your home—for planning things that would please others while attaining your own goals—for, oh, I can't express it—for creating places where others become their best. You have influence and grace and the respect of the most powerful in the nation ... and physics and engineering did not assist you."

"You are in the right of it there." She glanced with affection at her husband. "I believe, however, that it was my aim with a bow which began my career."

She must not let them drift away on a tide of reminiscence, the way older people tended to do.

"I want to emulate the best of men and women," she said earnestly, "and I believe I must begin in Geneva. What better foundation could I have than with friendships that began here, under your eye? That is all I ask, your ladyship. Your protection and chaperonage as I take my first steps along a path that, while they may not bring me to the heights you have scaled, at least may give me the kind of influence and respect that a lady deserves ... who has not been born to such a sphere."

Another glance between husband and wife. "How eloquent you are, Lizzie," her ladyship said. "And you have the right of it—I was not born to the sphere I occupy, either. Have you presented your case to Claire?"

"I have, and she says that you must be the arbiter of it."

"Then it appears that world peace hinges on our making an appearance. John, darling, do you object to five days in Warwickshire?"

"Only four," Lizzie interjected, as if less time in the company of Mr. Seacombe would be a benefit. "Lady Claire must return to London a day early. She is to be invested by the Royal Society of Engineers on the twentieth of July."

"In support of a young lady's aspirations, I suppose I can endure anything for four days," his lordship conceded with some reluctance. "It would break the voyage to Scotland quite nicely, Davina. I do not want you becoming fatigued."

"An air journey does not fatigue me in the least, and you must not fuss, dearest. But I confess that I do enjoy the Cotswolds, and do not forget that the Prince of Wales will be traveling thither at about the same time."

"Deuce take it, we're not invited to that confounded hullaballoo again, are we?" His lordship straightened in alarm.

"Every year, dear."

"Then by all means let us tell him we are engaged at Seacombe's. I shall consider myself lucky to have made the escape."

Lizzie hardly dared breathe, much less ask, but she felt driven to clinch the deal. "So you will come? On the fifteenth? We shall all go together?"

"Yes, drat and bebother it," Lord Dunsmuir sighed. "It is the lesser of two evils, and I shall call you to account for it one day."

"Oh, thank you, sir!" Lizzie leaped from her chair, hugged them both, and danced deliriously from the room before either of them could reconsider.

11

Lizzie gazed out the viewing port, and observed that on the ground below as they came in for their landing, four young men had abandoned a pair of girls on a blanket next to the river. Dressed in casual boating jackets and linen trousers, they galloped across the field to catch the landing ropes before the startled groundsmen could get there, and had *Athena* tied to her mooring mast and her gangway down before *Lady Lucy* was fairly secured.

Lizzie was first off the ship, to a raucous greeting by Claude, who swung her around in a hug. "I'm so glad you're here!" he cried. He set her down and indicated his three companions with a sweep of one arm. "These are my partners in mischief, but never mind that, you must come with us and settle our question at once."

"And what is that?" Lizzie said, laughing, allowing herself to be borne along by the boys with only the barest, tiniest bit of guilt at abandoning Maggie and Lewis and the Lady before they'd so much as set a foot on the ground.

Well, goodness, Maggie was as welcome as anyone. She could catch them up if she wanted to. Everyone knew Lewis was shy in company, so he would take longer to warm up, but by the time they'd finished supper, she had no doubt they'd all be the best of friends and merry as grigs.

"Simply this," Claude said, pulling her along. "Adolphus here says that when the old Queen dies, the crown ought to go to the Prince of Wales. But I say, and the pater says, that the prince is so ruddy ancient that it ought to skip him on grounds of simple economy, and go straight to Prince George—or someone more suitable."

"You know that won't do, Claude," laughed the young man in the enormous bow-tied cravat whom Lizzie presumed must be Adolphus. "You're bucking a thousand years of history and tradition. It will never happen."

"Of course it will." One of the girls joined in the conversation as though it had never been interrupted by the airships' arrival. "The Prince of Wales has got to be fifty or sixty at least, and his fast living and bad habits are going to make an end to him sooner rather than later. You can't deny it saves England a walloping great deal of money to simply skip him as a bad job, and move on."

"Move on to what, though?" Lizzie found herself saying. "If you don't observe the rights of succession, you're looking at a republic and ending the monarchy altogether, as they've done in France."

Claude whooped and slapped Adolphus on the knee. "She's got you there, cornered, tied, and served up for dinner, old chap!" He flopped onto the blanket and chortled in glee. "I knew you would fit right in, Lizzie, old thing!"

"Mind whom you're calling old," she said pertly. "As a college man, you're practically out to grass."

Far from taking offense, this sent Claude into a fresh paroxysm of laughter as he lay on his back on the blanket.

"Do introduce us, Claude, darling," said the brunette reclining closest to the picnic basket. "I want to know the girl who can arrive in a perfect wreck of an airship and trounce you so soundly without even breaking her stride."

"It isn't a wreck." Lizzie snapped to *Athena*'s defense. "It's the prototype ship for the Zeppelin automaton intelligence system."

"Goodness, what a lot of syllables," drawled the other girl, a blonde who rolled over and regarded Lizzie from under the brim of a straw hat so beautifully trimmed that Lizzie coveted it on the spot. "How exhausting."

"*Breathing* is exhausting for you, Arabella," the first girl said, and extended her hand. "Since an introduction is clearly beyond Claude, I shall do it myself. I'm Cynthia von Stade, Dolly's sister. I'm so pleased to meet you, after all we've heard of you from this wretch here. He's really quite smitten."

"Give me away, why don't you," came from under the boater with which Claude had covered his face, evidently worn out by his own humor.

"How do you do?" How she wished she had Cynthia's artless way of speaking, as though they were already fast friends. "Elizabeth de Maupassant, but do call me Lizzie. Everyone does."

"Elizabeth!" The Lady chose that particular moment of all moments to call her full name from across the field. "Come and pay your respects to our host, if you please."

Arabella giggled and Lizzie got up off the blanket, pulling her dignity around her, though she felt like a five-year-old being called in to tea. Fortunately Mr. Seacombe was as glad to see her as his son, though he was much more dignified about showing it.

"I am so glad to see you again, Miss de Maupassant," he said, shaking her hand in a firm grip. "And Lord Dunsmuir, Lady Dunsmuir, Lord Wilberforce, words cannot express how happy I am to welcome you to my home here in England."

Lord Dunsmuir shook his hand with a little more enthusiasm than he might have had he not known how closely he'd escaped the Prince of Wales's "hullaballoo," whatever that was.

"It is our pleasure, sir. And now, if you don't mind, I do not wish to keep my wife standing in the sun. She is in a rather, er, delicate condition."

Understanding dawned immediately. "Of course, of course. I have tea waiting inside, and perhaps a little drop of something stronger would not go amiss?"

As the little party paced away across the lawn, Lizzie took Maggie's hand as she made to join them. "Come on, and I'll introduce you to everyone once I get them all straight myself."

The languid Arabella Montgomery turned out to be the sister of Darwin Montgomery, a lad as lanky as she was petite. She and Cynthia had just finished their first year at Maison Villeneuve. "We shall tell you all about it," Cynthia promised. "The good, the bad, and the perfectly dreadful—by which I mean table service. You will make no missteps with us to look after you, have no fear."

"I don't think Miss Arabella plans to look after anyone," Maggie whispered.

"She was just being polite," Lizzie whispered back. "And don't call her Miss Arabella. Among equals, we just use first names."

"Equals, is it?" Maggie murmured.

She lifted her eyebrows in polite interest as Cynthia indicated the young man standing next to Arabella over at the river's edge, looking into the water through his amber spectacles as though he could see the fish fanning themselves at the bottom. "That's Claude's cousin Geoffrey, and somewhere hereabouts is his other cousin. Claude, darling, what's his name? The scientific one who always looks at you as though you're some species of baboon?"

"In my cousin's mind, that sacred organ being evolved far beyond those of the rest of us, I *am* a baboon," came from under the hat. "But for informational purposes only, his name is Evan Douglas." Claude removed the boater at last and sat up. "It's not likely you'll see him. He is engaged in Serious Work and does not have time for fribbles such as we."

Cynthia laughed at his capital letters and italics, and Lizzie smiled as well. "So instead of a madwoman in the attic, we have a perambulatory brain in the tower?" she asked.

"You have the right of it," Claude told her with a nod. "One does not cross the holy threshold without an invitation, which I have been waiting for these two long years." He shook his head sadly.

"Then you shall have to make do with us," Lizzie told him, tucking her hand into his elbow with such easy familiarity that Maggie looked shocked. "I do not care for heights, so receiving no invitation to the tower will not hurt my feelings in the least."

"And having to listen to his interminable lectures on mnemosomniography will not hurt your brain," Cynthia said. "What luck all round."

Claude groaned. "Must we discuss it? Such a crashing bore—the very name puts me to sleep."

"Just because you aren't invited to see his work doesn't mean someone else might not find it interesting," Arabella chided, gliding back to the blanket and seating herself gracefully. She gazed at Maggie as if she had just this moment noticed her sitting next to Lizzie.

Which was quite possible.

"Mnemosomniography is the study of imprinting dreams and memories upon some physical means of observing them," she explained, as if to children who did not understand how to hold a cup. "You are familiar with the way cameras work?"

"Of course," Maggie said. "But how do you extract an image from inside someone's head?"

"The difficulty exactly," Geoffrey said, joining them. "Hence the years of study."

He made it sound as if Maggie were stupid. Lizzie bristled. "It's a fair question. I should like to know the answer myself. *If* you know."

Cynthia bit her lip and twinkled at the twins. "Bella knows. Don't you, darling? I saw you come out of the tower a time or two last summer, did I not?"

Arabella merely raised an eyebrow as fine as a butterfly's feeler. "Perhaps." Then she turned to Maggie. "He has invented a machine that detects the images in the mind. His goal is to have them projected from the sleeping brain like the flickers at the theatre, but so far that eludes him. He has succeeded in securing one or two plates, however, from the minds of some of the villagers."

"Nightmares seem to work best," Claude put in. "Macabre, what?"

"They would be the most vivid, I expect," Lizzie said. Goodness, the things these people talked about. Most people, lying on a blanket by the river, would have nothing more interesting to remark upon than the quality of the food in the basket, or an estimation of the ant population in the meadow.

"That is what Evan says," Arabella remarked. "Perhaps you should volunteer to be his next subject."

—tawny eyes—

—a crack—

Lizzie blinked the image away, swallowed, and put on a smile. "Perhaps I shall."

৵৽

Dinner that night, while a merry affair, did not see them all as friendly as Lizzie would have liked. Mr. Seacombe sat at one end of the long, formal table, with Lady Dunsmuir, as the only married woman present, at the other. Lady Claire sat at his right hand, with Lord Dunsmuir upon his left and Lizzie next to him. But after that, rules of precedence seemed to be abandoned, which was unfortunate. Had Lizzie been in charge of seating arrangements, she would have put Lewis next to herself instead of next to Arabella, where the poor young man spent half the evening writhing in embarrassment at her careless sarcasm, too polite to give as good as he got and too unsure of himself to take up conversation with Cynthia on his other side and Geoffrey opposite.

Tomorrow she would see that girl put in her place, see if she didn't.

Between Lizzie and Maggie sat the mysterious Evan Douglas. Even superior brains, she supposed, must be fed at intervals. The conversation on the picnic blanket still in her mind, she turned to him after the first course had been removed.

"I understand you are the protégé of Mr. Seacombe, Mr. Douglas. Are you seeing success in your work?"

It took him a moment to respond, as though he had been somewhere else in his mind—somewhere quite a distance from Colliford Castle. "Hm? Yes … well, no. It varies."

Maggie came to her rescue. "The study of mnemosomniography seems fascinating—and difficult. I should think that one's success might be many years in coming."

Lizzie took the opportunity to examine him. He sat straight in his chair, not slouching as Claude did, and while he was dressed for dinner as a gentleman might be, in black tie and jacket, the tie looked as though it could be secondhand, and his shirt did not lie as smoothly as Claude's did. With rag picking in her past, Lizzie could spot such differences without difficulty, and concluded that Mr. Douglas had not come to Colliford prepared with dinner clothes, and had been forced to borrow some of Claude's.

"How long have you been working in the laboratory here?" she asked, when he did not seem inclined to respond to Maggie.

"Two years, more or less."

"And it is housed in the tower?"

"You seem well enough informed that these questions are rather unnecessary."

For a moment, Lizzie couldn't think of a word to say. Then, "Perhaps you might give us a little more information to work with."

"My work is not the subject of dinner-table conversation."

"Oh, come, Evan, don't be such a stick," Claude said, leaning around a bouquet of lilies to address him. "The ladies are curious, that's all. How often do you suppose they sit at table with someone of your scientific stature?"

"Quite often, actually," Lizzie said pleasantly to Claude, when the young scientist did not reply. "Mr. Andrew Malvern is rather a good friend, and we've spent many a day in his laboratory assisting with his experiments."

At last Evan Douglas had found something at least as interesting as the vistas in his mind—or his leg of lamb. "You don't say? I have enormous respect for Mr. Malvern, though of course our fields of study are very different."

Maggie spoke up. "We count several engineers among our acquaintance. Lady Claire is to be inducted into the Royal Society of Engineers on Friday. That is the reason we are returning to London a day early."

"Returning early?" Arabella murmured. "Such a pity."

The young man's gaze swung from Maggie to the Lady. "This Lady Claire, to whom I was just introduced? She is one of the co-inventors of the Malvern-Terwilliger Kinetick Carbonator?"

"Yes, and said Terwilliger is at present out in your park, aboard *Lady Lucy*," Maggie informed him, her generous spirit giving him the gift of knowledge she thought might please him. "He is a lieutenant serving under Captain Hollys."

Now Evan put down his knife and fork altogether. "You are having me on."

"She is not," Lady Claire said pleasantly. "Would you like us to introduce you after dinner?"

"I should like that very much. I had no idea Cousin Charles moved in such intelligent circles. I had been avoiding the party fearing that the current one had simply multiplied."

Lizzie raised her damask napkin to her lips for fear she would laugh out loud. Cynthia looked amused, and Arabella's expression had merely narrowed with something approaching dislike, as if she knew she had been slighted, but it was only to be expected, considering the source. Perhaps he had scorned her last summer, and the sting had not been cured by the attentions of someone else.

"I am sure Lieutenant Terwilliger would be delighted to meet you, Mr. Douglas," Lady Dunsmuir said. "Might I send for him and Captain Hollys to join us for coffee and brandy, Mr. Seacombe?"

"My dear lady," he said, raising his voice a little to accommodate the length of the table, "you must treat my home as your own, and issue both instructions and invitations as you see fit."

"Lovely," Lizzie said happily. She leaned past Evan to catch Maggie's eye. "Lewis will have someone to talk to."

"Is he having difficulty?" Evan looked about to locate the young man in question. "That person there, next to Miss Montgomery? He looks a most competent individual."

"He is, when he is in his proper sphere," Lizzie said. "At the moment he is a bit out of his depth."

"As am I," Maggie said.

"Why should you be?" His brows bunched under the floppy curls on his forehead, innocent of either comb or macassar oil, if Lizzie was any judge.

She shrugged. "We weren't born to … this. We have grown to it."

"What, precisely?"

Lizzie stiffened and attempted to get Maggie's attention behind Evan's shoulder. Now was not the moment for honesty—or for revealing their humble beginnings. That was the kind of information one shared with trusted friends, and while many in the present company were friendly, she could not yet say they were friends.

Or trusted.

Maggie waved a hand that took in the room, from the silver candlesticks to the oil paintings of hunting scenes hung on the high walls. "All this. Castles. Crystal. Cash."

"And yet you are here," Evan pointed out.

"Only by the grace of friendship and the kindness of Mr. Seacombe."

"What *were* you born to, Margaret?" Arabella inquired from across the table, leaning slightly to one side as the vegetables were served at her elbow.

Maggie, no—don't—no one wants the truth right now—

"Me and Liz, we was born under the sound o'

Bow's bells," Maggie said in the accents of their childhood. "We was proper alley mice, for true, until the Lady found us and took us in. Five years on, we become proper ladies, but I still don't know one fork from anovver like you lot."

Cynthia laughed in delight. "You precious thing! What a good accent she does, doesn't she, Geoffrey? We must get up a play or at least a tableau while we are here, so she can do it again."

"But I was—" Maggie began.

Lizzie cut her off. "She's an amazing mimic. She does Count von Zeppelin, too—so good you'd swear he was in the room."

"Go on, Miss Margaret," Darwin said. "Show us."

But Maggie was looking at her strangely, as if she didn't understand how badly Lizzie wanted the subject to change at all. "I would rather not," she said. "He is our friend and I should be a poor one myself if I were to make him the subject of ridicule."

"But it isn't ridicule. Mimicry is entertainment."

"You number Count von Zeppelin among your friends as well?" Evan asked.

"Yes, he is our sponsor at the Lycée des Jeunes Filles," Lizzie told him. "Or was. Mr. Seacombe is my sponsor now, I suppose." She smiled at that gentleman. "Thanks to his very generous bursary."

"Sponsor? Bursary?" Claude sat up, the better to understand, one presumed. "So you are dependent upon funds given or won to pursue your educations, then? Your families do not foot the bill?"

She had scrabbled out of the conversational pit,

only to be dragged back in by Claude, of all people.

"Really, Claude," Arabella said on a sigh. "One does not bring up such things at the table. Interesting though the subject might be."

"Maggie was quite serious, you know," Lord Dunsmuir said. "She and her sister and Lewis were street orphans long ago—and I thank God every day for it. If it had not been for them, we should never have seen our son again."

Willie, who had been permitted to attend a dinner mostly populated by young people, grinned at his father, then leaned in to turn an earnest gaze upon Claude at the other end, clearly anxious that the facts should be given. "Lizzie and Maggie and Lewis and me, we sang for our supper, and picked pockets, and slept on the rag-pile in the squat dockside. Until the Lady came."

"Rag-pile," murmured Arabella. "*Squat.* Fancy that."

"It's true," Willie told her. "When the Lady came, we moved into the cottage in Vauxhall Gardens, but it burned down. We had chickens and a garden and we learned our letters and numbers and how to make—"

"You and my wards can be proud of what you all have accomplished in such a short time, can't you, Lord Will?" The Lady stopped his speech so sweetly and with such a soft smile that no one would suspect his little lordship had been about to say *bombs.* "Yourself among them. Why, even now, your skill at mechanics puts you well ahead of other boys your age."

Willie beamed at this praise from the Lady. The

conversation then turned to school, and thence to summer holidays, and then to the prospects for game in Scotland that summer.

But for Lizzie, the damage was already done.

Cynthia and Arabella and Claude and the rest would despise her now. Because really, in their eyes what was she? A street sparrow in borrowed plumage, twittering prettier notes but still able to squawk in the vernacular of the wharves and alleys.

After all the trouble she'd taken to come here and make friends with these people, one speech from her own sister had destroyed it all. And like Humpty Dumpty, once you fell off the wall between the classes, there was no putting you back together again.

12

Only the utmost self-control kept Claire from leaping into the conversational fray in the defense of the people she loved, dealing setdowns like cards and putting that insufferable blonde in her place with such smooth violence she would never feel the cut until moments later, when she began to bleed.

Claire had been in Lizzie's place, oh yes, far too many times. It was not an experience through which she would ever willingly put her dear girl, but since it had to happen, at least it was in her company and that of Davina, who was on full alert as well. Claire would never have suspected that Lizzie harbored this desire for the approval of those she saw as her "betters." Not her feisty Lizzie, who shot first and asked questions later, who up until this period in her life, had not cared tuppence for the opinions of anyone outside her most trusted circle.

Claire had to own that she felt a little grieved at this evidence of trust and respect leaking out of the tight bond of that circle and dribbling onto those who did not entirely appreciate it. But she could not say these things to Lizzie. As Claire knew from her own experience, there were some things that could be taught in a lecture, and others that could only be learned through hard experience.

Growing a spine fell into the latter category. She had no doubt that Lizzie would prove up to the challenge, but still ... it was difficult to watch.

After an interminable six courses, during which the atmosphere of conviviality changed to reveal that Maggie's announcement had indeed affected the opinions of the Sorbonne set, the Dunsmuirs invited the company aboard *Lady Lucy* for coffee and brandy, rather than calling Tigg from his duties. The young scientist seemed interested in going, which pleased Claire immensely. Perhaps he was immune to atmosphere, and indifferent to status. Certainly one could isolate oneself in the pursuit of science—but there was a difference between choosing isolation and having it inflicted upon you.

She had not missed the subtle interplay between Maggie and Lewis that resulted in Evan's being included in their conversations and fun, even while he was ignored by several of the others. The circle of the Sorbonne set had its boundaries, too, it was clear—and they were etched in gold.

She was just making her way toward the terrace when Mr. Seacombe cleared his throat behind her. "Lady Claire, if I might have a brief word with you and Miss Elizabeth before we all go out to *Lady Lucy*?"

Lizzie, hearing her name, paused on the threshold of the French doors.

"Certainly, sir," Claire said, though she couldn't imagine why he might want to speak privately with them. She would have thought he would approach Lord Dunsmuir about some business deal or other, or take her ladyship aside to request some favor at court.

Indicating with a raised brow that Lizzie should come with her, they followed him into a large room whose shelves were lined with books. On each of the walls hung four huge portraits, from a man dressed in the lace collar and hose of Charles I's reign to a blond lady in a meadow that Claire could swear had been painted by Winterhalter, the man who could make any woman beautiful—the man, perhaps, who thought every woman possessed her own particular kind of beauty.

"Are these portraits of your family, sir?" Claire asked. She had not heard that he came of ancestry long established in England, but then, she knew next to nothing about him. That was the purpose of this visit, was it not? And besides, that was Blood thinking. To a Wit, ancestry was more of a hindrance than a help.

"Heavens, no. I bought the castle furnished from

the family that had been established here—and the furnishings included all the portraits. They lend the place a feeling of solidity, of timelessness, do you not agree?"

Claire murmured an assent. Was she the only one in the room wondering what had happened to the family who had to leave their home and heritage behind?

Seacombe went on, "The only one that belongs to me is that one there." He indicated the blond lady over the fireplace mantel. "That was my second wife, may God rest her gentle soul."

At last, something personal about him.

Claire studied the portrait. "She was painted by Herr Winterhalter, was she not?"

"You have a good eye, my lady. Yes, she was, in the flower of her beauty some time after the birth of our daughter." He paused. "Do you see anything to remark upon in her likeness?"

What on earth could he mean? Puzzled, uncertain as to what he meant to draw her attention to, Claire stepped back to take it in. The portrait was nearly life size. "Her eyes are as green as yours, Lizzie," she said at last. "It is an unusual color in a woman so fair."

"It could be her dress," Lizzie pointed out. "You know how my eyes change depending on what I'm wearing, and a rich green like that would do the trick—if you would let me wear proper colors." She gave her a nudge.

"When you are eighteen you may wear whatever colors please you," Claire said with fondness. "Until then, dark colors are not suitable."

She returned her gaze to the portrait. Something wasn't right about it. Not the painting itself—a lady seated in a glade with a castle in the distance was a common artistic conceit. But something about her gown ... or the way she wore it ... or the jewels ...

That was it. She was not wearing a gown at all, but a silk wrap tied with a wide sash under the bosom, parting to reveal a waterfall of lace and voile that both concealed and hinted at the curves beneath. This was a portrait of a mistress, not a wife. The kind of portrait that a man kept in his private rooms, not displayed in a library with someone else's very formally dressed ancestors, as though to mock and expose her.

Then again, Claire reflected, she did not have the artistic temperament. Perhaps she was reading too much into it.

"Ah," Seacombe said. "I had hoped you would remark upon her eyes. And there are other similarities, too—the shape of the brows, the pointed chin."

A chill brushed down Claire's spine, and she looked over her shoulder to see if the windows were open. But they were not. "Similarities, sir? Outside of the eye color, I do not see many. Even the lady's hair is different. Lizzie was once a proper towhead like that ... but her hair has darkened each year as she has grown up."

Lizzie's gaze upon the portrait had become fixed.

Seacombe poured a small glass of amber liquid. "May I offer you spirits, my lady?" When she declined, he knocked it back in one motion and poured another. "Eleven years ago, I lived in London with my little family. My first wife contracted a fever and died young, but I found happiness again with Elaine Seacombe, a gentlewoman whose family had made their fortune in the steamship trade between Penzance and France. While my first wife's father gave me my start, it was Elaine's fortune that turned the tide. When she told me of her condition, I was overjoyed that Claude, then only four, would have a sibling."

"A sibling, sir?" Here was the proof that would fend off the crisis she could see looming. For in any story that involved her wards, there must be twins. Not a single child.

"And in the course of time, she was born—a little princess as blond as her mother, with my thoughtful forehead and high cheekbones. And my short temper and quick wit, as it turned out."

She must be certain. Whatever the end of this story, it could have nothing to do with them—Lizzie, Maggie, their little flock. "One child, sir? Not twins."

Standing before the portrait, Lizzie turned to watch Claire—her stillness, her pale face enough to make Claire's heart contract with distress.

Seacombe's pleasant smile sagged into lines of sorrow. "You are quite correct, my lady, having anticipated the ending of my tale. Not twins. My beloved Elaine's younger sister Catherine, I am sad to say, was delivered of a girl at the same time—within days of my daughter's birth, but in circumstances so very different that the family's shame could not be measured. She did not survive the birth. But my wife's heart yearned for the sister she had known in the days of her youth, and she begged me to bring her child into our household, to be nursed and raised together with our own. I could never refuse Elaine anything, and so it was done."

Lizzie was now as white as the papers scattered upon the desk. "Sir, if you do not want to see me burst into tears this moment, you will speak plainly. Who is this story about, please?"

"I will come to that as quickly as possible, my dear. When the girls were five, Elaine took them on one of the company airships down to Penzance via London to visit her family. As they passed over London, the engines seized and the ship went down—into the Thames, in full view of a shocked and disbelieving public."

Claire gasped. "I remember that! It was in all the papers. Your wife and the children were among the dead? How dreadful."

It was a terrible thing to feel relief at such an end to the story, but if the children had not lived, then this was all a mistake—the maunderings of a man who had never recovered from his loss, who looked on a girl with a resemblance to his wife and could not separate the past from the present.

"Claude had remained home with some childhood illness—chickenpox, I think—so he alone was left to me." He turned to Lizzie, who had begun to tremble with repressed emotion. Claire took a step toward her, but Seacombe got there first and took Lizzie's hands. "All aboard were lost—and despite dragging the river and searching the banks, no trace of the children was ever found. I had lost nearly my entire family—or so I thought until I saw a young woman in Munich. A young woman of the age my Elizabeth would be now, who looked so much like Elaine that I thought I had seen a ghost."

"Her name was Elizabeth," Lizzie repeated while Claire's blood ran cold. "And her sis—her cousin's name?"

"Was Margaret."

Lizzie dragged in a breath, searching his face as though she could see right through to the truth. "I have no memories from before I was on the streets. Maggie doesn't, either. The first thing I remember is being ravenously hungry and Snouts offering me bread to eat. It had mold on it, and I threw it up before it properly hit bottom."

"Snouts?" he asked gently.

"The leader of the South Bank gang who adopted the girls into their ranks and enabled them to survive until we met," Claire explained. Her lips felt stiff, as if they could not form even simple words. "Maggie's tale at dinner was quite true. The older ones called the girls the Mopsies, until they grew old enough to pronounce their name without difficulty."

"Mopsies!" Rather than looking taken aback, he looked exultant. "Let me finish my story, then. Since my wife's family had no male heirs, during our period of mourning the Seacombes asked that Claude and I take that name so that the family heritage would be preserved. But before that …" His throat seemed to close with emotion.

Lizzie drew a ragged breath. "Before that, you

were—I was—"

"De Maupassant. You were so young that you could not pronounce our family name, my dearest girl, no matter how much your nursemaid coached you. It always came out garbled—and one of its incarnations was *Moppasee.*"

He cupped her cheek in one hand with infinite tenderness. "You are Elizabeth Rose de Maupassant—or Seacombe, if you choose—my own beloved daughter, whom I have believed dead all these years. Welcome home, my darling."

And he took Lizzie into his arms.

13

"I don't know what to say. How do I tell her?" Lizzie palmed the tears from her cheeks and wished in vain for a handkerchief. The world had turned upside down in the space of ten minutes—she was crying with joy, weeping with despair—she hardly knew whether she was coming or going, turned inside out or right side up.

For once, the Lady had no handkerchief, either, since she was wearing a sleeveless dinner gown, and was making do with the ruffle trimming the bottom of her petticoat. Mr. de Maupassant—Seacombe— Father—had left them alone together in the library for a few moments, but the Lady seemed as much in need of comfort as Lizzie did herself.

"I do not know. But you must think of a way."

"I can't think," Lizzie wailed. "I have a *father*, Lady. A father who is rich and successful and a mother who loved me. I have a *brother*." Her voice cracked and sank to a whisper. "But what I do not have any longer is a sister. Oh, Lady, how can I say that to Maggie?"

"It has made a wreck of me," the Lady said bluntly, hunting for a dry spot. "I shudder to think what it will do to her."

Which did not help in the least.

Lizzie hardly dared ask. "Are—are you angry?"

The Lady made a valiant attempt to pull herself together, abandoned the ruffle, and held out her arms. "That you have found your family? How could I be?"

Lizzie flung herself into them in a way she hadn't since she'd begun letting her hems down, and sobbed into her neck. "I'm so happy—and—and—so miserable!"

"Lizzie, what's wrong?" Maggie's voice came from the doorway, sharp with alarm. "They sent me back to see what was keeping you. Has something happened?" Maggie picked up her skirts and dashed over to the sofa, where she sank to her knees and slipped her arms around Lizzie's waist. Her amber gaze flitted from her to the Lady, widening with real fear as she saw the traces of tears on the Lady's cheeks. "Lady—Lizzie— please tell me. I can't bear it."

"It is Lizzie's to tell, if she can."

"What does that mean?" Maggie's arms tightened and Lizzie's heart broke that her sister—cousin—was already terrified, and she hadn't even got the words out yet.

You must do this. With love … and for love. Whatever comes after is up to Maggie.

She took a deep, shuddering breath and sat up, wrapping Maggie in a hug that lifted her up next to her on the sofa. "Mr. Seacombe has just told me some astonishing news."

"Bad news?"

"N-no … good news. Wonderful news. At least, I hope you will think so."

"No one else in this room seems to think so." Maggie's tone had not lost its edge of fear. "Lizzie, please. Spit it out, or I shall explode."

Another breath. "We have just learned that Mr. Seacombe is my father. Which makes Claude my half brother. And you my cousin."

She could feel the withdrawal already as Maggie's familiar hug loosened and she pulled back in shocked confusion. "I may as well be the cat's grandmother, for all the sense you are making."

"Mags. Look." She pointed up at the wall, to the picture of her mother, and as gently as she could considering her nose was still running, told Maggie the story. When she left out the bit about Maggie's own mother, the Lady shook her head. If the truth were to be told, it should be told complete. Claire added those details in the softest, most gentle tones Lizzie had ever heard her use.

But they still fell upon Maggie's reeling mind like the sharp pummeling of hail, if the way she flinched was any indication. "I don't understand. Is he saying that ... we are not twins?"

"No. Born within a week of each other, but not twins."

"Not sisters?"

"Cousins. Our mothers were sisters, who loved each other very much."

Maggie gazed up at the portrait, her face slack and disbelieving. "And your mother was a fine lady who got her portrait painted, while my mother was a—a desert flower who died having me?"

"She was *not* a desert flower," the Lady said firmly, though how she could sound so positive, Lizzie didn't know. The Lady knew as much of the circumstances as Lizzie did—which was next to nothing. "We do not know her situation, but a girl of good family would not take up that life. She was forced—or there was a secret marriage—or there is some other explanation, you may depend upon it."

It was clear Maggie did not believe her. "Who was my father, then? What is *my* name?"

"We don't know," Lizzie said, wishing that didn't sound so damning. Wishing she had let Father tell her. "But your name is the same as mine, since Mr. Sea— Father adopted you."

Maggie's mouth trembled and she rose from the sofa. "Father? You're calling him Father now, are you, after meeting him only three times in your life?"

"He appears to be what he says he is, darling," Claire said softly. "Her birth certificate was in his desk—and you girls were close when you chose your birthday. Lizzie's is March twenty-second."

"What about *my* birthday?"

"March twenty-fifth. That is information that only Lizzie's father would have—and it dovetails perfectly with what she remembers."

"But I don't remember it, and you say I was there, too!" Maggie cried. She turned to Lizzie, pleading. "You don't remember, not really. He could be feeding you a line of codswallop to—to—well, I don't know why he would, but he could be!"

"That is just the reason we believe it to be true," the Lady said. "Mr. Seacombe has no reason in the world to claim Lizzie as his daughter—being perfectly cognizant of her past—other than the fact that she really is."

"But what about me?" Maggie wailed. "What is going to happen to me? To us?"

"That, I fear, is the crux of the matter." The Lady's face grew bleak. "What may be enormous good fortune for Lizzie—to be reunited with her family, to have a home, things that any compassionate person would not begrudge her—is the cause of equally enormous grief for me." Her lips trembled no matter how much she pressed them together. She swallowed and went on, "I do not know how I shall bear it, if we are to be separated."

"We shan't be separated!" Lizzie said fiercely. "We're a flock. Nothing will change. Maggie and I simply have firm and sensible reasons to go to finishing school now, and we will come back to England during holidays just as we always have."

"No, we won't." Maggie couldn't seem to stay still. She paced the Persian carpet, her skirts whipping around her ankles as though she kicked them. "You'll come here for holidays, or Paris, or the Antipodes—wherever he and Claude are. Of course you will. You'll want to be with your family." With what appeared to be an effort of will, she added, "I would, too, in your place."

"But why wouldn't it be your place, Mags?" Lizzie leaped up from the sofa to stop her frantic pacing. "Father said that he adopted you as his own. We were both with our mother when the airship went down. He has found not just one daughter, but two."

"I was not the one he asked into the study to tell the happy news."

"That was because you'd already gone ahead to *Lady Lucy*. I'm sure you were next."

"I don't think so. Why would he want me? It appears I'm not even related to him, and it's not very likely that a promise he made to his wife sixteen years ago is going to hold now."

"You're wrong. He's not like that." Maggie's intuition and knack for observing people were often right, but Lizzie knew in her bones that they were not this time. "Come on. We'll ask him. He's gone out to the ship to tell Claude and everyone else. We'll ask him and you'll see."

Lizzie pulled them both along with her across the expanse of lawn to the broadmead by the river where the airships were moored. As they mounted *Lady Lucy*'s gangway, they could hear the sound of applause, and a whooping sort of cheer. And then, as they reached the doorway to the grand salon, they stood transfixed.

Claude, all nearly six feet of him, capered with delight, whirling about the room like a dervish. In one glance, he saw Lizzie, dashed over, and swung her around so that her silk skirts flared out like a bell.

"Elizabeth! My sister! It is you—I knew it would be—found at last!"

She had not spared a single thought as to his feelings about their father's revelations. Her only concerns had been for Maggie and for the Lady. But this! There could be no doubt about her half-brother's thoughts on the matter now.

"I'm so happy!" He crushed her to him in a hug that would set permanent wrinkles in her bodice—but she didn't care. She hugged him back and laughed with contagious joy. This was the kind of welcome that could warm the very cockles of a lost lamb's heart—the kind of joy that finding the lost ought to bring.

And with no warning but a cloud of light perfume, Cynthia von Stade engulfed her in a hug of her own, and then she was being patted on the back by Darwin and Evan and Geoffrey and wished every joy as though she had done something marvelous. Even Arabella leaned in with a cool kiss to say, "I knew there was something more to this party than charity." Behind it all stood their father, beaming with happiness, and over there by the coffee service was Lady Dunsmuir, her lips parted in astonishment, an empty cup forgotten in her hand.

Lord Dunsmuir was seated on a sofa under the viewing port, trying to explain to Willie what had happened. And there, next to the decanters of spirits, stood Captain Hollys and Tigg.

Tigg knew nothing of her feelings—nothing of her future. But from the other side of the salon, over Cynthia's bare shoulder, Lizzie could see it in his face. She knew without a doubt that he was already saying good-bye.

৵৽৽

For the next two days, Lizzie's emotions flung themselves from the depths of despair to the heights of joy—sometimes within the space of a few minutes. Despair when Tigg turned away from the celebration and went back to his duties in the engine room—clearly a ruse, because the engines were not running—with hardly more than a word to her. Joy when Father sent the pigeon notifying Maison Villeneuve in Geneva of the change in her name and advising them that she would require a private room and a personal maid when she arrived in September. Despair again when Maggie decided once and for all that she would not go to Geneva under any provocation and she hoped the maid would be a better friend, if Lizzie was going to be so stuck-up as to go along with such a ridiculous plan.

All in all, it was quite a relief when the day came for everyone's departure. Now she and Maggie would have some quiet time together to talk. They could ride, and ramble through the park, and even go boating, since it appeared Claude was going to leave his skiff here for the summer. Lizzie walked into the room they shared, ready to suggest they might do any one of these after the Lady lifted, to find Maggie laying the last of her blouses in her valise.

"Mags, what are you doing? You don't have to change rooms, you know. There is plenty of space in here for both of us."

"I'm not changing rooms. I'm going to London."

For a moment, it felt as though Maggie had landed a roundhouse punch in her solar plexus. She could hardly get a breath. "But—but why?"

"It's what we had planned."

"But everything is different now."

"Different for you, maybe. Not for me. Are you telling me you're not coming to the Lady's investiture?"

It hadn't even entered her head. Not once.

And worse, Maggie saw it had not. "Don't you think that after all she's done for us, you might see your way to doing something for her?"

"I—I—"

"I packed your valise, too."

"I can't go. Not now."

"Why not? Why can't you take two days to be with her for something that you know perfectly well means everything to her? While all these wonderful things are happening to you, can you take a moment to remember how momentous this is for her?"

Did no one understand? "The Lady is always doing momentous things. She won't miss me."

"She will. And even if she doesn't, I will."

"As much as I'll miss you here. And in Geneva." Maggie concentrated on tucking the lace collar of the blouse into place just so. Lizzie tried again. "Stay for a month. The rest of the month. It's only ten days. I need you with me while I get my feet under me—while I get used to all of this." Despite herself, her throat closed up. "I need my sister to scout with me, the way I always have."

Maggie left off fiddling with the valise and straightened. "Your cousin, you mean. Come to London, and then I'll come back with you."

"I can't. Father and Evan are entertaining some lot of scientists tomorrow evening and I'm to act as hostess."

"They are? When did this come up?"

Lizzie waved a distracted hand. "I don't know. I suppose it was always up, and then I happened and everyone forgot."

"What was he going to do for a hostess before?"

For goodness sake, why was she playing the Spanish Inquisition? "I've no idea, and I don't care. It's an honor to be asked—to do something a lady would do, not a child—and there's an end to it."

"There's the heart of it, you mean," Maggie said, and fastened the clasps on the valise.

"What does that mean?"

With a sigh, Maggie laid the jacket of her traveling suit over her arm and picked up the valise. "Come and see me off, at least, if you can walk that far without getting your feathers ruffled?"

"My feathers are not ruffled. I am perfectly calm. Tell me what you meant."

"I simply meant that you're in a bigger hurry to grow up than I am. You want to be a lady. That's well and good—certainly Cynthia and Arabella have proven that it's blood that counts there, not accomplishment. And now, apparently, you have the blood, so you can be the lady. Good for you."

She pushed past Lizzie, who struggled with a dozen retorts to this, none of which could make it out of her gaping mouth. By the time she managed, "It's not that way at all!" Maggie was halfway down the grand staircase, with its portraits and busts set in niches to remind one that there were better things to look up to in this world than the method of getting up or down.

Maggie gazed at her across a gulf so large that her voice echoed against the marble. "One of the first things the Lady ever told us was to put others first. That's the mark of a true lady, not what's on your birth certificate or how much money your family has. She has always put us first, Liz. Don't you think you can return the favor and do the same for her?"

Her father came along the gallery just in time to hear, freezing Maggie in embarrassment upon the stairs.

"I am glad to know that your former guardian instilled such noble principles in her wards." He tucked Lizzie's hand into the crook of his arm and they paced together down to the foyer.

By the time they reached the bottom, Maggie's blush had faded and her back was straight as she turned to face them.

"And your cousin is quite right, Elizabeth," he went on, looking earnestly into her eyes. "I will not take it amiss if you decide to go to London for this event ... though I must say your absence will be noticed."

Exactly! "Maggie, Father needs a hostess to help him far more than the Lady needs me standing in some big audience. No one will notice my absence there."

"Lady Claire will. I will."

"But not in the same way as it might be here," Seacombe said before Lizzie could reply. "The hostess's chair will be empty, and I am afraid Claude will not fill it nearly so graciously. Many of these scientists do not know the civilizing influence of ladies at table—to say nothing of the gentle spirit of a true home. But of course you must do as you think right. The decision is entirely yours."

Was this not what she had wanted for weeks now—to create the kind of influence for good that Lady Dunsmuir did so effortlessly? Here was her opportunity, and she must take it. "I am staying, Maggie. You must give Lady Claire an extra hug of congratulations for me."

Maggie would understand some day, and until that day, she would show patience and grace and forgiveness. Those were the qualities of a lady, too.

None of which helped in the least when Claire hugged her at the bottom of *Athena*'s gangway and Lizzie saw the tears swimming in her eyes. "Are you sure you will not come home with us, Lizzie? There is still time to fetch your valise."

It took all her conviction that she was in the right to say, "Quite sure, Lady. My place is here, where I'm needed—and—and I want to know my family better."

The Lady's dear face turned slightly paler, but despite it, she nodded slowly. "I hope you will write should you want more of your clothes or books. And I will expect you at Carrick House on the first of August, when Mr. Seacombe leaves for the shooting, so that we can buy your clothes for Geneva together."

"Yes, Lady. I'll look forward to it."

"Good-bye for now, then, darling."

Lizzie couldn't ... quite ... let go.

"Send a pigeon if you need me," Claire whispered into her hair. "You know the code for *Athena*."

B1LL4 B0L7. Oh, yes. All of them knew it. They had memorized it years ago, just in case.

Maggie and the Lady boarded ... the gangway swung up ... the groundsmen released the ropes. *Athena* fell up into the sky, past the treetops, past the castle towers ... and beyond all hope of calling her back again.

14

The long dining table seemed even longer with the Dunsmuirs, the Lady, and Maggie gone. There had to be thirty feet of gleaming damask tablecloth, with islands of bone china and place settings and glasses marooned at intervals along its length, and floral arrangements of fragrant lilies and roses separating one side from another like continents. Lizzie, had she been in charge of the arrangements this evening, would have seated everyone at one end so that they might have a proper conversation.

But she was not in charge. Yet.

The butler pulled out the chair at the far end opposite her father and waited for her to seat herself. "This is your place now, Miss Elizabeth, as the daughter of the house," he said. "We understand that you have been reunited with your family. I hope you will permit me to say that the staff and I are delighted."

"Why, thank you, Mr.—I mean, Kennidge," she said, so touched that tears sprang to her eyes. "How very kind of you."

She would have said more, but Claude took that moment to lean in and call down the length of the table, "Pater, we're off to Newquay tomorrow to see the new sub-marine cable cars. What fun to whizz about underwater! May we have *Victory*, or will you make me slog it out on the train?"

Their father craned around the flower arrangement to gaze at him, confused. "I thought you were staying the week, and racing here on the Colley?"

"Water's too low," Geoffrey put in before Claude could speak. "And it's too hot—the ladies don't want to crew. There will be good fun at Newquay, though. Can't say it's too hot under the sea."

Wait—they could not be thinking of going? And leaving her here all alone? Well, as alone as one could be with one's father and a staff of a dozen at least?

Her father said as much, and Claude laughed. "You brought it up last night, so don't go blaming me because I agree it's a brilliant idea."

"But Claude, I didn't mean for you to go this week—practically this instant. What will Elizabeth do without all her friends—and without you?"

All my friends have already gone. But no, that was disloyal and untrue.

"What about it, Lizzie?" Claude asked, waving his

fork to get her attention. "Want to come down to Newquay with us and see the latest in sub-marine engines? They're going to see if they can get to Bristol, underwater. If we lift in the morning, we should be there in time for lunch—and the marina puts on a topping spread."

"I—well, I hardly—" Good heavens. It would be horribly rude to abandon their father. Every bit as rude as Claude abandoning her. And besides, she could not think of anything less appealing than being under the water. The thought of it closing over her head horrified her. But she could certainly watch from the deck of the marina. "I am to be Father's hostess when the scientists come tomorrow. I couldn't possibly go until the day after, at least. Why don't you put it off until then?"

"Barometer's dropping," Geoffrey said to his salad. "Won't get away if we don't lift tomorrow, don't you know."

"Rather unsporting of you, Lizzie," Arabella drawled. "Do come. What do you want with a lot of grisly scientists, anyway?"

As if she didn't know perfectly well that Lizzie numbered several scientists among her friends. "I told Father I would, and so I shall," she replied quietly.

"That's the spirit," Father said. "She stands by her word. A valuable quality in a young woman."

Claude merely grinned, and Lizzie waited for their father to put his foot down and insist that his son stay. They needed time to get to know each other—to become a family. In a few days' time the Prince of

Wales would come to his country home with his eldest son and what the papers had taken to calling the Three-Feathered Court—his personal circle, separate from that of the Queen or even that which he inhabited with Princess Alexandra—on his way to Scotland. Her father and Claude would join the royal shooting party and she would return to London—and two weeks after that, she would be on her way to Geneva. Time was short, and she had years of it to make up for.

"Oh, very well, if you must go," Father said. "I'll have the crew alerted for an early departure—say, nine o'clock?"

Arabella groaned, and her brother nudged her. "Chin up, Bella. You can nap on the way."

Lizzie dropped her gaze to her own salad, for fear they would see the shock and dismay there. She felt as though she were sinking into her chair ... down through the floor ... into the cellar, where people kept things they didn't have any use for—or would use sometime in the future, but not now.

If she protested any further, six pairs of eyes would train themselves upon her, and six minds would come to the rapid conclusion that she was a baby and a self-centered one, to boot. *A lady thinks of others before herself.* Claude would come back—this was his home, after all. Or one of them. They had years and years to get to know one another.

She was fortunate, really. She would have Father all to herself, with the exception of Evan, who rarely stuck his head out of the laboratory unless there was the imminent prospect of food. She would get to know

Father, then. He could tell her about her mother and about her past. She was hungry to know every detail—how her mother looked when she'd held her as a baby, whether she preferred green to blue, as Lizzie did, and what kinds of flowers were her favorites.

Yes, all things considered, maybe this was the best thing that could have happened. Claude had had their father all to himself for eleven years. Now it was her turn.

The next morning, according to plan, the Sorbonne set straggled aboard the Seacombe airship, *Victory*, with the maximum of fuss and bother and a minimum of organization. Lizzie watched them with some amusement. One week in the company of the Lady and Arabella would learn to pack everything once, in the proper order in her trunk—would possibly not even *have* a trunk, for the Lady travelled light. One simply did not need shoes in every color to match every single gown one owned. Captain Hollys would never allow Darwin and Geoffrey to lounge about on the lawn instead of assisting sisters and friends. And Tigg … well, Tigg would not be swanning off to Newquay and leaving her here at all.

A pang of homesickness reverberated through her, and she decided she would write letters this afternoon. It had only been a day, but there had been so much left unsaid between her and the ones she loved best that she would not waste any more time in communicating it.

Cynthia ran over to hug her when it appeared everything at last was loaded into the ship. "Are you sure you will not come?"

This was the second woman who had asked her that in as many days, but the answer was still the same. "Quite sure. Do send a postcard, though, won't you? I should like to see a picture of the engine, at least."

"I shall, then, if that is all you wish. Will we see you before September?"

"I will be here for ten days, and then I return to London. I must order my wardrobe, you know." Goodness. How Maggie would laugh, and remind her that even five years ago, neither of them would have dreamed one could say such a thing.

Cynthia clapped her hands. "We are, too! Oh, do give me your card. We must meet in town—put our heads together at the modiste's and have lunch in Piccadilly—perhaps take in a fashion show or two. Monsieur Charles Worth is exhibiting his most famous gowns, you know, for the first time ever. One mustn't miss it."

Lizzie had no idea who Monsieur Worth was, but she nodded as enthusiastically as if she did. "I haven't a card, but we live in Wilton Crescent. Number twenty-three. You are welcome to call at any time, Cynthia."

"Wilton Crescent, is it?" Her eyebrows rose coyly. "Aren't we the fashionable ones. I shall be delighted to call." She kissed her on both cheeks, in the European way. "Until then, dearest."

Arabella gave a languid wave and the two of them climbed the gangway, assisted by Geoffrey and Darwin, who appeared to be able to stir themselves for that much, at least. And then with a cry of "Up ship!" *Victory* lifted, leaving Lizzie alone in the company of the groundsmen and her father.

She smiled as she joined him. "I hope they have a pleasant flight."

"I'm sure they will." He offered her his arm. "The barometer is indeed dropping, which makes me a little concerned for the flight of our scientific guests. But Cowell over there assures me that as long as they arrive by midafternoon, they should avoid the worst of the storm currents. Will you join me for another cup of coffee, my dear?"

"With pleasure," she said, happiness flooding in to fill the empty spaces all these rapid departures had left inside her.

The breakfast table had already been cleared of the mess left by the Sorbonne set, and magically, two places re-set with a coffee service. Either someone was listening at the windows for the least whim of the master of the house, or he habitually returned for coffee at mid-morning. If the latter, perhaps he would not object if she made it her habit, too, though coffee was not one of her favorite beverages. Perhaps she might stand near an open window and muse upon the possibility of chocolate for herself to see what would happen.

"So, my dear." He waited for her to pour him a cup, then her own. "We are to keep each other company. I should very much like to hear of your life between the day I last saw you at five, and the day I saw you again at sixteen."

"I will need more than the space of a cup of coffee for that story, Father. And there are parts I do not wish to dwell on, even for your sake."

"Understandable. But perhaps we might begin with how you met Lady Claire?"

Lizzie hesitated. Yes, he was her father, but at the same time, the Lady's secret life was just that—secret. While much of it might be in the past, there were still loose threads that extended from that time to this, and every inhabitant of number twenty-three knew how to keep mum on the subject. If the Lady didn't deal with you herself, Snouts would. His patience was much thinner than hers, and his methods less civilized.

"We were street sparrows, Maggie and I," she began. "Lady Claire had opened a school in Vauxhall Gardens, hard by the bridge, and we heard from some of our mates that a body could get a good meal there. We went, thinking that at any moment we would be beaten and turned away, but instead she took us in, fed us, and offered us a cot. The next morning, she began to teach us our letters and numbers."

"How commendable."

"Our lessons progressed to table manners and ethics, and then to physics, mechanics, and chemistry. And then when it was discovered that one of our number, Weepin' Willie, was actually Lord and Lady Dunsmuir's kidnapped son, our lives changed again, and through them we met Count von Zeppelin. He encouraged Lady Claire to study in Munich, and of course by then she had made us her wards, so we went, too."

"It seems I owe Lady Claire a great debt."

"We all do," Lizzie said softly. "I can't bear to think what might have happened to Maggie and me if we hadn't met her. We'd likely be Whitechapel chippies—or dead."

He shuddered and set his cup in its saucer rather forcefully. "I'm sorry, my dear, but to hear such words upon your innocent lips distresses me."

"I'm sorry, Father." There were many worse epithets she could have used, but to say *desert flower,* an expression used only by Texicans, would have brought up their adventures in the Americas, and that was skating a little too close to other people's secret lives— including her own—for comfort. It was much easier to tell him the story of Weepin' Willie, and of his dramatic return to his parents.

"So that is the secret of your familiarity with the Dunsmuirs," her father said, draining his cup. "It is very good to know. Upon such connections a glittering social career is often based, from what I understand."

"Oh, yes," she agreed eagerly. "Lady Dunsmuir has already offered to sponsor us for our come-out in two years' time."

"Has she?" A glow of approval suffused his face. "How very kind of her to take a motherless girl under her wing."

"Well, at the time we were not really motherless. Lady Claire is more of a—an elder sister, but as our guardian, she stands in the place of a mother from time to time. I am quite certain she and Lady Dunsmuir put their heads together on the subject behind our backs."

"You speak of *our* and *we*, my dear. Are you including Margaret in your thoughts of the future?"

What a question. How could she phrase this so that he would understand? "She is my sister in every way that counts. We have been like this—" She crossed her third finger over her forefinger. "—forever. As you say, practically since birth."

"But she is not, in truth, your sister."

"Well, no, but certainly by all other ties, if feeling and experience mean anything."

"Your loyalty to the girl is commendable, my dear, but do you see your relationship continuing?"

"Of course."

He gazed at her, as though marshaling the right words to say. Once back in England, with its kinder systems of illumination, he had put away the amber, multi-lensed spectacles. Now his gaze held hers, tawny and somber.

—tiger eyes—

—smoke, and the floor falling—

"Elizabeth? Have I said something to distress you?"

She blinked and gripped the edge of the table—something firm to hold on to while she battled a sense of vertigo. "No ... no, I think I may have had too much coffee. It has made me dizzy."

He rose at once, and took her hands to guide her from her chair. "Then you must lie down in your room. Let me call a maid."

"No—no, Father. I am quite all right. I think I might just step out into the garden and walk a little in the fresh air."

"Do whatever you think best. I do not want my hostess taking to her bed, after she was so selfless as to give up a trip to Newquay in order to assist me with my guests."

With a smile, she made her way to the grand salon and then out the open French doors to the terrace, where she breathed deeply of the soft morning air. Several wide flagstone steps took her down into the garden, which seemed in disarray despite the efforts of the two gardeners she could see beavering away in the shrubbery.

The roses smelled beautiful, though, and as she made her way around the Queen's Tower, she found herself descending into the moat. Here was clearly where the cut flowers for the table arrangements had come from. The air was heavy with scent and the somnolent buzzing of bees. Butterflies wavered from rose to lily to lavender, with no particular destination in mind, much like herself.

At the second tower, she climbed the slope, wondering if there was a kitchen garden on the fourth side of the castle, and if so, if there might be chickens. She missed the company of the hens. Perhaps if there were none, Father would let her bring some home, and she could have her own flock here, as Lewis and Granny Protheroe did at Wilton Crescent, and the Lady did wherever she happened to be.

"I say, make up your mind. Are you coming or going?"

Lizzie looked past the drapery of honeysuckle and

ivy growing on the tower wall to see Evan Douglas standing on the flagged step of what she supposed must have been the old postern gate, back when these towers were meant to defend actual occupants, not merely the bastions of science.

"Neither," she replied, his bluntness freeing her rather neatly from the constraints of civility. "I'm exploring."

"One usually has a destination in mind for that."

"If one did, it would be called *traveling*, not *exploring*."

His lips twitched. "Point to you. I thought you'd gone to Newquay or Cowes or wherever it was that lot were off to."

So he did listen to the dinner conversation, even if he hardly ever participated. "No, I'm to act as hostess this evening, when the scientists come, remember?" Perhaps he would be different tonight, with his own kind at the table.

"I do now. You're to be our sole civilizing influence, then, I take it."

"I shall at least endeavor to keep you from smoking in the dining-room."

"Good luck there. You'll be lucky if they use their napkins—to say nothing of spoons."

The image made her laugh. "Come now. It can't be that bad. *You* seem fairly civilized."

"That's only because I have to sing for my supper and be on my best behavior."

"Sing for your supper? Do you mean with your experiments?"

He kicked a stone away and sat on the step, his hands dangling between his knees, heedless of the fact that the back of his white laboratory coat would be dusty when he got up. "Yes, that is what I mean," he said, gazing moodily down into the moat. "Cousin Charles is sponsoring me to conduct the research, but that means that when there is something to write up, he gets the credit, not I."

"Has there been something to write up?" Lizzie sat on a mossy rock close by, wondering if it had fallen from the tower a century or two ago—or perhaps been dropped upon an invader's head.

"A small monograph on the two images I've managed to capture. The Royal Academy of Technology and Science was not impressed. I did not make it into the monthly journal—not even in the Notes in the back."

"But you will, in time," she said, trying to encourage him. "If effort and application lead to success, then of course you will. You must be patient."

He turned his gaze upon her. His eyes were the blue of the bachelor buttons that grew on the roadsides, and his brows were strongly marked under the riot of curls falling onto his forehead. "What an odd field genetics is," he said, apropos of nothing.

"I find it rather fascinating," she said at once, feeling quite chuffed that here was a subject about which she knew a little. "At Gwynn Place, in Cornwall, where we've spent the last few summers, Polgarth the poultryman is breeding a special strain of chicken—they're calling it the Carrick Orpington. Maggie and I were able to assist him using what we had learned of the subject at school."

She realized with a sinking feeling that this would be the first year since they had met the Lady that they had not gone down to the St. Ives estate for the summer. No wonder things felt so out of joint.

"I'm glad to hear it. Perhaps you can explain, then, how Charles managed to produce a daughter like you and a flibbertigibbet like Claude."

"We do have different mothers," she reminded him, unsure of whether or not to be pleased. It might not, after all, be a compliment. Nor was it exactly the kind of polite conversation a gentleman might have with a young lady. But no one was listening, were they?

"There is that."

"And nurture, you know, has as much to do with how someone turns out as nature. Claude would likely be an entirely different person if he had spent five years on the streets of Whitechapel, scrabbling and thieving and trying to stay alive."

"Is that how it was for you?" She had his entire attention now. "Margaret was not merely playacting?"

"Worse. I do not like to dwell upon it."

"So your memories and dreams, then ... they might be particularly vivid, given the material upon which they cogitate?"

"Sometimes they are." Sometimes she woke, screaming, with the snarling faces of Billy and Albert and the other members of the Billingsgate gang hanging over her, their hands scrabbling at her skirts, and in the dream, no help or hope in sight. In reality, she owed quite a lot to Snouts and Jake.

She shook the ugly images from her mind. Her dreams since returning from Bavaria were much stranger—water, falling, that silly children's tune perpetually in the background—but no less frightening.

"Would it be an imposition if I asked you to help me?" His gaze had not moved from her face. A gentleman would have looked elsewhere to give her time to compose herself. But Claude and the others had already established that the young scientist was not a gentleman.

"How?" she asked. "Are you going to put me in your machine and extract my memories? Are you quite prepared for what you might find, Evan Douglas?"

"I am never prepared for the endless puzzle that is the human brain," he said slowly. "But if you are willing, I should like it very much if you would consent to be a subject. It does not hurt ... and I am afraid I have rather run out of people able to help me. Geoffrey said he might, but he is halfway to Exeter by now."

From here, she could not see the front of the castle, the gardens, or even the broadmead from which the airships had lifted. She had nothing to do but tidy the room she had shared with Maggie, no one to talk to except her father, and he likely had estate business to take care of in between rafts of guests.

No one needed her except this disheveled young man, who at least spoke to her as though she had a brain in her head, though his delivery could use a little refinement.

"All right," she said. "Why ever not?"

15

Filled with curiosity, Lizzie followed him into the tower. It took a moment for her eyes to adjust from the bright summer day to the enormous, dim interior, which was illuminated by electricks strung along the stone walls about ten feet from the floor, and further up, by the arrow slits where archers might have fired during a siege. The floor the archers stood upon, however, had been knocked out to accommodate the size of the scientific equipment.

"Shall I explain what you are looking at?" Evan asked.

"I presume that enormous thing is the mnemosomniograph. Goodness, what a mouthful. It is almost as long as that machine is tall. May I simply call it the *dream device* and be done?"

Again, he almost smiled. "A reasonable plan. So, before you is the table upon which the subject—you, for instance—would repose, either in a state of meditation or sleep."

She tilted her head back in an attempt to see where the coiling cables went into the body of that enormous glass globe suspended above their heads. "I would not be able to sleep with that above me, I am quite sure."

"I could read my baccalaureate thesis to you, if you like."

She laughed in sudden delight. If only Arabella could see him now. "And they said you had no sense of humor."

"Just because one possesses different qualities does not mean one is devoid of them."

"Of course not. I am pleased to make the discovery. We shall get on swimmingly now."

"I thought we were getting on already. You have not made a single disparaging remark and it has been all of ten minutes."

"Oh, I am sorry. You must have me confused with Arabella. One blond girl is very much like another, I suppose."

"I could hardly find two more different. And you are not really blond, you know. Your hair is more a honey color."

Goodness. At this rate he would begin reciting poetry.

"So this is the table, and those are the cables. Why is that glass globe suspended up there? I won't even ask how you got it up there—one could fit a piano inside it."

"We built it inside the tower. That is an aggregation chamber, based in part on the Malvern-Terwilliger Kinetick Carbonator. One needs a lot of power to create the equivalent of a flash charge on a camera. And since floor space in towers is limited, we have spread vertically rather than horizontally."

"I see. And those massive flumes?"

"They speed the particles of light to the substrate upon which the subject's memories or dreams are recorded." He walked behind a screen and came back with a square plate rather like the ones that slipped into the backs of cameras in a photography studio. "These contain the chemical substrates. Eventually, my technology will progress to the point where a continuous series of small plates can be made as the dream progresses, and then illuminated one after the other to replicate the dream exactly as the sleeper experienced it."

"Fascinating. But if you do not mind my asking, what is the point of all this? Why capture people's dreams and memories at all?"

He laid the plate upon the table. On the other end of the table sat a heavy metal helmet—goodness, is that what one wore while attempting to sleep? That would make it even more impossible, unless there were a pillow concealed inside.

"Because the conscious mind can be most unreliable. Imagine Sir Robert Peel's policing force, for example. Five different witnesses to a murder could give five different accounts of the perpetrator. But if their dreams and memories were freed of the conscious mind's tendency to edit and preserve itself, the police might obtain a more reliable image of the murderer—and they would have a better chance of catching him."

"I see," she said slowly. "Is that the only use for it? Is Father sponsoring these experiments solely for the public good?"

He smiled and touched the helmet, which bristled with wires and cables and a long hose that ran into the body of the larger device. "Many of our country's advancements began as a way to accomplish one thing important to one individual. It is not until later that one sees how it may benefit many."

"And what does Father want to accomplish?"

"He wishes to preserve as many memories of those he loves—or has loved—as possible. Apparently Cousin Claude remembers very little of his own mother. Nor, I imagine, do you remember much of yours. Or am I mistaken?"

She gazed at him, marveling anew at the things she was learning about her father, who had been a stranger only a few short weeks ago. "No. You are not mistaken."

"He possesses no images of Claude's mother. That is why he went to the trouble of having your own mother's portrait painted. But once this device becomes fully able to do what he envisions for it, he will submit himself upon the table and hope that I can harvest some images to give to Claude."

Lizzie found her throat closing with emotion, and it

was a moment before she could speak. "I should very much like to assist you, then, Evan. I should like to help make that a reality for both my father and my half-brother."

He gazed across the table at her, and a long dimple creased his cheek. "I am glad, and your father will be, too."

"Shall we begin now?"

His dismay as he perceived that she was serious was almost comical. "Oh no, no. It takes a day to prepare the device for a subject, and with the crowd coming this evening I cannot even begin. I am to present a paper on it after dinner, and I must finish a few final notes."

"Tomorrow, then?"

"They will tour this tower tomorrow morning, and return to London in the afternoon. But if I work part of the night, I could have everything ready by the next day."

"How can I assist you?"

He reared back as though retreating from her in sheer incredulity. "Assist me? I think not."

"I do not see why you should say that. My sister—cousin—and I made a walking coop with hydraulic legs, powered by the lightning cell invented by Dr. Rosemary Craig, when we were ten. I am quite capable of lending my lily-white hands to this effort should you need them."

"Rosemary Craig." His voice was hushed, the way some people spoke of Her Majesty—or God. "One of the greatest minds of our time."

"I am glad you agree. I shall tell her you said so, the next time I write."

Oh, she'd done it now. He goggled at her in such surprise he could not speak for a full thirty seconds. "You—you know Doctor Craig? Personally?"

"Yes, of course. She assisted us with the walking coop. That was before she set out on her travels, and long before she took up residence in Edmonton, of course."

She had quite winded him now. "I must say, Cousin Elizabeth, that you astound me on a regular basis."

"For goodness sake, if we are to be related, you must call me Lizzie." She tried to roll the dream helmet up to get a look inside it, but the bolts on the outside prevented it. "You should come out of your tower more. Clearly your sphere of experience is in need of expansion, if you judge me by so low a standard."

"I have not judged you at all, except to observe that you have rather a livelier mind than most, with fewer plates of metaphorical glass between it and the rest of the world."

What an odd way he had of saying things that she was not entirely sure were complimentary. She gave up on the helmet and wandered around the edges of the equipment.

"I should be honored to be mentioned in the smallest capacity to Doctor Craig," Evan said, returning to the subject at hand. "I will not presume so far as to speak of my great admiration for her achievements, but perhaps you might present my humble compliments in your next letter."

"I shall indeed. I was going to write letters this afternoon, in fact."

"Oh, don't go yet."

She had no intention of going yet. "I do not see the telescope. Where is it?" She looked behind the equipment, and then up at the glass globe.

"It is not in here, but up on the top floor—the parapet, I suppose you would call it. But no one is permitted up there except your father."

"And you, I presume."

"No, not even me."

"But we are family. Surely that restriction applies to the staff and guests, not to us."

She was quite certain he snorted, but since he had gone behind the screen to replace the plates, she could not be sure. "It certainly does apply to family—can you imagine the result if Claude decided to fiddle with the second most powerful telescope in England?"

Look—here was the base of a stone stair that wound up the walls of the tower in a steep spiral. She began to climb.

He came out from behind the screen and saw her. "Miss—Lizzie, no! What are you doing?"

"I am quite sure that particular rule does not apply to either of us," she called down. "I am going to see the telescope so that I may converse intelligently with our guests if the subject should come up this evening. And so should you."

"Lizzie!" His boots scraped on the stone steps as he

began to climb after her. "I beg of you, come down." When she ignored him, he climbed faster, his steps falling in a syncopated rhythm with hers. "Botheration, girl. Do be careful. There is no railing because I do not want any extraneous metal objects in here that could wreak havoc with the conductivity of the current. If you fall, the damage will be permanent."

"I have no intention of falling." To someone who had grown up on the dockside catwalks, to say nothing of *Athena*'s rigging, climbing a set of stairs fixed into a stone wall that hadn't moved in a thousand years was child's play. Or so she told herself.

Up and up they climbed, until she reached the point where she could look down no longer, and focused on the curving radius of each step. Not for worlds would she admit to him her fear of heights, which had not begun to affect her until she'd come level with the great glass globe. No matter. She had started this, and she would finish it.

At the very top, the steps ran up into the ceiling, but with half a dozen to go, she saw a lever set into the wall, obviously to open the door. She pulled it down and with a smooth clicking of gears in good working order, the floor above retracted into a deep slot in the ceiling, leaving an opening like that of a trap door.

She stepped through, into the breezy sunlight.

Lizzie could not bring herself to look over the parapet at the ground some two hundred feet below. But even if she'd had no fear at all, her astounded gaze would have been drawn to the huge barrel of the telescope protruding from the brass dome built on top of the tower.

Evan emerged from the trap door and lifted his face to the sky as though he had not seen it in some time. Then he crossed to the parapet and gazed out at the Cotswold hills, with copses of trees folded lovingly into their valleys, and a village not far off with stone cottages, thatched roofs, and a church spire. All of which she could see quite comfortably from the base of the telescope, thank you. There was no need to join him at the embrasure.

The breeze snatched at her skirts and tossed them flat against her legs. Before it threw her hair over her face, she pulled open the door—which was not locked—and let herself into the dome.

The apparatus that governed the telescope's angle and direction of sight was equally huge. It looked like a cross between a gyroscope and the insides of an exceedingly large watch. Extending out of the complicated array of gears for turning and aiming it was the brass barrel, the tip of which was visible from the outside through a slot in the dome's roof.

"We are going to be in so much trouble if we are discovered." Evan closed the door and gazed up in awe. "Great Caesar's ghost. Look at the size of it."

"Why do you suppose Father has forbidden it to anyone?" She mounted the steps to what she could only call the pilot's chair, and seated herself on the leather seat. The ocular assembly was too tall for her, as though a man usually sat here, so she gave it a tug. On well-oiled and silent bearings, the assembly lowered itself to her eye level, bobbing slightly, and she looked through it.

Nothing.

How very strange. "I can't see anything."

"Of course not. There are no stars or planets visible at nearly noon."

As if she did not know that. "I should be able to see sky, at least," she said impatiently. "But it is all black. Does it require electricks in order to operate?"

"If you move and allow me to sit there, I will tell you. And if we are discovered, it is much better that I should take the blame than you."

She descended the steps and traded places with him. "Why should you do that? We are in this together, it seems to me."

Settling himself into the seat, he said, "Because firstly, I am the elder, and secondly, Charles tasked me with the responsibility to see that no one comes up, given that I am here most of the time. So you are safe."

He applied his eye to the viewing assembly. Frowned. Raised his head and gazed at the controls as if they were an equation that could be solved with sufficient concentration.

"I told you." Lizzie tried not to sound smug, without success.

"There are no electricks up here, so it cannot require power. The engine powers the directional assembly only, it seems. The telescope itself is separated from it, and it appears the vertical aim is accomplished with this hand crank. So why ...?"

"Perhaps there is a cap on the end of it."

"Perhaps you are right. We may be required to remove it—but for now, I suggest we remove ourselves. Come, Lizzie. We need to go down."

"Just check," she begged. "Have a look outside while I lower it. I should love to see the village, at least, if I cannot see the stars, and this may well be my only chance. Please?"

"Very well," he said after some mental struggle. "But only for a moment. If Charles should happen outside and see that the barrel has been moved there will be hell to pay."

Once the door closed behind him, Lizzie lowered the telescope's barrel using the hand crank, which made the gears and wheels within the gyroscope circle and adjust. Her hands fell naturally onto two levers somewhat similar to the driving bar in the Lady's steam landau. What were these for?

Gently, her lower lip between her teeth, she moved the lever just an inch toward the barrel.

Nothing.

Another inch.

Another set of gears engaged and began to turn. Lizzie nearly choked on her own indrawn breath, and pulled on the lever to make them stop.

But they did not. Once engaged, it seemed the process must be completed.

With a whimper, she pushed the lever all the way forward when it began to shake with the demand that she do so. The next set of gears engaged, and then a drive chain, and with a sliding *thunk!* the side of the telescope opened and a gleaming brass arm swiveled in her direction.

She could not have moved if she tried. She was frozen on the leather seat, cold alarm moving over her skin at what she had done.

The arm clamped onto a cylindrical object that had just slid heavily down a chute next to her, removed it, and inserted it into the slot in the side of the telescope barrel. The brass door in the barrel slid shut with a clang and the arm ratcheted back whence it had come. A light glowed in the ocular assembly.

She put her eye to the eyepiece and saw the bright blue of heaven.

She could still hear Evan's boots on the stone outside as he circled the barrel, trying to see what was at the end of it as it tilted up to the sky. There was no cap. No, whatever had been blocking her view was gone now, because what it needed had been supplied.

In the ocular assembly, on the side of the bright field of vision it allowed, a brass wheel engraved with tiny capital letters clicked into place.

ARMED

Lizzie's spine lost its ability to hold her up, and she wilted back against the leather seat, immobile with horror.

This was no telescope sitting on top of the tower, waiting for a clear night and a gentleman hobbyist's leisure.

It was a bloody great cannon.

And she had just loaded it.

16

Evan must not know that Lizzie knew what the tele-scope really was. If he already knew, she might be in danger. If he did not, then she did not want to endanger him.

Quickly, she returned the tilt of the barrel to what it had been before, adjusted the ocular assembly to its previous height, and hopped down from the seat. She had just stepped outside and closed the door behind her when he reappeared from around the back of the dome.

"There is no cap that I can see, Lizzie … why … what is the matter?"

She could not help the color of her complexion, nor its clamminess. But she could use it. "I—I did not want to tell you before, but ... Evan ... I have a terrible fear of heights. I'm afraid I can't conceal it any longer. I—I need your help to get down."

"Good heavens, you goose." He passed an arm about her waist and assisted her over to the trap door. "Pride has got many a good scientist into trouble, but I would never have suspected it of you."

"I'm sorry," she whispered. She took a few unsteady steps down after him and would have fallen to her knees in thanks when the trap door slid shut above them if there had been anything to fall upon.

"Hug the wall," he ordered from a few steps below her. "You must be brave, Lizzie. I cannot carry you. All I can do is provide a cushion to land upon, and even that may not save us both if you fall."

"I shan't fall." She concentrated on the cut stones in the tower wall, her shaking hands running over the cold edges where they fit together, feeling her courage return with every step downward toward the ground and away from that cannon.

Did Evan know what it really was? Was he being paid to keep it a secret—to keep people out?

No, that could not be. He had followed her up as blithely as she, more like an older brother anxious for the well-being of a naughty child than a villain determined to keep her away from a terrible weapon.

Her original instinct for silence, drilled into her by her years under Snouts's protection, did not fail her. She refused his escort into the house, making light of her feminine weakness until she reached the safety of her room. Then she flung herself upon the bed while her legs twitched and trembled with the tension of that climb down the tower wall.

That, and the urge to flee.

If Evan were innocent of the telescope's true purpose, she would do everything in her power to keep that knowledge from him. The greater question was, what on earth was it doing up there? Why was her father passing it off as a telescope when it clearly could never be used? What if someone heard about the "second most powerful telescope in England" and actually wanted to look at a star or two? One of the scientists coming that afternoon, for example. Would he simply tell them it was undergoing maintenance and could not be used at present?

And for goodness sake, what was it being used *for?*

She must find out. She could not believe that a man as kind and generous as her father would knowingly keep a weapon of that size and power on his roof. Perhaps he had been deceived. Perhaps he thought it was a telescope, and had simply never had the time to climb into the pilot's seat and actually use it. Perhaps there had been a mix-up in the order, and someone in—in the Texican Territories was presently puzzling over a giant telescope in a crate instead of the cannon they had been expecting.

Oh, how she wished Maggie were here!

The two of them had ferreted out many a secret over the years, and solved a mystery or two as well. Even the Lady had laughed during their first Christmas at Wilton Crescent at her lack of success in hiding the presents from them. With Maggie here, at least she would have someone to talk to. Someone to tell her she was crazy for thinking ill of a man who had done so much for her. Someone to soothe her mind, which never failed to leap to the worst conclusions—a habit she tried hard to break but in which she had seen little success.

No, she could not think ill of her father. It was a mistake, that was all—a mistake of colossal proportions, mind you, but it was the only explanation.

Well, except for the one that suggested her father wanted to shoot something out of the sky.

Lizzie tried to stop her mind from going there, but she could not. She and Maggie had not survived the streets of Whitechapel by blinding themselves to facts. If something walked like a duck and quacked like a duck, in all probability it was a duck. How many times had Snouts told them that? And how many times had he been proven maddeningly right?

Stop thinking in this way. It is disloyal to your family.

But she could not. The image of that cannon concealed on the roof of the tower haunted her.

All right, then, if you must betray by your thoughts a man who has gone to such lengths to bring you back to him ... what does one shoot out of the sky?

Pheasant.

Not with a cannon. Try again.

Aeronautic conveyances.

Yes. Airships, rocket rucksacks, pigeons—

Lizzie sat up straight on her bed, and swung her feet to the floor, as if the glossy walnut planking could steady her.

Father had said he'd sent a pigeon to Geneva, telling them of her change in name and requesting a lady's maid for her. But pigeons did not fly to fixed addresses. That was what the tube system was for. Pigeons flew to moving recipients, like airships and steamships. The only reason *Athena*'s pigeon came to Wilton Crescent was because Lewis had illegally monkeyed with its guidance system to protect the Lady's most confidential correspondence.

Why had Father sent a pigeon instead of a tube? To rendezvous with a ship bound for the same location? But *Victory* had been moored right here when he'd sent it. Lizzie got up and began to pace the Persian carpet.

You can't solve that one, my girl. Back to cannons.

All right, then. One could shoot ships and things out of the sky. But why would one want to? The only ships that passed by this deep in the country—far from the industrial shipping lanes—were private ones, like *Victory* or *Athena* or the one the Prince of Wales would undoubtedly use to come to his estate.

She ran into a wall, both literally and figuratively, and turned for the door. There was no point in thinking this way, ducks notwithstanding. None of it made any sense, just as that pocket watch that was a bomb had made no sense until her father had explained what it had been intended for. She simply did not have enough information—and would not, until she could talk with someone.

She needed Maggie. If she sent a tube now, her sister would get it this evening, and board a train in the morning. By this time tomorrow, she could be sitting here with her, talking it over and trying to decide if it would be better to sit tight and not think crazy thoughts, or to get down to the business they were both best at—keeping a watchful eye out while poking their noses where they didn't belong.

Quietly, in as ladylike a fashion as she could manage, Lizzie drifted through the silent house to the morning room, where there was an escritoire, ink, and stationery. The fact that it bore the family crest of those who had lived here previously made her a little uncomfortable, but when one needed paper this urgently, one ignored such niceness.

Dear Maggie,

Please forgive me for being such a toplofty gumpus. It has only been a day, but I miss you dreadfully. I was stupid, and I'm sorry.

Something has come up here at Colliford and I need you with me, as soon as you can get a train. If you get the 7:15 from Paddington you'll be here in time for lunch. I can't put it in writing, but ... bring raiding rig. And my antigravity corset. I could have used it today.

Please don't tell the Lady. I may be able to explain you to Father, but I will not be able to explain her—and besides, she will only worry, or worse, come like lightning *rather than harmless as a cloud.*

Please, Mags. I believe I may be going crazy,

and I should like you to tell me not to be a stupe-nagel.

All love,
Lizzie

She sealed the sheet in an envelope so it couldn't be read by whoever happened to collect it at Wilton Crescent, and set the code. With a pneumatic slurp, the tube was sucked away. She checked to see that nothing had arrived in the other slot, and then heard the lunch gong.

She and Evan were the only ones to come to the table, but this time, she refused to sit thirty feet away. She picked up the entire place setting and walked the length of the table to re-set it all on Evan's right.

"Miss Elizabeth," Kennidge said, shocked. "Is the setting not satisfactory?"

"When we are *en famille*, Kennidge, I should like to be seated together from now on. How can I get to know my family when I am forced to shout down the length of the room?"

Kennidge permitted himself a smile, and bowed. "Yes, miss. It shall be as you say. And, er—the pickle fork goes to the *outside* of the salad fork, miss. Like this."

It was the first time she had ever given household instructions. It felt very satisfying—but she must not let the feeling of power go to her head. The Lady had told them often enough that servants were simply men and women like themselves, earning a living, and were to be treated with the respect and civility one would give an equal.

After lunch, Evan returned to the tower and she listened to the servants moving about the silent house. With every hour that passed, she became more and more edgy, listening for the sound of a tube arriving even though she knew it could not come before midnight at the earliest. The thought of the telescope—cannon—gnawed at her, and the sharper the thought of it became, the more it seemed that her father must know what he was housing on his roof.

He dealt in arms. She knew that because he'd told her, in Munich. He'd had that bomb in his pocket to show to Count von Zeppelin. His story seemed wildly dangerous—if not utterly improbable. Looking back now, the Lady had to have been right, and Lizzie had been blinded by her need to believe in him and had not been willing to admit it.

What if, as she had suggested, something had tugged the pin out during the dancing? What if he had pulled too hard on the chain or dropped the device? Why on earth carry a bomb about your person when you knew it was live and could kill you and everyone within ten feet of you?

Oh, this way lay madness. She hated not knowing the answers to questions. And what was more, she hated having to ask them. To admit the possibility that she might have been deceived.

Lizzie found herself back on the second floor, outside her father's study, which was next to the morning room. The door was closed, but she knew he was out on the estate with his manager. Perhaps there was something in here that could shed some light on the subject before she began screaming from tension and sheer frustration.

She went in, careful to close the door behind her. It was the only entrance, but two long windows with burgundy velvet curtains overlooked the front drive. One of them stood open, the curtains gently billowing and brushing the carpet. Outside, the wind was coming up, and clouds scudded across a sky that had been clear before lunch.

She wouldn't stay long. Perhaps only long enough to glance over his desk.

It was very clean, as though the maids had dusted only moments ago, and held nothing but a blotter and an inkwell.

She'd stay only long enough to open a drawer or two, then.

The top ones held pens, stationery, peppermints, two letter openers, and bits and bobs of pencils and string. Both the middle ones held what seemed to be account books. She riffled the pages and didn't see anything more exciting than the price of cigars and a replacement propeller for *Victory*. These must be his personal accounts, not those of the estate. Claude's tuition and books, seven pairs of shoes—seven? Good heavens, Claude was nearly as bad as Arabella. A silk scarf, cufflinks from Bond Street. Yawn. She flipped some more pages, but they were blank.

The deep bottom drawer on the right held a bottle of spirits, though why he should bother when there was a full array there on the sideboard was a mystery. When she shoved the drawer back in with her knee, it stuck.

"Bother. Come on, you." What was the matter with it? It had come out easily enough. She ran a hand under the drawer above to check the clearance, and felt something soft. With pages. Held to the underside of the drawer above by a pair of thin leather straps. Good grief, did he think this was a particularly good hiding place? Willie could have found a better one. "So, Father, what have we here?"

She drew out a leather-bound book. Another account book, from the look of it, but its contents were utterly different. Metal parts and gears. Gunpowder. Brass barrel, two hundred pounds sterling. Columns of figures that looked like estimates of distance versus velocity, multiplied by several different weights of projectiles.

Outside, she heard the musical chugging of a steam landau and for one crazy moment, she thought the Lady had returned to collect her. A quick look out the window squashed that idea—it was her father, unfolding himself out of the passenger side while a man who must be his estate manager leaned over the acceleration bar to converse through the window.

Lizzie dashed to the desk and slid the book back into its holding straps, then lifted the bottom drawer a little in its track as she shoved it in. It slid into place with a clink of the contents inside. She wasted no more time, but ran out of the room and down the stairs, and was waiting with a smile when her father came in the front door, removing his gloves and hat and placing them in Kennidge's care.

He leaned down and kissed her on the forehead. "Now, here is a sight to warm the heart. What have you been doing with yourself today, my dear?"

The Lady said that the truth was always the best course—except when it might result in bodily harm or the betrayal of a friend. But one did not have to tell the entire truth—or even the majority of it. "Evan showed me the dream device, and I have volunteered to be a subject for him before the week is out."

"Have you?" He led the way into the library, where he poured himself a thimbleful of spirits. "That is both brave and kind, to help your cousin in such a way."

"The only trouble is that we cannot work for two more days, until after the scientists have gone."

He poured another thimble. "Our loss is somewhat mitigated, then—I have been informed that the weather is too unpredictable and the entire party have put off the trip."

Disappointment clashed with relief. "Then I shall not have to be your hostess?"

"Not for a few days. Why, were you nervous about it?"

She shook her head. "Between Lady Claire, Lady Dunsmuir, and the Landgrafin von Zeppelin, Maggie and I are well versed in etiquette. In fact, I think we could pour tea into a thimble balanced upon the nose of a spaniel and not spill a drop. No, I had been looking forward to it. I shall merely continue to do so."

"Good. Well, I must catch up with the newspapers,

now that I am to be at leisure today." He settled into a chair, where the afternoon editions were already neatly stacked on a table at his elbow.

She hovered near the door. "Father, how did you hear that the scientists were not coming?"

He looked up, distracted, from the racing news. "I suppose I received a tube. I cannot remember, but I do remember feeling quite put out for your sake. I believe you missed your Lady Claire's investiture today for nothing, to say nothing of the excursion to Newquay."

There had been no tubes, and she had been listening all afternoon. "Does the estate manager's house have its own tube address?"

"Hm? Of course, dear."

"Then you got the news about the scientists there?"

"No. Here. What the deuce does it matter? I am trying to resuscitate my mind after a distressing afternoon looking at tumbledown tenants' cottages, and I do not wish to be pestered." He took a breath as he tried to control his tone. "Forgive me, my dear. I dislike a badly run show, and that is what this estate has become. Be an angel and go and tell Evan he may begin his experiments on—with—you as soon as he pleases."

"Of course, Father." She crossed the room to kiss him, but by the time she reached the door again, he had disappeared behind the paper.

Grimly, she took herself outside, where the wind was as fractious as a small child in a temper, slapping her skirts this way and that, and tugging on her hair.

Point one: Her father knew he had a cannon on the roof, and had overseen its construction himself in some detail.

Point two: There had been no tube. Either the scientists were coming still, or they had never been coming at all. What proof did she have, after all, that they were expecting guests? The servants had not been dashing about with bed linens and flowers, nor was there activity in the kitchen that would suggest the preparation of a large meal. The entire castle, in fact, seemed to be resting on its elbows in quiet relief after the Sorbonne set's departure, not building up a head of steam to manage a new influx of guests.

Conclusion: Her father was lying to her in matters great and small. The question was, why? What was going on here at Colliford Castle ... and why, she wondered with a chill as the clouds massed and hid the sun, had he maneuvered everything so that she was here all alone?

17

Evan Douglas, while taken aback at the change in plans, was quite willing to make adjustments and alter course. "If I do not have to waste the evening worrying about collar points and dessert forks, I can spend it preparing the mnemosomniograph. If you assist me, Lizzie, it is entirely possible that we could begin in the morning."

While she had been looking forward to acting as hostess for the very first time, underneath it all Lizzie felt a loosening of tension. For if even one of the scientists brought up the subject of telescopes, she knew herself only too well. She would not be able to resist asking questions about it, and she would slip up, and then her father would know that she knew.

A LADY OF RESOURCES

The fact that she knew nothing would not keep her out of trouble, if he was going to these lengths to keep the cannon a secret.

She spent the evening fetching and carrying for Evan, and then upon his advice, took a hot bath in the clawfoot tub and drank a mug of warm milk and honey in bed. This was supposed to calm her mind and clear the slate, as it were, for the experiments the next day.

A scientist might be able to go to sleep and save his dreams for the next day, but she was too excited about what might happen upon the dreaming table to do so. She fished a couple of books out of the bookshelf next to the bed to see if reading would help to put her to sleep. It often worked with history textbooks, to say nothing of philosophy.

They were children's picture books. *Mother Goose. Little Playfellows. Aesop's Fables.* And as she turned the pages, time seemed to recede and turn back on itself. It was not the same room, nor the same bed. But these were the same books.

Her books, Maggie's books, from their life before.

She could almost feel the warm arms of her mother around her, almost hear the soft voice as she read Lizzie's favorite, "The Ant and the Grasshopper." She'd never had much patience with silly Grasshopper, when even tiny birds knew that you had to save up for the winter. Ant's patient industry in the face of Grasshopper's derision had stuck with Lizzie, even when she'd long forgotten its source. Maybe Ant was why she'd steal two pieces of bread when it was much more dan-

SHELLEY ADINA

gerous than one. Or hide a bit of cabbage or a wrinkled apple in the squat, just in case a day passed
where they couldn't scrounge enough for everyone.

Before long, the soft echo of her mother's voice
reading still in her mind, Lizzie fell asleep.

৯৯৯

*"Charles!" Lizzie woke with a start in the cozy
cupboard bed where she and Maggie slept aboard the
airship. Her mother had slid the doors shut so that if
there was rough weather, they would not fall out. Lizzie
loved the cozy space. Sometimes she and Maggie would
play in here, though Mama would be very angry if she
knew they had brought a candle in earlier to see by.
Lizzie slid the door open a crack as their father strode
into the cabin, where Mama was tidying up the books
they had brought. She thought they were asleep. Maggie
was, but Lizzie wasn't.*

"We did not expect to see you—how did you—"

*"I imagine not. There are enormous advantages to
owning laboratories that produce such things as veloci-
thopters and aeroscopes. I simply landed upon the fuselage and entered via the ventral hatch. Our gallant
captain does not even know his employer is aboard."*

"But why?"

*"You are not a stupid woman, Elaine, and sadly,
not a devious one, either. Did you think I would not
follow you?"*

*"I do not know what you are talking about. I am
simply taking the girls to visit my family. Why on*

earth would you follow us?"

"Via London?"

"I thought we might do a bit of shopping before we went down to Penzance. Really, Charles, the girls are asleep. May we continue this conversation elsewhere?"

"It does not matter now whether they sleep or not. Sit."

"I shall not."

"Sit, or I will make you."

Mama's navy-blue skirts rustled as she sank into the seat under the viewing port. "The speed of the velocithopter has addled your mind."

"No, it has cleared it. I know what I must do. Whom have you told?"

"No one. I have nothing to tell anyone—with the possible exception of the clerk at Fortnum and Mason."

Lizzie's eye, pressed to the crack, widened as Papa pounced on Mama like Cinders the cat on a mouse. "Playing at ignorance will gain you nothing. You were listening at keyholes last night, weren't you?"

"No. You are hurting me."

"What did you hear?"

Mama muffled a shriek as Papa did something Lizzie could not see. Cold fear showered through her, held her immobile, surged in her small body like a wave.

"I heard you and your friends," Mama gasped. "I— I cannot believe this of you. The Prince of Wales—and Prince George—why, he is hardly more than a boy!"

"They are heirs to a throne that is redundant— scions of a family that is rotten to the core."

"You are mad."

"I am perfectly sane. I am a patriot—one of many—charged with a sacred duty to England."

"Assassinating a young man and his father is hardly sacred!" she snapped, then groaned when Papa twisted her wrists behind her back.

Why was Papa being so unkind to Mama? He loved her and brought her presents. And who was this boy who was causing all the trouble between them?

"When this country is a republic with a responsible government, you will see. Or perhaps not. Because I cannot allow you to betray me, you see, my dear. I cannot allow little birds to twitter to London magistrates and members of Parliament."

"What are you going to do, lock me up?"

"No. That would be inhumane. Good-bye, Elaine. We could have been happy for many years if you had not run away."

"I could not allow my girls to stay another moment in that house with you," she hissed. "Beast. Madman. Murderer ...."

৩৽৽৻

Lizzie swam out of the dream, choking and gasping. The sheets were damp and tangled around her legs, and she pushed them away frantically, trying to escape.

Escape. No. She did not need to escape. She was safe in her room at Colliford Castle, and she had had a nightmare.

A LADY OF RESOURCES

Lizzie slid out of bed and went to the window, where she opened the latch. Rain pattered on the stone sill, and the cool exhalation of the ground as it welcomed the moisture was scented with mint and lavender.

Safe.

It had been so real. So detailed. She could still feel the hard wood of the cupboard door as her cheekbone had pressed against it.

Had it been a nightmare? Or a memory?

A memory … in which she had seen her mother's face. No, that couldn't be right. She had never had such a memory. The first time she had seen that face was in the portrait over the fireplace in this very house.

But if it were a dream, would Mama not be wearing the only dress Lizzie had ever seen her in—the dressing gown over the frothy white nightclothes?

As clearly as she recalled the cupboard door, Lizzie's mind recalled the navy silk traveling suit her mother had worn, complete with the bustle draped in a fashion that had been obsolete for a decade. A fashion that did not permit her to sit comfortably on the narrow bench beneath the viewing port.

Not a dream. A memory.

But what had happened afterward? Why had Father twisted up her wrists like that and deliberately hurt her? What boy had they been talking about—His Royal Highness? Surely they could not have meant Prince George, the Prince of Wales's son?

Her father—assassinating father and son because they stood in line to the throne? But it had not happened. Prince George was alive and well, and in fact was planning to join the Prince of Wales in Scotland for the hunting party, if the *Evening Standard* had its facts in order.

Dream or memory? Whatever it had been, it had murdered sleep for Lizzie, well and truly. It must be long past midnight. Perhaps a tube had arrived and with the staff gone to bed, there was no one to hear. She buttoned a summer dress over her batiste nightgown, shook a moonglobe into luminosity, and padded down the marble staircase barefoot.

A tube waited in the slot in the library.

Dearest Lizzie,

You are the toploftiest of gumpuses (gumpi?) and of course I forgive you.

I shall be on the 7:15 train. The Lady has not yet returned from the revels at the Society (!) so she will not hear me leave. I have confided in Lewis, however. Someone must know where we are, and by the time the Lady extracts the story from him, we will have solved whatever it is that has your wig in a welter.

Love, Maggie

৯৩

"Bundle your hair into this cap," Evan said, handing her a small garment halfway between a mobcap and what one might wear sea-bathing. "It will protect your head somewhat from the metal interior, and your hair will act as a cushion. Do you see now why I asked you to leave it down?"

Obligingly, Lizzie tucked her hair away and arranged the cap comfortably. He handed her a teacup filled with a milky liquid. "What is this?"

"Something to help you sleep, but watered down quite a lot so that you wake in only an hour or two instead of tomorrow morning. It may have some other physical effects, but they wear off quickly."

She drank it down—it tasted bitter and slimy—and then Evan guided her onto the table, where he fitted the dream device over her head. "Is Father going to come watch the experiment?"

"I do not know. He mentioned something about visiting the tower at breakfast, but perhaps he wanted to check the telescope. He had better do that either before the experiment begins or after it is concluded. I do not want you to be disturbed."

"I hope it is after—and that he will not notice the telescope has been moved."

"He has not been up there in some time. I doubt that he will remember how he left it, and our bad behavior will go unremarked. Are you comfortable?"

"As much as one can be with a diving helmet on one's head." The last words came out a little slurred. The aforesaid head seemed to be floating off her shoulders.

"Good. Now, I shall lower this visor and I will not be able to hear you. Nor shall you be able to hear me.

We will communicate with hand signals and a slate."

She nodded, and the visor slid down. Her breathing sounded loud in the confined space, and before long, the metal in front of her nose would show the condensation from it. At a gesture from Evan, she lay back and swung her feet up. He slid a bolster—covered in chenille, no doubt filched from one of the many bedrooms in the castle—under her neck and shoulders to support them.

And then she slid into unconsciousness the way an airship crashed—a long, slow glide and a soft landing.

؟؈ؽ

Mama's voice was only a whisper, but Lizzie in her cupboard could hear it clearly. "Murderer." Beside her, Maggie stirred and rolled over, but Lizzie could not move.

"So dramatic, Elaine. Nothing has happened yet."

"What do you plan to do with us?"

"That is well in hand."

"Charles, think of the girls. They are only five, for God's sake. They are innocent."

"I do think of the girls, but when one looks at the longer view, I have all I need in Claude. Girls cannot run businesses, nor can they inherit, especially once I secure a peerage. It is a pity you did not give me a son, like Louise."

"I know what happened to her, Charles. I know, and if you do not leave now, I will tell what I know. It is all written down, and a word from me will see that

the papers get it."

"And who will hear that word?"

"I shall scream."

"I have no doubt you will." He advanced upon her. "But for the sake of the girls, I suggest you do not. Will you terrify them so?"

"You may do as you like with me, but leave them alone." Mama's courage was beginning to crack.

"I am afraid not. You see, I know that Elizabeth is awake in that cupboard, and that little pitcher has particularly big ears. No, I am afraid this must be a family affair."

"What do you—what is that? Charles, what is in that syringe?"

And then Papa pounced upon Mama again, and she tried to scream, but then her body went limp, and something dropped to the floor that Lizzie could not see.

Papa advanced upon the cupboard, and Lizzie pressed both hands to her mouth. Mama lay upon the floor. What was wrong with her? Why was she sleeping there and not in her bed across the cabin? Mewling noises emanated from between her fingers, and Lizzie tried to choke them back. Some deep instinct told her she must be quiet, he must not see her—

Too late.

His tawny eye pressed to the crack in the cupboard door. Only a crack, but she could see the malevolence and the triumph there.

"Do not move or speak," he whispered, "or your mother will die." And then he was gone.

Frozen in terror, Lizzie huddled under the quilt. When the smell of smoke crept into the cabin, she sniffed the air. Oh, no. Even she and Maggie knew that meant something dreadful. Fire on an airship meant it would crash. They must not crash!

She must disobey Papa and wake Mama, hurry hurry.

She slid the cupboard door open with both hands and leaped out, shaking Maggie with all the terror that had kept her motionless a few minutes ago. "Maggie! Wake up! There is a fire!"

Maggie rolled to a sitting position. "What? Where?" She coughed and clapped her hands over her nose. "Fire!"

Lizzie dropped to her knees next to Mama and shook her shoulder, the silk slippery under her fingers. "Mama! Wake up! Mama!" But she did not. Mama's face was waxy pale, and her mouth hung open, filled with spittle. "Mama!"

Lizzie could hear the flames chuckling madly now, and without warning, the floor dropped away underneath her. She screamed and lunged for Maggie. "Get the Captain. He must help Mama!"

They tumbled into the corridor, where men were dashing up and down, handkerchiefs over their faces. "Run!"

"Where?" Maggie pulled her ruffled nightdress up over her nose, coughing uncontrollably. "I can't breathe, Lizzie."

Lizzie grabbed the sleeve of an airman in mid-flight. "I want the captain! Mama is sick!"

"Get in your cabin, missy." He shoved them both back into the cabin. "You're like to get trampled."

"But—"

The door closed with a bang and smoke seeped in over the top. The floor dropped out from under them again and Lizzie screamed. This flight in the airship, which had begun as such a treat, was horrible! She was never flying in one again. The floor canted at an angle now, and Mama rolled over and over, landing up in a heap against the base of the sleeping cupboard. "Mama, wake up, please wake up."

Maggie climbed onto the window seat and gasped, which made her choke again on the smoke. "Lizzie, look! The river!"

The burning ship made orange and red dance on the surface of the water far below. They skimmed right over the top of London Bridge—

—London Bridge we're falling down—

—and the water rushed up, faster and faster. Instinct made Lizzie pull on the latch and the window swung into the room, came off its hinges, and shattered on the steep slope of the floor.

"Jump, Maggie!"

"No! Mama—"

"The water will wake her up and she will swim up to find us. Jump!"

Holding hands, they leaped out into the burning dusk, and no one alive saw them go.

৽৽

"I believe she is returning to consciousness. We must remove the helmet."

Lizzie swam up through the water ... no, the night ... oh, how cold the water is ...

"Lizzie?"

Something tugged on her hair, and she opened her eyes to see a vast dimness with a large glowing ball above her. The sun? Was she still under the water?

No, not the sun. Glass. And walls. The tower. She was in the tower at Colliford Castle. None of it was real.

And yet ... all of it had happened. She knew it as surely as she knew her own name. Her mind reeled, her head pounded with the worst headache she'd ever had, and she sagged back against the bolster with a groan.

"Lizzie, can you speak?" Evan hovered over her, his voice low and full of concern. "I am going to take the helmet off."

The heavy metal would have scraped her ears had they not been covered by the cap. As it was lifted away, she tried to lift her arms to the strings to get the cap off. They would not move.

"Let me assist you." When he removed the cap, her hair tumbled over the bolster and hung over the side of the table. "I do apologize. One of the effects of the elixir is that there is some temporary paralysis of the limbs afterward. Do you feel any other effects?"

"Headache. A dreadful one." To say nothing of the creeping horror still surging in her bloodstream—a horror she was powerless to act upon because she could not bloody move.

"I am sorry to hear it. It is the elixir again, I am

afraid. All my subjects report the same, but apparently one feels better after a large glass of water, so I come prepared. Here, drink this."

He slid an arm behind her head and she guzzled the glass down and nodded for more. The second one went down more slowly, but she finished it, too, and her head seemed to clear a little. The horror of the memories, however, did not.

For they were memories.

The crack—the tawny eye—

Oh, yes. She had been having flashes of a memory so deeply buried that it was not until she had seen the author of her grief and fear again that it had begun to bubble to the surface. And between her childhood books and the elixir—opium, she had no doubt—the memory had been freed altogether.

"Is Father here?" she whispered.

"I would not miss this for the world." Her father stepped out from behind the screen, and her stomach plunged in fear. "How do you feel, my dear?"

"Better." She tried to sit up, to move her legs or arms, but the most she could do was wiggle her fingers. She must play the innocent, the invalid. "Or perhaps not."

"Do not exert yourself. Sometimes it takes as much as an hour for the subject to recover fully from the elixir. When Kennidge agreed to be our subject, such was the case."

"Did it work?"

"Yes, we were able to get one of our successful plates from him."

"I beg your pardon—I meant did it work on me?"

She prayed it had not. How foolish she had been to agree to this! For if even one plate showed an image— a single moment of those memories—then her life would be worth even less than it had been on that fateful day when she and Maggie were supposed to have died.

Maggie!

Now she lay rigid, struck motionless by terror. Even now Maggie was probably alighting from the train and looking for the trap Lizzie had sent. What had she been thinking? How could she have been so foolish as to drag her sister—cousin—into this, simply because she was frightened and wanted company?

Oh, how selfish she had been! Now Maggie's life would be in danger, too. There would be no explaining to Father—de Maupassant—she could no longer think of him as any sort of parental figure who could bear her mother's name—that unlike Lizzie or her mother, Maggie had neither seen nor heard anything that could incriminate him.

For he had more to lose now.

But she and Maggie had much more to live for.

"Lizzie, you must rest until the effects of the elixir have worn off," Evan said. "While you recover, Charles and I will process the plates and see whether my recent improvements to the mnemosomniograph have been effective."

She must run. While they were busy, she must find a conveyance and get to the train station as fast as she could. And then what? There was no return train to

London until this evening. Well, no matter. If they had to walk all the way across the Cotswolds, they would be safer than staying here. As soon as this wretched paralysis wore off, she would act.

Now she could wiggle her toes inside her kid boots. One foot flopped to the side, and with a great effort, she brought it to the vertical.

The examination of the plates seemed to take ages. Not that she would complain, for each minute that passed brought some small return to mobility. Now she could circle her ankles. And lift her arms.

Patience. Knees?

Muscles tightened in thighs and calves, to no effect. She curled her spine forward, but could not manage to sit up.

From behind the screen, Evan exclaimed, "I think we have something!"

Come on. Come on, body. Do not fail me. I must … get … up …

No matter how she struggled, her legs would not move.

"Lizzie, you are a wonder!" Evan called. "We have three clear images!"

Oh, Lord, help me now, for I am alone.

"What do you think produced such high quality?" de Maupassant asked him.

"Since the laboratory conditions were identical to those of the other subjects in every respect," Evan said, excitement in his voice, "I cannot help but attribute it to an excess of emotion on the part of this subject. Er, of Lizzie. It is common knowledge, after all, that the young girl is an emotional, dramatic creature."

Ooh, if she only had the use of her legs, she would march over there and show him just how dramatic it would be to have one of his precious plates broken over his head! Her thigh muscles twitched, and she lifted her left knee.

Victory!

Almost. Her right knee would not so much as bend.

The curtain was pulled back and Evan and de Maupassant walked out, the former carrying the plates. "Look, Lizzie. Can you sit up?"

She would not look at her father. Instead, she fussed with her skirts, which had ridden up a little in her efforts to move various body parts. "I don't know."

"Do not overexert yourself," Evan cautioned her. "Only look. Can you identify this image?"

She did not want to look. But de Maupassant had already seen them, hadn't he? He knew who she was, and that she was the only witness to the murder of her mother and every other poor sod on that ship that evening. Reluctantly, she looked at the ghostly image on the plate in its brass holder.

A figure in bustled skirts, dark against light, with pale hair, lying face down. Above it, an oval floating in midair. Ah. The viewing port.

"Does your conscious mind recognize this scene?" Evan asked gently, holding it before her with one hand while attempting to plump up the bolster on which her head rested with the other.

Snouts's voice whispered in her mind. *When in doubt, play dumb. Once they underestimate you, you have the upper hand.* It had served the Lady well. She could only hope it would do the same now.

"A—a doll?" she said weakly. "A dressmaker's mannequin?"

"Perhaps," Evan said thoughtfully, "though one would not think such things would elicit strong emotion. What about this one?"

She stared at the plate for some time before she understood the dreamy image floating thereon. "That is Maggie, very young, asleep under a quilt."

"Ah." Evan exchanged a delighted glance with de Maupassant, whose face remained fixed in a pleasant smile. "That bears out my theory, at least, though the mixed results are a disappointment. And the third?"

The last image was stark—the very embodiment of what her mind had been trying to tell her for weeks. A dark field was bisected by a vertical ray of light, and in that light hung a human eye, with a round lens tilted down over it. A lens that would turn a hazel eye tawny.

Her breath died in her lungs as her entire body stiffened with the chill of fear. She must not—she must not look at him—

But like the rabbit exploding out of its hiding place when stillness would have saved it, she could not stop herself from meeting her father's gaze.

"Do not move," he said softly.

The predator had stalked and found her. In the echo of the words he had used on that terrible night, she knew with utter certainty that if she could not find the resources within herself to outwit him, neither she nor Maggie would survive a second time.

"Hallo, the tower," came a familiar voice from the door. "Are you all in here?"

Evan and de Maupassant whirled with identical expressions of surprised annoyance. "Margaret?" de Maupassant managed at last, blinking as though his eyes and ears played tricks on him.

"The same," she said cheerfully, coming in wearing her smart brown traveling suit with the velvet facings on the jacket, her eyes sparkling with pleasure that had certainly not been there on the occasion of her first visit. "Kennidge said you were all here and that Lizzie was to help you test the dream device. Have you begun? What have I missed?"

You would think she had merely overslept, not

journeyed all the way from London and probably climbed out of the trap two minutes ago.

"Margaret, first, you are just in time to view the first set of plates along with Elizabeth, and second, what on earth are you doing here?" Evan asked. "Surely you haven't gone all the way to London and back so quickly?"

"I have, actually. I attended Lady Claire's investiture—which was terribly exciting for her and Mr. Malvern and terribly dull for ordinary mortals like me—and then I found I missed my cousin so much that I repacked my valise and set off. I do hope my unexpected return is not an inconvenience? I would have sent a tube, but the decision was rather sudden, and—"

"No, not at all." De Maupassant had recovered his manners, pulling them on like a cloak. "In fact, the scientists we had been expecting were delayed due to the weather, so you find us happily *en famille.*"

"But where are Claude and the others?"

"Gone to Newquay," Lizzie said. "Maggie, do help me sit up. I cannot lie here and speak to the glass globe above us."

But try as she might, Lizzie could not master her disobedient muscles well enough to sit up, and finally Maggie and Evan were forced to let her relax upon the table again, her shoulders against the bolster.

"Would you like to see the plates?" Evan said eagerly, thrusting them under Maggie's nose before she had a chance to reply. "Lizzie says that this one depicts you. Can you credit it?"

Maggie peered at the image rather as one might

peer through the fog on a particularly bad London night. "Not at all. Me? I do not believe it."

"Like dreams, I suspect the images may be subject to interpretation," de Maupassant said easily. "Now, Evan, we cannot leave poor Elizabeth lying here indefinitely. I suggest we remove her to a proper bed so that she may recover in comfort. The Queen's Tower is nearest."

"The Queen's Tower?" Evan said blankly, dragging his attention away from his plates with difficulty. "Why not simply take her to her room?"

"I believe I just explained why. Come, boy. You are young and strong and you may devote five minutes to the well-being of your cousin, surely?"

Evan's cheeks flushed above the youthful growth of beard he had clearly forgotten to shave this morning. "Of course. I do apologize. Lizzie, if you will pass your right arm about my neck, I will endeavor to lift you."

Lizzie had been close to many a young man—in dance class one could hardly avoid it—but it was a different sensation to be cradled against someone in a relatively supine position. She was not altogether sure she liked it—or rather, she would like it more if she were surer of his motivations and knowledge.

Maggie followed them inside the house and along the corridor to the Queen's Tower, which, since it had usable rooms for guests, had not had its doors bricked up in the same way as the science tower. "We could not have house guests opening the wrong door at a crucial moment in the experiments," Evan explained. "Here we are. Just one more stair and your journey will be over, Lizzie."

"I fear it is much more work for you than for me," she said as Maggie preceded them up the stone stairs, which wound around a central pillar. At the landing, Maggie pushed open the heavy door and Evan carried her inside.

"So this is the room where Her Majesty slept," Maggie said, turning in a circle as Evan laid Lizzie upon the embroidered coverlet and plumped up the down pillows behind her head and shoulders. "It is very fine, is it not, Lizzie?"

It was indeed. Midnight blue curtains embroidered with stars hung on either side of a curved window. An easy chair was pulled up next to the fireplace—laid with wood ready for the match—and curved shelves filled with books and curios had been fitted cleverly along the walls. On the side opposite the bed with its rich hangings was another, smaller door. "Where does that go?"

"Up to the parapet," Evan said. "It is of a height with the other."

"You may leave it closed, Maggie," Lizzie told her. "I shall not be exploring parapets anytime soon."

"There is a water closet in this alcove here behind the curtain, which was once used for storing arrows. Maggie, perhaps you might get Lizzie another glass of water? I must return to my plates and see what else I might bring up for you to look at."

He clattered down the stairs much more quickly than he had come up bearing her, and when Maggie brought her a glass, she drank the water gratefully. At this rate, she was going to need that water closet—but her headache was gone, and she was feeling much less fuzzy.

"How long before you can walk?" Maggie asked. "I must say, I don't like the idea of you being laid up."

"Nor do I." Lizzie tried her knees again, and this time, they both bent together. "Look, I could not do this a few minutes ago."

"Try sitting up."

But no, the muscles in her back would not allow it. She would have to be patient, no matter how much the inactivity—and the risk—irked her.

"While you're lying there," Maggie said, sitting on the edge of the bed, "you might as well tell me what is going on."

"We're in trouble," Lizzie began. "It started with—wait, someone's coming up."

"Kennidge, maybe, to see if Your Majesty would like tea in your room?"

"If I drink another drop, it will be you carrying me to the water closet."

The door opened and Lizzie's stomach plunged once more at the sight of de Maupassant. "I see you are comfortable," he said from the threshold.

"As comfortable as one can be when one cannot move, and is in a strange room."

"I thought you would enjoy seeing the Queen's Tower while you recover. I hope you enjoy your surroundings for as long as they are necessary."

"I'm sorry—what?" Necessary? What was necessary was that the last of the recovery process should not take much longer. As soon as her legs would bear her weight, they were getting out of here.

He gazed around the room, settling at last on the narrow door up to the parapet. "When she and the Prince Consort stayed here, Her Majesty had just survived one of the several attempts there have been on her life. She found it very comforting that there is only one way in and out of this tower. With a guard on the parapet and one at the base of the stairs, it was quite possible to give the royal couple complete security at very little expense."

"Well, fortunately, no one wants to make an attempt on us," Maggie said with a smile.

His gaze moved from her to Lizzie, and held. "Quite. What a shame you will not be able to tell your relations in Penzance that you slept in the bed of a queen."

"What on earth do you mean?" Lizzie tried once more to sit up, and found that she could lean on her elbows.

"I informed the servants you are staying up here for a lark, before you leave to see your mother's family," de Maupassant said. "It will mean fewer questions, particularly since His Highness is expected to arrive at his estates tonight. In mathematics, this would be called an elegant solution—solving the greatest number of problems using the fewest number of operations."

Maggie gazed from him to Lizzie. "I am afraid I am completely lost, Uncle Charles."

"You are no such relation to me," he told her with blunt, careless cruelty, and Maggie's breath caught.

SHELLEY ADINA

Rage ignited in Lizzie's helpless bosom. How dared he take that tone with Maggie, who was a thousand times the better person!

And in that moment, as though the fizzing fury inside her had ignited her mind, all the pieces fell into place and the reason for the cannon on the roof became clear. "You are going to try again," she whispered. "I am surprised you didn't do Her Majesty in while she was sleeping here."

"It would be difficult to explain that away satisfactorily," he said. "However, given the fact that His Highness's arrival is typically feted in grand style, with fireworks in the village and a seven-gun salute in the park of his estate, the situation will be quite different. Made to order, in fact."

"What on earth are you talking about?" Maggie demanded. "Lizzie?"

She had nothing to lose now by playing dumb. Her father intended to do away with them both no matter what she said. "He is going to shoot the Prince of Wales's airship out of the sky when it flies overhead this evening," she told Maggie in a voice devoid of anything but contempt. "That is no telescope on the roof of the science tower. It is a cannon, and he is going to use it to murder the prince and his son under the cover of the fireworks."

De Maupassant's moustaches twitched in a smile. "Clever girl. Climbing about like a kitten on the drapes, were we? Poking our whiskers in where they don't belong?"

"I was bored."

"You're very much like your mother. She was not bored, but curiosity certainly killed that cat."

"It did not. You did. I saw it all."

Maggie's face was a study in horrified confusion as she looked from Lizzie to de Maupassant.

"Yes, I know. What luck that you *volunteered* for the dream device. I should not have liked to force you against your will—it would have been very difficult to explain to Evan, whose scruples are rather deeply entrenched."

"You *wanted* me as a test subject, then."

"Oh, yes. From the moment I saw you in Munich and realized that the girl I thought safely at the bottom of the Thames was not only alive, but grown up, it was necessary to know how much you remembered. A perfect subject for the dream device. When you spiked my guns the first time, I realized that force must be replaced with guile. How fortunate for me that your need for family was as great as my need to draw you close to me."

Maggie's eyes widened. "The pocket watch."

"Yes. I did not expect you to use the skills you developed on the street. One doesn't, does one? Getting it into your hands proved easy, but still you eluded me."

Lizzie was finding it difficult to breathe. "That bomb was intended for me?"

"I had originally planned to offer it as a graduation gift. Clumsy, I admit, and with unfortunate collateral damage, but it was all I had in my possession on short notice."

If she had opened it that evening, in her room with

Maggie and the Lady, all three of them would have been killed. Her choosing his pocket to pick instead of any other man's had saved their very lives—and the bully-boys had met her intended fate instead.

"I shall do better this time," he added.

"In a pig's eye!" Maggie lunged for the door, but he was ready for her. Stepping outside, he slammed it shut, and she crashed against it. They heard the lock turn, smooth and well oiled.

"Good-bye, my dears," he said through oak planks at least an inch thick. "You shall have a fine send-off this evening."

Lizzie roared, low in her throat, and threw herself from the bed to go to Maggie's aid.

One leg worked. One did not. She fell awkwardly on the carpet, blinded by tears and rage at her own stupidity. Why had she not seen it sooner? Why had she not run this morning, when she had the chance?

But if she had, then Maggie might be the one all alone up here, waiting for the moment of her death.

Lizzie crawled across the carpet to her, and together they huddled against the door. In fact, it felt very much like the night they had crawled out of the water and crouched weeping on the river steps, helpless and wondering where their happy lives had gone.

19

It took all of the next hour to tell Maggie everything she had learned and remembered—and nearly all of that time for her body to restore itself to its normal working order. But Lizzie had had a day to come to grips with the knowledge that de Maupassant had already tried to kill her twice. Maggie was making a valiant attempt to recover, but it was clear that her loving heart was having a difficult time accepting it.

"I cannot believe it," she whispered every few minutes, pacing from one side of the tower room to another. "How is it possible for him to conceal from people that he is raving mad?"

"Not mad," Lizzie said with withering scorn. "A *patriot.*"

"And your mother found him out after his first attempt on the princes, and took us away."

"Perhaps the attempt confirmed what she could not believe—that somehow, he had killed Claude's mother, too. In any case, she fled, he followed in the velocithopter, set the airship afire, and flew away to safety like the coward he is."

Maggie stopped pacing and came to sit next to Lizzie on the window seat, which gave a fine view of the surrounding country. "And the most amazing thing of all is that I do not remember any of it."

"Nor did I, until I picked up one of the books in our room and realized it was one of our own, from that life." Aesop had revealed much more than proverbs to live by. "My dreams told the truth—and unmasked a villain. As soon as he saw the plate showing Mother on the floor of the airship, my hours were numbered."

"We must stop him."

"I agree. I am not sure just how yet."

"What about Evan? Surely once he knows the facts, he will help us."

Lizzie ran a finger along the seam of the window, which was fixed in its frame and did not open. Naturally. "Much as I like him, I do not know how much he knows. And until I do, I cannot trust that he won't betray us—even inadvertently."

"So we are on our own, then."

"We have been in this position before. Or have you forgotten Resolution?"

"In Resolution, we were not locked up in a tower like a pair of madwomen."

"Well, we've managed to evade him twice so far—the third time is the charm."

Maggie got up. "Right. If the Lady were here, she would tell us to catalogue our resources and then use our imaginations."

"If the Lady were here, we wouldn't be in this position," Lizzie admitted grimly. "I was stupid to tell you not to tell her. Utterly stupid—on that and several other counts."

"It's all right." Circling the room, her cousin smiled at her. "One doesn't expect one's father to be a murderer. It's not something you can plan for." The smile faded. "Oh, Lizzie. I'm so sorry. That was a horrible thing to say." Maggie's eyes filled with tears—not at the thought that they had only a few hours to live, but at the idea that she might have hurt Lizzie's feelings.

Lizzie crossed the carpet—rejoicing in the simple fact that she could, with working legs—and hugged her. "It's only the truth. I've had a little time to see him for what he is ... and me for what I'd let myself become. How could you have put up with me?"

"Because I know you. I know that you would cry into the rag-pile years ago, thinking that I didn't hear, because we had no mother and father. I saw how you looked at the other girls' families in Munich—your longing for that kind of life was plain on your face."

Lizzie clutched her hand. "Oh, please tell me the Lady doesn't think I—"

Maggie shook her head. "She doesn't have a father, either, remember? And her mother spent how many months trying to marry her off to Lord James Selwyn against her wishes? The Lady understands about family—warts and all."

"*She* is our family," Lizzie said fiercely. "We chose one other. We are a flock and nothing is going to change that ever again."

Maggie fingered the hangings on the bed as though estimating their weight. "What about Claude?" she asked. "And Evan? If they prove to be innocent of this affair, will you claim them?"

"If they prove to be as deceived in de Maupassant as I was, I will be happy to claim them as family, and so will you. Claude is my half-brother, and Evan is our cousin, after all. But never again will I live with them, or think of them the way I think of you and the Lady and Snouts and—and Tigg—" She choked at the thought of Tigg, who was somewhere in Scotland with miles of wind and moor between them. Tigg, who was laboring under the delusion that she had chosen any number of people over him.

"Lizzie, do not break down on me now. We must be strong, and consider our resources. Look. Do you think we could pull these hangings down and use them to let ourselves down the wall?"

Self-control had never been one of her virtues. Maggie was right. If she went to pieces with grief and fear and disappointment, then Maggie would, too, and they would never be able to think their way out of this situation. "It's a two-hundred-foot drop, Mags."

"And these are only twelve-foot drapes. Is there anything in the water closet?" She emerged a moment later, crestfallen. "Nothing but a commode, and a bowl and ewer with water. At least he was that considerate."

"And there isn't so much as a pair of compasses or a tweezer on these shelves with which I might pick the lock." Lizzie searched behind the books and curios. "Though if he comes back, we could use this chunk of amethyst to conk him on the noggin." Getting that close to the madman was only a last resort. She opened the narrow door on to the equally narrow stair up to the parapet. "Come on. Maybe there is something up here."

They emerged onto the stone circle of the parapet, where the wind grabbed their hair and tossed their skirts behind them. "The sun is going down," Maggie said. "When is the Prince of Wales's ship expected?"

"When it is dark enough for fireworks?" Lizzie wished she had paid more attention to the dining-room conversation of Claude and the Sorbonne set. "I don't know. All we know is that it's this evening."

She walked to the waist-high parapet and gazed over the castle roofs at the other tower, where the barrel of the telescope protruded from the brass dome. "We have two tasks, don't we? To scuttle that cannon so it can't fire and bring the ship down, and to get away from here so he can't find us. The question is, how are we going to accomplish them?"

Maggie leaned over the parapet as far as she could, examining the sheer stone wall. "You'll have to put on your antigravity corset and fling yourself off, because we certainly aren't going to be climbing down. I thought medieval towers were supposed to have vines and missing stones and footholds and all those helpful things."

"If I had my corset, I would. But if it's in your valise, it may as well be in Munich, for all the good it will do."

"But it isn't." Maggie straightened and began to unfasten her suit jacket. "I've got it on."

Lizzie gaped at her.

Off came the jacket. "Here, undo the buttons on my waist, will you? I put it on over my own, and until this moment had completely forgotten about it."

Lizzie had the sudden urge to laugh, and if that was hysteria, then so be it. She took the green brocade garment that she hadn't seen since her final examinations, and tossed it to the flagged floor. It bounced about four feet in the air until Maggie grabbed it.

"Careful. It'll go over the parapet and then where will we be?"

Where, indeed? "Why on earth did you wear it? I expected it to be in your valise with your raiding rig."

"Have you seen how the porters on the trains here treat the luggage? I couldn't very well risk my valise being tossed on the platform and having the blessed thing go bouncing off down the line or up onto a roof, now, could I? It was put the corset on or leave it at home."

Swiftly, Lizzie re-wrapped it around her cousin and began to hook up the front. "What are you doing?" Maggie protested, pushing at her hands. "I brought it for you."

"You may have done, but you're going to wear it. You're going to go and get help."

Maggie stared at her. "You're not suggesting—"

"I am. You're going to do exactly what you just said—jump off this tower and get word to the Lady. There is just enough time to send a tube and for her to lift and fly here. Perhaps she can even intercept the royal ship."

"And what are you going to do while I am taking headers off towers?"

"I shall scuttle that cannon."

"And if you're discovered?" Maggie's cheeks were reddened by the wind and by incredulity. And fear. "What then?"

Lizzie took her hands and squeezed. "Then at least I will know that you are safe, and you'll see that de Maupassant is brought to justice."

"I know what you are doing, you rascal. You shall not send me to safety and stay here to be killed, Elizabeth Rose. We go together or we do not go at all."

Lizzie shook her head and invited Maggie to put on her embroidered waist. "I do not know how the repenthium will behave. Sending you to safety—I do not even know if you will survive the drop." She stopped attempting to dress her. "No, on second thought, *you* must scuttle the cannon and *I* will jump. Take this off at once."

Maggie pulled away and reached behind herself to button her waist. "I will not. If you are going to risk your life with your father, then I shall take the same risk with the fall, and we will settle up the safety question when we are both far away. Here, do me up, will you? I can never get the ones in the middle."

Maggie was right. It was Hobson's choice anyway—

either course was as likely to get them killed. As she fastened the buttons, Lizzie said, "Remember your angles in geometry?"

"As if I could forget. I nearly went mad. What has that to do with anything?"

"The repenthium will cause the bounce at an angle opposite to the surface toward which it is forced. If you go straight down, you will come straight up, and that will do us no good at all. If you land on the far slope of the moat, you will bounce straight into the castle walls, and—and, well, I do not want to think about that. So you must endeavor to come down on the inner slope of the moat, bounce outward, and land somewhere in the park, there." She pointed.

"Two hundred feet, you said?" Maggie asked, her gaze flickering from one point to another as she calculated angles, weight, and trajectory.

"Approximately. Oh, Maggie, let me do it. I cannot bear the thought of you—" She could not finish.

"Then do not think of it. How do I stop the bouncing?"

Lizzie swallowed and controlled the urge to break down and weep once more. "Reach up under your waist and remove the bones of repenthium one at a time until you can control your landing. The channels in the corset are open at the top—I ripped out the ends of the seams one afternoon after the Lady had to rescue me with a very large butterfly net."

"Is that where that came from? I wondered what on earth she was experimenting with. All right, then. There is no time like the present, I suppose."

Together, they leaned over, and Maggie examined the slope of the moat. "It looks possible."

"Surprisingly so, for something impossible." She hugged Maggie to her, feeling the hard casing of two corsets around her slender form. "Do not die, Mags. I could not bear it."

"The same to you," Maggie whispered. "Once I send the tube, I will return to help you."

"How?"

"I do not know—but I will use my imagination. You must focus on that cannon."

Maggie took as deep a breath as her two corsets would allow, and climbed into one of the embrasures. A final calculation and—

"Maggie, one last thing."

With a loud exhalation, she stepped back from the brink. "Yes?"

"Make sure you curl up and fall horizontally, knees to chest, so the greatest number of bones repel the earth."

"I'm glad you remembered that now instead of a second from now."

"In fact, why don't you slip one out of the front and give it to me. I just had an idea."

Maggie reached under her batiste waist, and after a second of fiddling, threaded a thin rod of repenthium up through her embroidered collar and handed it to her. "Here you go. Chin up. See you later tonight— we'll enjoy the fireworks together."

Lizzie handed her the suit jacket, and she slipped it on. Then she stepped to the edge, flexed her knees ... and leaped straight out into the empty air.

If she had sent the one she loved best in the world to her death, then she could not turn her face away like a coward.

Lizzie leaned over the parapet and watched Maggie's body plunge toward the inner slope of the moat. For one dreadful second it appeared as though Maggie would hit the wall—and then she rolled to her back, spread her skirts, and the air caught them enough to change her trajectory and take her to the slope of the moat. She pulled her legs in just in time, the repenthium repelled its target a good four feet from the point of impact, and Maggie flew up into the air in a huge, arcing bounce that took her over the moat, over the garden, and into the park.

Another bounce barely took her to the top of a maple tree.

And Lizzie could not even see the third bounce. She must be taking the rods out two at a time, controlling her motion at the risk of increasing impact. Where was she? Had she hit a tree? Miscalculated and broken her back on a rocky outcropping? Lizzie's eyes dried in the wind at the top of the tower as she stared out into the park, desperate for some sign.

And then, a small brown blob stepped into one of the distant grazing meadows for the draft horses, and waved. Once—twice—and Maggie ducked back under the trees and was lost to sight.

Lizzie dissolved against the cold stone, weeping in relief and gratitude. She went to church with the Lady but had never been the religious sort. However, if there was ever a moment to give thanks to forces greater than herself, now was that moment. *Safe. Oh, thank you, Lord, she is safe!*

When her sobbing quieted enough that she could think again, she wiped her face with the ruffle on her petticoat and got to her feet.

Now, then—the first order of business was to get off this tower. She crossed it and leaned over the other side to consider her course. Going back into the bedroom was useless, and scaling the walls impossible. Her only option was to do as Maggie had done, and jump down onto the roofs of the castle, which sloped this way and that, with battlements and walkways and odd bits of crenellation on the ridges.

It was clear that no one had been up to look after

the roof in at least a decade—drifts of leaves had piled in the corners, and that directly below, freezing winters appeared to have caused some of the blocks to separate as ice expanded and contracted in rotting masonry. She would have to choose her landing site carefully, or she would turn an ankle. Or worse.

There. The ridge of the slate roof directly below her flattened out in a foot-wide walkway, presumably so that a workman could get over to the eaves to clean them. It was the only flat landing place that she could see, but she would need to be very careful. If she leaned too much one way or the other, she would go tumbling down the steep roof, and who knew where she would land? She had enough memories of the catwalks and roof hideaways of Whitechapel to know that keeping one's head was just as important as keeping one's footing.

How strange that she was able to keep her head, now that she thought about it. She, who could not look out of a second-story window without feeling as though the whole house were bending to toss her out of it, who could not fly in an airship without becoming violently ill, had been bounding about on this tower two hundred feet in the air for half an hour without feeling a thing.

Had the dream device had an unexpected side effect? Had the deeply buried memories been what had caused her fear of heights—and now that they had risen to the surface, her body had no further reason for nausea?

She would think about that later, with Maggie and

the Lady, over a restorative cup of tea. For now, she must concentrate on her escape.

Lizzie tucked the rod of repenthium beneath her feet like a skipping-rope, held on to both ends, and leapt from the parapet.

She landed heavily, awkwardly, one foot on the walkway and the other sliding dangerously off onto the pitch of the slates. In grabbing for something— anything—to stop herself from losing her balance and sliding away down the roof, she dropped the rod. Gasping, her hands wrapped around a stone crenellation, she watched it skate away and finally go sailing off the roof into the kitchen garden far below.

Ten rods of repenthium could cause a body to be repelled from two hundred feet. One rod could barely do the job from twenty. Something to make a note of during the aforesaid cup of tea.

Lizzie tested her knees and ankles, thankful that the only damage was to her stockings. Well, and a scrape on the side of one calf, which was sure to stop bleeding in a minute or two. With a closer view of the rooftops, she cast around, getting her bearings.

The cannon tower was as smooth and featureless as the Queen's Tower, so scaling it was out of the question. To scuttle the weapon, she would either need the corset to bounce herself up there—not an option now—or descend to ground level and go in through the laboratory.

What were the odds that both Evan and de Maupassant had left it empty? And if they had, that they had left it unlocked?

As she gazed at the tower, thinking, a movement on the parapet made her heart leap. Her stockings gave up the ghost entirely as she flung herself flat on the walkway behind a stone chimney. Cautiously, she raised her head and peered around the chimney to see her father leaning on the parapet opposite, smoking.

Had he seen her?

No, it did not seem so. He appeared relaxed ... a man whose problems had been solved and who had only to wait until the next set floated into view. After a moment, he flung the stub of his cheroot away with a careless flick of the wrist, and disappeared from sight. But before Lizzie could make up her mind to rise, the barrel of the cannon lifted above the parapet, then lowered. Lifted, swung to right and left, and lowered.

He must be testing the guidance mechanisms, making sure everything was operational. Which meant he had already discovered that the cannon had been armed. Not that it mattered. She had just saved him a moment's work, that was all.

But he was occupied. If she was going to move, it must be now.

She climbed down the slope of the next roof on stone trim formed like stair steps—with a roof on one side and empty space on the other. Jumping on to a level spot, she realized she must be on the roof of the gallery on the third floor, which traversed the distance between the two towers. She took off at a run, hoping that if there was a maid dusting in the gallery, she would think the sound merely the racing of rats in the wainscoting.

But what was this? She fetched up against the tower, panting, and stepped back a little to look it over. The arrow slits were at eye level here, as if the slates on which she stood had once been the floor of a wing that no longer existed—as the floors in the tower no longer existed so that the dream device might be housed there.

If this had been a floor, could there also be a door?

She circled the wall, acutely aware that the sun would be down in an hour. Clouds massed in the west, gilded on their edges as the sun behind them splayed its rays across the sky like a crown. Surely it was a sign that she would succeed and the princes would be safe. Oh, if only she had more than her bare hands to work with!

Consider your resources, girls, and then use your imaginations.

She must not give in to fear and despair. She must behave as the Lady would, and use her eyes and hands to help herself.

The cannon tower, unlike the other, had become overgrown with ivy and honeysuckle over the years. Not all the way to the top, sadly, but at least to this level, which was sheltered a little by the bulk of the house. She circled as far as she could around the front closest to the face of the curtain wall, pulling away the ivy, to no avail. Then, on the back side, directly under the barrel of the cannon twenty feet above her, she found it.

A door. It must lead to what had been the third floor of the tower—the last before the trap door. Stiff fingers located the handle, and she pushed with all her might.

Locked.

Blast and bebother it!

Oh, if only she had the Lady's lightning rifle! She could put a hole in this door that even the Cudgel, one of their old enemies, who was built like a pig, could climb through. She could face her father down without fear just before she blasted that cannon to bits, and everything in the laboratory under it—and this whole wretched castle that pretended to be a home and was not by any stretch of the imagina—

Wait. Hadn't Evan said that the dream device was powered by a cell similar to the one in the Malvern-Terwilliger Kinetick Carbonator? That he had, in fact, cribbed the design for his own purposes?

The breath went out of Lizzie's lungs and she sagged against the ancient door. The ivy nodded around her shoulders and brushed her cheeks, with its musty green scent that smelled like secrets kept and hiding places offered to small children.

She did not have to get all the way up to the parapet to scuttle the cannon. She did not have to face her father, who had already proven he was capable of cold-blooded murder. All she had to do was lock the trap door and then blow up the cell in its great glass globe below it. The floor of the parapet would not stand the blast, and everything on top of the tower—dome, cannon, and murderer—would come tumbling down inside it.

She had to get off the roof and into the laboratory.

If Evan was there, she would remove him by whatever means necessary, even if it meant rendering him unconscious. And then she would lock her father on the roof with his weapon, and see how he liked being the one in prison, with death staring him in the eye.

જી∘જી

A tube landed in the slot at 23 Wilton Crescent with a pneumatic hiss and an accompanying stampede of feet to see who would be the first to get it.

Claire smiled and immediately yawned, and was ashamed of herself. Fancy getting up at one in the afternoon, and still lounging in a loose tea-gown on the comfortable sofa in the library at teatime! But she deserved a day to lie about after the triumph of last night.

She had dreamed of her entry into the Royal Society of Engineers for so long, and the reality had been even more wonderful than the dream. To advance down the central aisle, seeing the smiling faces of her guests and her colleagues alike ... to mount the stage and receive the formal brass chain of membership over her black graduation robes from the Prince Consort himself, he being the Society's royal patron ... to see her name on the program and know that it would be engraved upon its own plate in the Society's great library in London ...

Claire sighed in quiet, glowing satisfaction. It had been a triumph, and it was not over yet. Andrew was coming at eight to take her to dinner, and then tomorrow they were asked to the home of one of the board members for a reception for the new inductees.

It would have been lovely, of course, if Mama and Nicholas could have come up to town for the occasion, but Mama, much to her own astonishment and Sir Richard Jermyn's jubilation, was in a delicate condition and was on no account permitted to travel. Claire could hardly credit the news. On the positive side, Mama would now be plunged back into motherhood, and it was devoutly to be hoped that her attention would be fixed there for the next eighteen years at least. Claire would be free to live her life secure in the knowledge that her mother would be too tired to meddle in it any further.

Lewis appeared at the door. "Two come for you, Lady."

She held out a hand for the letters, one of which was curled in the shape of the tube, signifying a longer journey than merely across town. "Thank you, Lewis. Will you and the others join me for tea? I heard a rumor of orange chiffon cake. Is it true?"

"Mrs. Morven says so, Lady. She knows it's your favorite. I'll round up the others and let her know you're ready."

She opened the envelope with the least amount of curl.

Dearest Claire,

It has come—the day I have waited for so long! The day I may write and tell all my friends that Pe-

ter and I have fixed a date at last—and I hope that after four years of patient waiting, you will not find it too short a notice.

Our wedding day is the fifteenth of August. There! I have written it in ink but I am determined it will be in stone—I will not be obliged to move it out one more time. The ceremony will be at eleven in the morning, at Holy Trinity, with a breakfast afterward in Cadogan Square.

Claire, we have talked about this and dreamed about it together on many occasions, but I must have your answer by return. Will you be my maid of honor—for sure and for certain, as we used to say when we were schoolgirls? Mama has my bridesmaids lined up from every possible branch of the family—eleven, can you imagine anything so silly?—but I have held firm that there is only one person who will stand beside me at the altar, and that is you.

Please let me know soonest. I promise I will not make you wear pink.

Your own,
Emilie Fragonard (soon to be Livingston)

Claire could not help the joy that warmed her heart at the thought of Emilie being married at last. If any woman had shown the patience of a saint as her intended readied Selwyn Place for them and brought it back from a near ruin to a producing estate, it was Emilie. Claire would write this very evening with an emphatic yes, and then wouldn't Mrs. Fragonard stamp up and down the stairs and abuse the housemaids!

But it could not be helped. Claire had been responsible for seating Emilie and Peter next to one another at dinner several years ago—the night that both their lives had changed, in fact—and she would reap the happy harvest of the seeds that had been sown then.

Still smiling, she ripped open the thin post-office paper most often used by people who did not possess stationery.

Lady,

I am at Colliford Castle and you must come with all haste. Lizzie's father is a murderer, and she is his next victim. So is the Prince of Wales.

The telescope on the tower is really a cannon, and he plans to shoot down the prince's airship tonight. We are going to prevent it.

Please come.

Maggie

Claire leaped to her feet and the sheets of paper scattered like snow in a gust of wind. "Snouts!" she shrieked, dashing out of the room. "Lewis! Quickly!"

The two of them materialized in the hall, Snouts with his mouth full of the cake that hadn't quite made it to the library. "Lady, what's wrong? Is there a mouse in the book room?"

"No, but there is a rat in the castle. Arm yourselves with everything you have to hand, and meet me in the mews in ten minutes. We'll drive out to *Athena.*"

She was halfway up the stairs when Lewis got his mouth moving. "*Athena,* Lady?"

"Yes. Quickly, now! We are flying to Colliford Castle to rescue the Mopsies from that murdering Seacombe and we must lift within half an hour."

She dashed into her room and flung open the trunk that stood at the end of the bed, perpetually packed and ready for a sudden departure. Her raiding rig lay on top. If she had not been shaking with rage and fear for her girls, she would have rejoiced in the occasion to put it on again.

The Lady of Devices had not made an appearance on English soil in quite some time. The man who had precipitated her appearance was going to regret it for the rest of his very short life.

Lizzie balanced on the point of a gable and scrambled in through the open window of one of the servants' rooms on the fourth floor. Thank goodness it wasn't November, or raining, which would have meant locked windows all over the house. Now to leave the sash just the way she'd found it, and nothing else disturbed. She let herself out of the room and made her way downstairs on quiet feet.

Maggie's valise still sat on the floor of their room where the footman had left it. She rifled through it quickly and found her cousin's raiding rig, which she had not taken the time to put on. Lizzie wrapped the leather corselet about her waist, cinched it closed, and checked inside the square, flat case hanging from it by a brass catch. Matches. Some firecrackers for distraction. A handkerchief and two sticking plasters. A pound note. And under it, one of the smaller of their collection of lightning cells, assembled at various times over the years because of the Lady's insistence that they never forget how to do it.

Maggie thought the oddest things necessary. Never mind. Though she could not see a use for any of these things just now, the heat of the moment might call for any one of them.

Looking this way and that, Lizzie crept out of the bedroom and down the back stairs to the kitchen garden. The kitchen maid straightened up from the lettuce she was picking when she saw her.

Blast!

"Good afternoon, Miss Elizabeth. Have you come looking for your tea?"

"No, thank you, Dorie. But I did lose something out here—a corset bone. Black, with a blue tinge. Have you seen something answering that description?" She gazed up at the roofs far above, attempting to calculate where the rod might have come down.

"Pardon me, miss, but why should a young lady's corset bone be out here in the garden?"

Lizzie gave her a smile filled with mischief. "It was meant to be a joke on my cousin, but it seems to have turned into a joke on me, since I cannot find it."

Dorie did not look as though she understood the joke. Gamely, though, she walked slowly down the row of lettuce, and Lizzie did the same in the carrots and radishes, then cast a wider net over the squash, pumpkins, and herbs. There were plenty of stakes, but they were all canes, not black metal. Then Dorie frowned at the neatly staked tomatoes, which had just come into flower. "Wait. Here is something." She plucked it from the plants and held it up. "Is this it?"

Far from bouncing off the ground, the rod had become wedged in the bushy, slightly sticky tomato plants, which gave it no solid surface from which to be repelled.

"It is!" Lizzie took it, and pushed it down between her corselet and her blouse. "Thank you. What good eyes you have."

"Mam always told us to eat our carrots. Are you sure you don't want your tea, miss? Mr. Seacombe is up with his telescope and don't want to be disturbed, but Mrs. Kirby can have something ready for you young ladies in a trice."

If she forced anything into her stomach in the state she was in, she would toss it right back up. "No, but thank you for your kindness."

"All right, then. Mrs. Kirby says dinner is at eight o'clock—unless you'd want to dine earlier, since you're going to Penzance tomorrow?"

"No, no. We usually dine at eight. There is no reason to change it. Thank you, Dorie."

Lizzie retreated back along the castle walls, attempting to look as though she were enjoying a botany excursion while hugging the stone to avoid being seen from above. How strange that the staff behaved exactly as though everything were normal. Mrs. Kirby, the cook, did not know that she and Maggie had been locked in the tower, and in fact was expecting them at dinner. Surely her father did not plan to let them out for that? What would he do, swear them to silence in front of the servants?

Not likely. He was going to shoot down the prince's airship, put paid to her and Maggie, and then saunter down to eat his filet of sole as though nothing in the world was wrong. Why, their bodies would probably rot in the tower and not even be discovered until the next royal visit—because he would simply say this evening that they were resting, and tomorrow that he had taken them to the station himself and seen them off to Penzance.

Oh, he was a clever-clogs. But no more clever than she and Maggie—and they had been trained by the best. The fact that she had told someone she planned to be at dinner would come up eventually, as would the fact that Maggie's valise still sat in their room instead of in the Queen's Tower. Doubt at these inconsistencies would drift into the minds of the staff. Doubt was a thin line to hang a life on, but it was all she had at the moment until she could weave something better.

Lizzie slid around the curve of the cannon's tower and paused outside the door. Silence, except for the breeze that was freshening across the fields and in the trees. Those clouds were piling higher in the west, and something in the air told her there would be rain again tonight.

Oh, please let the Lady arrive safely. Please let Athena weather the journey and bring us help.

I can't do this alone.

She allowed herself only a moment to despair. Because she could not avoid the truth—for the moment, she *had* to do this alone. She must do what she could, and hope it would be enough. Even if rescue never came and she died in the attempt, anything was better than an ugly end locked up alone in a room the Queen had found so safe and comforting.

Safety and comfort, Lizzie had learned, all depended on who held the key to the door.

Speaking of which …

She slipped inside and removed the old-fashioned key from the lock, tucking it inside the pouch on her corselet. If anyone were to lock people up, it would be she.

Was Evan here?

The laboratory stood empty, but from behind the screen came the click and slide of glass and brass. Lizzie gritted her teeth. Why couldn't he have gone to the house for his tea as he had every day she'd been here? Why did he have to become caught up in his experiments today, of all days?

Holding four or five plates, he came around the screen and saw her before she could dart up the steps encircling the walls and out of his line of sight. "Lizzie!" he exclaimed. "Are you completely recovered? I thought you and your sister were resting in the Queen's Tower."

"Yes, I am recovered, thank you. Maggie is resting after her train journey, but I'm not fond of idleness during the day—there is too much to interest one, don't you agree?"

"I work at all hours of the day and night, and in here, you know, midnight and noon look much the same. I say, are you quite all right? You look as though you'd been dragged through a hedge backward." His gaze fell to her stockings, which she should have changed when she was in her room. Bother! "Have you fallen? Would you like to sit down?"

"No, I'm quite all right. I have been studying botany outside, and slipped into the moat. Evan, how much are you acquainted with my father's telescope, really?"

He set the plates on the dreaming table and gazed at her, puzzled. "Not at all. As I told you, no one but Charles is permitted up there—and it was sheer good luck that you and I were not discovered."

"Evan, I must tell you something."

"Certainly. Here are some more of your plates. You can tell me whatever it is, and then you can tell me what these images mean."

He spread them out, and for good or ill, Lizzie made up her mind. She pointed to the middle one. "That is another image of my mother on the floor of our cabin in the airship that crashed. She had just been injected with a syringe of something fatal by my father."

"That is encouragingly specific and—*what?*"

"This one is London Bridge as we flew over it, moments before the ship crashed. My father set fire to it, you see. Maggie and I were the only survivors, but only because we jumped out of the viewing port at the last moment before it went into the river."

His jaw sagged open and he stared at her as though she had gone utterly mad.

"It is quite true, Evan," she said steadily, holding his appalled gaze. "My father killed my mother that day the airship crashed in the Thames, because she had discovered that he and others had been plotting to assassinate the princes next in line to the throne. And since I was the only witness to Mother's murder, he plans to kill me, too. Today, in fact, after he shoots down the Prince of Wales and Prince George as their airship passes overhead. He will use the cannon up there on the roof that everyone believes to be a telescope."

Under this fresh shock, poor Evan's mouth snapped closed and he took a step back from her, fetching up against a counter containing a cast-iron sink and a Bunsen burner. "You are hysterical," he finally managed. "Or I am dreaming. And since the second is not true, the first must be."

"That is poor logic and you know it," she said crisply. She held up the plate showing her mother's prone body. "How else do you explain this?"

"It—it is a dressmaker's mannequin, as you said."

"I only said that because my father was standing right there and I did not want him to know that I remembered his crime. But it was already too late. He locked Maggie and me into the Queen's Tower, you know, and told us what he planned to do with us. We weren't resting at all. We were prisoners."

"You are not a prisoner now." He seemed to grasp this inarguable fact with relief.

"We escaped. But he is already up on the tower, preparing the cannon for the prince's airship. We must stop him, Evan, and I need your help."

He gazed at her. Took another step back. "Are you quite sure you are well, Lizzie?" he asked gently. "If you have been out rambling so soon after recovering from the elixir, it is entirely possible that you are suffering from heat stroke."

"I am nothing of the kind. Evan, you must believe me. Why else has he isolated me here and contrived to send everyone but you away? He needed to know how much I knew—how much I remembered of my mother's death. He needed you for that, to operate the mnemosomniograph. Once he succeeds in killing the princes, he will come for me and Maggie—and you, for that matter. You are the last witness to today's events."

"There have *been* no events."

"But there will be. I armed that cannon myself, by accident, when we were up there. A missile the size of that gas canister on the counter dropped into the barrel. I remembered the Sorbonne set talking of republicanism, and then last night I dreamed of my mother and what my father had done. It all fit together. "

"Why in God's name didn't you tell me?" But he didn't look as though he believed her. She held his gaze, but in her peripheral vision, she saw him reaching behind his back.

"Because I did not know whether or not you were aiding him in his efforts at anarchy."

"Now you do go too far." He smiled disarmingly.

"Anarchy? He has been known to criticize the monarchy, and half the students in my class at university toyed with republicanism, but it is a far cry from that to shooting royals out of the sky."

"If it did not mean your being killed, too, I would encourage you to go up there and see for yourself. He is testing the cannon's undercarriage as we speak."

As she said the last word, she balanced her weight evenly on the balls of her feet, and when his hand tightened on a vial of elixir and he lunged at her, she was ready.

Swinging to the side, she snatched up the canister of gas for the Bunsen burner, and when he staggered past her, off balance, she pirouetted as gracefully as a dancer and swung it at his head with all the force she possessed. *Thank you, Mr. Yau.*

He went down like a rock, and the vial shattered on the stone floor. The thick and bitter elixir that had disabled her for most of the day spread in a pool, seeping inexorably toward him.

Well, that would be one solution, if he ingested some of it. But if she managed to cause an explosion, he would not survive it. She was not convinced that he knew anything of her father's activities—that incredulity could not have been manufactured. He was simply loyal to his patron, whom he had known for some years, and had only met her a few days ago. She could be a raving lunatic, for all he knew.

Right, then. Lizzie grasped him under his armpits and, huffing and blowing, half-dragged and half-rolled her cousin out the door of the tower, down the steps, and into the grass. He was dreadfully heavy for such a slender person. She made him as comfortable as possible, considering he would have a huge goose egg on his head tomorrow, and returned to the laboratory, locking him outside.

And locking herself inside with the man who had wanted her dead for eleven years.

22

Lizzie climbed the steps, watching her footing more carefully the higher she went. The rod of repenthium tucked in her bodice would not help her in the least if she were to fall more than about ten feet—and the parapet was far higher than that. About fifty feet up, level with the great glass globe and the power mechanism for the mnemosomniograph, she paused and sat on a stone step, her back against the cold wall, to examine it.

He might be a fine scientist as far as the realms of the mind went, but Evan and whoever had put this together were dreadful engineers. Lizzie's gaze followed the cables around in an enormous, messy coil, in and out of the power cell and thence into the globe where the charge would be aggregated. Disabling the entire apparatus would be fairly simple, but how was she to create an explosion that would lift the parapet clean off the tower—without killing herself?

What she needed here was one of Tigg's ignition clocks. Or a fuse that could be lit from a safe distance. Some explosives. She would even be happy with a firelamp.

But none of these helpful inventions were available to her. She climbed a few steps more. Perhaps if she had a view from above the apparatus, she could see a way to create a blockage in the circuit. If only it were not so dim up here! The electricks running along the wall were all very well to guide one's feet up the steps, but they were clearly not meant to allow people to see into the dream device's power structure. There must be a way to lower the entire mare's nest down to where it was light. How else could Evan see to maintain it?

Looking up, searching the dim reaches, she saw the pulleys bolted into the stone and reaching from one side of the tower's interior to the other, which she had completely missed before. Who noticed pulleys, after all, unless one needed them? It looked like a two-man affair, however. Up there by the trap door was one set of levers, and the second set was at the bottom of the steps, affixed to the wall.

Hm. If she jimmied the largest conductive cable on the top of the power cell, it would build up a charge with no release into the rest of the mechanism. While the charge built to explosive proportions, it might give her just enough time to scramble down the stairs and get out the door before the glass globe went incandescent and blew up.

Excellent. But without help—Maggie, for instance—to work the pulleys, she was going to have to climb down onto that tangle of cabling like a monkey and do it in midair, as it were. There were plenty of ropes. It was possible—certainly no more difficult than all the climbing she and Maggie had done up and down the coaxial ladders on *Athena* and *Lady Lucy.*

She would just position herself there, near the top, where she could shin down that rope—

From directly above her came the click and whir of the trap door's mechanism as the door slid back into its horizontal housing. A bar of red sunset light plunged down the stairs, illuminating her crouching there with cruel clarity.

"Why, Elizabeth," her father said pleasantly, after a moment. "How very resourceful you are. Do come up."

Fear froze her in place—fear and the frantic churning of her mind as she considered and discarded twenty different ways of escape. The ugly truth was that she had taken a risk coming up here—and had lost. If she had stayed down on the floor of the tower, she could have slipped out the door and been gone before his eyesight adjusted and he descended the stairs. Yes, he would have found Evan unconscious outside, which would have tipped him off that the jig was up, but at least she would not be trapped here like a mouse under the paw of a very dangerous cat.

"If you do not obey me," he said, "I shall come down and kick you off that step."

There was no help for it—and no hope but one. Maggie was still out there somewhere, and she would not let her down. If all had gone according to plan, by now the Lady would be on her way. All Lizzie had to do was play stupid and afraid—not much of a stretch, as it happened—and stall for time. Help would come.

She did not want to think about what would happen if one of the hundred things that could go wrong had gone wrong … and all had *not* gone according to plan.

She got to her feet, dusted off the back of her dress, and mounted the steps through the floor of the parapet. De Maupassant closed it behind her and leaned against an embrasure, the wind riffling his hair under his bowler hat.

"I am exceedingly curious to know how you come to be here and not there." The bowler tilted in the direction of the Queen's Tower.

She pressed herself against the stone out of arms' reach. "I—we knotted the sheets together and I let myself down onto the roof."

"You alone? How selfish of you."

"S-someone had to pull the sheets back up, otherwise they would be seen from here."

"So Margaret is still within?"

"Yes."

"I am relieved to hear it. Though there is nothing to stop her from climbing down, since she can see that your game is up if she chooses to look outside. I hope she will not, however. I shall simply shoot her off the wall like a spider." He pulled back the lapel of his tweed hunting jacket to reveal a pistol in a holster under his arm.

Lizzie's blood seemed to congeal in her veins. "Sh-she will not. She will be afraid you will shoot me."

"A wise young lady. Also most perspicacious. There is nothing to prevent my shooting you now, save for the subsequent inconvenience of disposing of your body."

Lizzie briefly considered apologizing for that, then discarded the idea. She might not have much at this moment, but at least she still possessed her dignity.

The sky was still bright with the glow of sunset, and the wind had cooled to announce that rain was on its way. On the wind came the far-off sound of cheering, and a Catherine wheel blossomed in the darkening sky far to the south. A chrysanthemum of light cascaded around it.

"Ah," de Maupassant said. "The Prince of Wales is come. They are giving him a fanfare in the villages as he passes." He snorted in disgust. "Fools."

"Will they do the same here?" she managed to ask.

"Oh, yes. Any excuse for a show. It keeps the serfs entertained and for a few moments, they forget their servitude to this bloated, greedy monarchy."

"Why do you hate the Queen and her family so much?"

One eyebrow rose in condemnation of the violence of her language. "I do not hate them, my dear. They mean nothing at all to me. What I hate is their greed and their robbery of the coffers of this nation to finance their comfortable way of life while the poorest among the people starve."

"The Queen has done much for the poor—she always has, since she took the throne."

"I am surprised that, having lived on the streets and tasted poverty, you should defend her."

"She is a very nice woman. I've met her."

He regarded her without interest. "Bully for you. I am not interested in personal relationships. She represents a tradition that must end, and the sooner it does, the faster this country will embrace an elected head of government."

He was deluded at best—and barking mad at worst. Did he not hear the cheering, see the fireworks? The people were embracing their future king, not her father's misplaced patriotism.

"Come, Elizabeth. I have been considering all my options, and I believe I have hit on the perfect solution."

She backed away, but the further she went, the faster the circular walls of the parapet would bring her back to him. "And what is that, sir?"

"I have decided that I will not fire the cannon and bring that ship down."

She hardly dared believe her ears. "You will not?"

He smiled, and in the fading glow, she saw no kindness in it. "No, my dear. You will."

ॐ

In an agony of fear and impatience, Claire gripped *Athena*'s helm with both hands and peered out the viewing port. Twenty miles north of Oxford and an eternity yet to go. "Snouts, is there no way we can increase her speed?" She gave him no chance to reply before she raised her voice. "Nine, increase engine power at once." The sound of *Athena*'s engines, already laboring at the top end of their ability, did not change. If dear Nine had been able to speak, he would likely have had some choice words for her.

As it was, Snouts appeared in the gangway from the engine room with a few words of his own. "I'm no Tigg, Lady. If you can't get any more out of these automatons of yours, then it's certain I cannot."

"We must be in time. We simply must." But if they were not, then perhaps a smaller, more agile device could help. "Snouts, we must send a pigeon to the Prince's ship. We must tell them to divert their course at once and fly east until the danger is averted."

"And His Highness will believe you, Lady? Does he trust your word?"

"He has never met me, unlike his father. Just do it, Snouts. It is a slim hope, but we cannot live with ourselves if we did not use any means at our disposal to avert this tragedy."

He ran back down the gangway to the hold, and five minutes later, a pigeon shot away into the gathering dusk ahead of *Athena*'s bow.

"Come on …" she urged her ship, which had given her so much—a home, independence, inspiration. Her hands were damp on the helm, and she wiped them one at a time on her black skirt. ".Just a little bit more, darling, for the sake of our girls ..."

৵৽

"I will not do it," Lizzie said as soon as she could speak. "Just try and make me."

She might be shaking with rage and incredulity, but he merely smiled with the utter confidence of the truly mad. Reaching under his jacket, he pulled out the pistol and waved it at her with casual negligence. "Really, Elizabeth? Is that a dare?"

"It is. I would rather die than have a hand in killing my future king."

"It is easy enough to say so, I'm sure. But answer me this—are you willing for Maggie to die? Or your cousin Evan?"

Maggie was safe, but Evan was not. De Maupassant had only to divest her of the key and there would be nothing to prevent him from walking outside, discovering poor Evan lying there unconscious, and shooting him right there in the grass.

Worse, he would make her watch him do it.

"Where is Evan, by the way? He has strict instructions not to let anyone up here, but if the arming of my cannon is anything to go by, it seems he already has."

"I expect he has gone to the house for tea. We were up here yesterday. I did it. I armed the cannon by accident. Which was how I came to discover it was not a telescope. Evan does not know."

"If you armed it, then it is even more appropriate

that you should fire it. Come along. We haven't much time, if the fireworks are any indication."

The first of the welcoming fireworks had already gone up in Colliford village, and in the distant sky, Lizzie could see a tiny set of horizontal lamps … the running lights of the *Princess Alexandra*. To the west, thunder grumbled and a fork of lightning flickered in the massed clouds, quick as the tongue of a snake.

De Maupassant grasped her upper arm with his free hand and frog-marched her across the parapet to the cannon. The brass dome had been tucked away into its housing, and the snout of the cannon pointed south. He shoved her toward the steps. "Get up there."

"I will not! I—"

He backhanded her across the side of the head and fireworks burst behind her eyelids. "I said, get up there or I will beat you insensible."

The illogic of this did not occur to him, but the threat of it was plain to her. She stumbled up the steps and collapsed into the seat of the cannon.

"Aim it. You will track the ship until it is within two degrees of the cross-hairs in the eyepiece, and fire when it crosses the center line. Is that clear?"

"I will n—"

He hit her again, and her head clunked against the arm of the assembly that loaded the barrel of the cannon. The pain made her fold in half, holding her head, and a howl of agony escaped her lips.

"Cry all you want, but if you do not take aim in the next five seconds, I will shoot you where you sit, and the devil take the consequences."

Despite her brave defiance, Lizzie did not want to die. She wanted to live, and see Maggie and the Lady again, and begin the sixth form back in Munich in September. She wanted to make something of herself—something that would erase her father's name from the face of the earth and vindicate her mother, whose very memory was being shamed in this house as they spoke.

The first thing she would do after that cup of tea was burn that portrait.

Her jaw rigid with fury, Lizzie straightened, and as she did, the corset bone tucked between her corselet and her blouse poked her in the ribs.

The *repenthium* corset bone.

Her gaze locked on the slot in the barrel where the missile rested, ready for her to fire. She straightened, her head ringing, the side of her face on fire where he had struck her. "All right, Father. Please do not hurt me any more."

He let out a breath of satisfaction. "Of all the things I have noticed about you, Elizabeth, your good sense is uppermost."

She took the guidance mechanism by its handles and pushed. The great gears and clockwork assemblies of the undercarriage began to rotate, and as she applied pressure, the barrel of the cannon swung slowly to the left and upward, tracking the course of the airship as it sailed closer. The moment the barrel came between her and her father and blocked his view of her hands, Lizzie moved.

She pulled the rod of repenthium out of her corselet and yanked the lever that slid back the door in the barrel. There was the missile, ready to do its deadly work. She lifted it—ten pounds at least, it was—and hastily wrapped the corset bone around and around its tip, tying off the ends in a knot that she flattened out as best she could.

Then she slid the door shut, put both hands back on the guidance handles, and put her eye to the eyepiece.

Ten degrees.

Eight.

Five.

Two.

The *Princess Alexandra*'s golden bow passed between two marks in the eyepiece … centered …

"Now, Elizabeth, blast you!"

Fireworks exploded into the sky, the sound of cheering soaring into the air along with bright colors of red, gold, and green. Lizzie wrenched the firing lever back and her father's cannon roared and spat out cold death into the festive night.

23

Ahead of *Athena* sailed the majestic bulk of the *Princess Alexandra*, passing over the village already welcoming its future ruler with fireworks and snatches of "God Save the Queen." Her pigeon had clearly not been taken seriously. Now she must focus solely on Colliford Castle, isolated in its park and the next landmark over which the royal ship would sail.

Between the fireworks and the last of the sunset, Claire had just enough light to make out a tiny figure as it burst out of a door near the top of the telescope's tower—a figure with hair the color of Brazil nuts and wearing a chestnut suit that had been made for her in Munich.

Maggie—alive!

"Snouts, bring her around over that long, flat roof," she commanded, relinquishing the helm to him and freeing the lightning rifle from the holster on her back. "I am going to let down the basket."

"Can you see Lizzie?"

"Not yet, but—great Caesar's ghost!"

From the top of the tower, the telescope that was not a telescope spat fire, illuminating the slender figure in the white dress at the controls, and the darker, bulkier figure with one arm extended.

Claire's blood stopped cold in its frantic course as she stared across space from Lizzie to the royal airship. The missile raced toward it, powered by a rocket that had been ignited in the bowels of the firing mechanism. Closer—closer—it would take the gilded gondola amidships—and then, at the last possible second, it veered aside. Once, twice, it bounced along the gondola's keel—and then it found its direction. Its deadly speed had been halved, however, and it raced through the sky to plunge into the River Colley. It exploded with violent force, a plume of water cascading high into the air.

"Praise God and all the little angels!" Snouts shouted. Had Claire's mind not been otherwise occupied, she might have marveled at this—she had never suspected Snouts of harboring any affection for the royal family at all.

But her mind was wholly occupied. They had only minutes to effect a rescue—if not seconds. "Snouts, Lewis—he has forced her to fire on the princes at gunpoint—and he will not like being foiled!" Claire pushed the power switch of the lightning rifle to the active position as she ran out of the gondola. "Four, open the lower hatch!"

She reached the hatch below in record time—three gasps of breath, in fact—to find that Four already had it open. She snatched up a safety line and clipped it to her leather corselet, then pulled her driving goggles down over her eyes to protect them from the wind. Snouts was bringing them around in a tight circle, but *Athena* could not adjust her course quickly enough. Lizzie was being marched over to a door let into the floor of the parapet, and before Claire could speak to countermand her own order, they disappeared from sight into the bowels of the tower. He would shoot her inside, and Claire could do nothing!

But outside, clinging to the ivy twining up the tower, her feet on the coping, Maggie wrenched open the door outside of which she was concealed, reached within, and dragged Lizzie outside onto the roof. Both of them leaped to the door to shut and lock it—oh, well done, Maggie!—but Seacombe was too quick—and physically, more than a match for the two of them. Inexorably, he pushed the door outward until the girls must yield or be unbalanced and pushed off the roof to their deaths.

"Snouts! Tighter!" Claire shrieked. They would not make the turn in time. The lightning rifle hummed, already at firing pitch.

Holding hands, both girls fled across the roof, legs pumping, skirts flying up before and behind as they fought the mismatched stone and slate. But Seacombe did not follow. For he did not need to.

Claire's worst fear came alive in front of her wide, horrified eyes as he raised his pistol, aimed it with the casual negligence of the superior marksman, and fired.

The gun spat a foot of flame, and Maggie fell forward, her own momentum and that of the bullet carrying her across the roof to land in an untidy heap against an embrasure, a host of dead leaves flying up around her.

Claire screamed in pain and rage, and time—her pulse—the very rotation of the earth—slowed to a crawl. Her mind calmed as it iced over with the sheer necessity of ridding the world of this menace. Her focus narrowed to a single target, and she brought the lightning rifle to her shoulder. Sighting through the lens, she observed the moment when Seacombe became aware that he and Lizzie were not alone on the castle rooftop—that an avenging angel sailed overhead with grief in her heart and cold accuracy in her eye.

Lizzie flung herself upon her cousin's body, screaming, as Seacombe swung the pistol around and brought it to bear on the open hatch of *Athena*.

Claire pulled the trigger and a bolt of blue-white light sizzled across forty feet of empty space, catching him full in the chest. Tendrils of light splashed outward over his jacket, his trousers, his head, and his bowler hat fell off. Before it hit the rooftop on which he stood, his eyes bugged out and evaporated. All his clothes fused to his body as it slumped to the rooftop, fell, and slid down the long pitch. It caught briefly on a stone rain gutter, flipped over it, and plunged a hundred feet to the ground, where it rolled into the shadows that had already filled the moat.

Overhead, the black clouds that had sailed in to intercept the course of the two airships, broke with all the fury of a hot summer storm.

"Four, ready the ship for mooring!" she shouted. "Lewis, winch me down!"

Lewis, panting from running from one end of the ship to the other, leaped to the winch and Claire flung herself into the basket.

Maggie could not be dead. God would not have given her into her care and then torn her from her at the hands of a madman.

And—and blast it all—she simply would not allow it!

With the basket still four feet from the roof, Claire leaped over the side and landed in a crouch, the rifle still in one hand, then gathered up her skirts with the other and ran. Overhead, lightning leaped out of the sky, thunder cracked with a ground-shaking concussion, and the heavens opened up and wept.

৩৵৵

"Maggie—Maggie—please don't be dead! Please, Maggie!" Blinded by tears, Lizzie crouched next to her cousin's body, terrified to turn her over, yet desperate to know if that beloved heart still beat, if the life she valued more than any other was housed yet in this dreadfully still form.

Around her, thunder crashed and lightning lit up

the rooftop as she gently pulled on Maggie's shoulder and rolled her to her back. Her right arm flopped to the ground, as inanimate as clay.

Every lesson Lizzie had ever learned in anatomy and biology clean fled her brain in her panic. Pulse? How did one check a pulse? How—

"Is she alive?" A feminine voice. A rush of wet skirts. The scent of roses and cinnamon. Who—? "Lizzie, you must pull yourself together," the Lady said in a rush, already pulling Maggie's jacket aside, her hands frantic on her chest, her ribs, her shoulders. "Is she *alive?*"

Lizzie's mind seemed to snap back into operation as though a switch had been thrown. "Lady, de Maupassant—!"

"—is dead. I shot him. Dear heaven, Lizzie, is Maggie—what on earth …?"

For there was no blood. There should be blood— Maggie's wet blouse should be running with it. The only blood she could see welled from a cut on her forehead where she had struck the wall in her forward momentum.

And then Lizzie's frantic hands encountered something hard under Maggie's waist. Hard and rectangular and utterly out of place. Not a corset. Then what? She yanked the batiste out of Maggie's waistband, raised it up, and stared.

"Lizzie, what in heaven's name is that?"

Lizzie's mouth hung open, and it was only with difficulty that she got it shut and working again. She drew the objects—for there were two, one in front and one in back—out from under Maggie's clothes. "They—they are mnemosomniographic plates. Dream plates. But why ...?"

The glass of the one in her right hand was cracked all the way across from the force of Maggie's landing upon it. The one in back bore a dent as big as a robin's· egg in the brass backing, and the glass plate had been shattered altogether. Glass tinkled under Maggie's body as they lowered her gently to the slate.

"Lizzie?" came a whisper, faintly under the sound of the wind and driving rain. "Lizzie, are you alive?"

She dropped the plates and gathered Maggie into her arms, hot tears welling in her eyes and running down her icy cheeks. "Mags! You're alive! Tell me where it hurts, darling—are you hurt?"

"My back—something awful."

"And no wonder," the Lady said softly, gathering them both into her arms, her own face awash with rain and tears of joy. "Maggie, dearest, did you really use those plates as *armor?*"

"I couldn't think of anything else." Maggie's voice strengthened with every word. "They were lying on the dream table so I just snatched them up in case he was armed." Her eyes widened and she tried to sit up. "Is he—Lady, watch out—"

"He's dead, Mags." Lizzie helped her sit up. "The Lady got here just in time."

"You got my message, then," Maggie breathed. "The postmistress was dreadfully annoyed—she was just closing up to go to the fireworks and she—" With a gasp, she exclaimed, "The princes!"

"Safe," the Lady said. "For some strange reason, the missile veered away from the ship at the last moment, and plunged into the river. They will have a bathing-pool there now, I daresay. It was quite the spectacular excavation."

Lizzie might have laughed in sheer relief if her blood hadn't still been thundering through her veins in the aftermath of terror. "I wrapped it in a corset bone," she said, "while de Maupassant wasn't looking. From my antigravity corset. It was repenthium—that useless element with the bad reputation."

The Lady's and Maggie's eyes both widened in such comical astonishment that this time, Lizzie did laugh. She laughed and laughed, until finally she began to cry. But it was a good kind of crying. Sometimes life was such a wonderful gift that laughter was simply not adequate for the occasion. And like laughter, tears could be shared with those you loved.

"Lizzie," Maggie said softly through her own tears, "the plates—they were the ones of your mother. I was in a hurry and—oh, Lizzie, if they were the only images of her that you had, I am so sorry!"

Lizzie shook her head, and wiped her cheek with the flat of her hand. "Don't ever be sorry. My mother gave her life to save us all those years ago. Don't you think it's wonderful that her memory was the very thing that saved your life tonight?"

"Her memory, and your own resources," the Lady said tenderly, smoothing Lizzie's wet hair off her face, and touching Maggie's cheek as if she were infinitely precious. "I can think of no better legacy a woman could leave the children she loved, can you?"

And as the Lady and Lizzie helped Maggie to her feet, Lizzie had to admit that she could not. Perhaps she would not destroy her mother's portrait after all. In fact, if the Lady agreed, it would fit rather nicely over the mantel in the drawing room at Wilton Crescent.

SHELLEY ADINA

Epilogue

The Evening Standard
July 23, 1894

TREASON RESULTS IN SHOCKING DEATH

In an act of treason that has shocked the nation and
shaken the Empire to its core, it has been discovered
that industrialist and financier Charles Seacombe,
born Charles de Maupassant before he changed his
name to evade capture and questioning for the murder
of his wife, has made an attempt on the lives of Their
Royal Highnesses the Prince of Wales and Prince
George of Wales.

The motivation behind this dreadful act has its roots in the tide of republicanism that has swept the colleges and streets of England. Far from being a harmless belief to be argued over in lecture halls and public houses, this sedition has culminated in action upon the part of de Maupassant and persons unknown. These miscreants attempted to launch what is believed to be a bomb at the *Princess Alexandra,* His Highness's personal airship, as it bore him and the newly wed Prince George to his country estate and thence to Balmoral in Scotland for the grouse season.

The bomb, this newspaper may report with unbounded relief, was successfully diverted, and in the course of a summer storm which passed over the neighborhood at the same time, de Maupassant alias Seacombe, on the roof of his house, was struck by lightning and instantly killed.

Lady Claire Trevelyan, lately inducted into the Royal Society of Engineers and resident of Belgravia, while travelling to visit friends along the same route as the royal party, was witness to the entire shocking scene. "It was my observation that heaven itself intervened to save the heir to the throne," she said in an interview together with Lady Davina Dunsmuir, close confidante and representative of Her Majesty, from the Prince's summer estate. "God may not be an Englishman, but I venture to say that our beloved country must have a special place in His heart."

Private funeral services are being held for Charles de Maupassant alias Seacombe at an undisclosed location in order to avoid the risk of public demonstrations.

৩৯৫

Two weeks later

"I see that you are not wearing black." Lizzie sat up on the blanket spread on the broadmead in the shade of *Athena*'s deceptively shabby fuselage, and gazed at Evan and Claude.

"I see that you are not, either," Claude observed, all traces of his usual insouciance and humor gone. The Sorbonne set, alarmed at the prospect of actual notoriety, had fled back to Paris, leaving him alone to face the consequences of his father's actions. Alone, that is, except for his half-sister and cousin, who had returned to the castle to help him clear out.

Evan was watching the workmen down the river, who were busy digging out the crater caused by the missile and turning it into a bathing-pool, as the Lady had predicted. Lizzie had suggested it to Claude herself, though none of them would have the pleasure of swimming in it. Colliford Castle was to be sold, and as far as any of them were concerned, the sooner the better.

"I find it very difficult to put on mourning for the man whose only object since I met him was to take my life." Claude winced, and Lizzie touched his arm. "I am sorry, Claude. I know you loved him."

"I feel a perfect fool," he said bitterly. "How could I not have known the kind of man he was?"

On the other side of the picnic basket, the Lady finished slicing the first of the Colliford orchard's peaches, and handed half to Claude and half to Maggie. "Do not blame yourself, Claude. You are not alone in this—I was once engaged to a man who had an entire country fooled. The important thing to remember is that he did love you, and you loved the father in him, though the man was flawed."

Claude nodded, his gaze cast down, and took a reluctant bite of the peach.

"Lady Claire is right," Evan said. "I'm in the same boat as you, old chap—on the leakier end, at that. After all, *you* did not attempt to force opium elixir down your sister's throat against her will." He sighed, his shoulders drooping under his seersucker jacket.

"Evan Douglas, if you do not stop moping about that, I shall drag you over to the river and drop you in," Lizzie said. "And you know I can do it."

Evan gave a rueful smile and touched the back of his head, where the goose-egg had long since subsided. "I do indeed. But I hope I made up for it in some small degree by seeing your mother's portrait safely aboard *Athena* just now. When do you plan to lift?"

"Soon," the Lady said. "After lunch." She gazed about, taking in the castle sleeping in the sun, the gardens, the river. The sweet smell of cut grass and the roses dozing in the moat wafted to them on the summer breeze. "Such a shame. This was a home, once. But I suppose now the new owners will be obliged to deal with the thrill-seekers who come to the gates to stare."

"I am half tempted to change my name," Claude said miserably. "But I suppose I must think of my grandparents and my responsibilities to the Seacombe shipping enterprise. They will be depending on me now."

"If you are to remain a Seacombe, then perhaps I should become one," Lizzie said. "You are my half-brother, and I certainly do not want to carry *de Maupassant* and all the horror associated with it for the rest of my life. Is that not so, Maggie?" The Mopsies, in great decisions and small, stuck together.

"No, it is not," Maggie said.

The Lady straightened in surprise, and Lizzie felt a shock, rather as though someone in the river had dashed water on her.

"I don't know what name I am entitled to, nor anything about the Seacombes except what I've been told," Maggie said, a little defiantly. "I am half tempted to choose a name for myself. One of the Lady's family names, perhaps. *Maggie Carrick* has rather a nice ring to it, don't you think?"

The Lady's gaze warmed. "I do indeed—though you must think carefully on such an important decision. During a trip to Penzance, perhaps?"

"Capital idea," Claude said, showing the first signs

of animation all afternoon. "I must go in any case to see the grands—been putting it off far too long. We shall beard the Seacombe lions together."

"Together—but not alone," the Lady said firmly. "With the Dunsmuirs at Balmoral for the shooting, Tigg is free until they decide to return. If you are going down to Penzance after Emilie's wedding, then I should feel easier if he went with you."

Lizzie's heart gave a bound, and to hide it, she touched Maggie's fingers and redirected the subject, hoping no one would notice the color in her cheeks. "Whatever name we choose, Mags, it's up to us to bring honor to it at least, if we cannot make it memorable."

Evan gave a bark of laughter, and the Lady smiled. "My dearest girls, if anyone can make a name—or anything else, for that matter—memorable, it is you. Now, if someone does not cut that orange chiffon cake and give me a slice, I shall expire of sheer longing."

Lizzie squeezed Maggie's hand and amid the laughter, reached for the silver knife. In a world that was full of discovery, of friends and enemies, and of bewildering change, it was reassuring to know that there were some things one could always count on.

THE END

SHELLEY ADINA

A Note from Shelley

Dear reader,

I hope you enjoy reading the adventures of Lady Claire and the gang in the Magnificent Devices world as much as I enjoy writing them. It is your support and enthusiasm that is like the steam in an airship's boiler, keeping the entire enterprise afloat and ready for the next adventure.

You might leave a review on your favorite retailer's site to tell others about the books. And you can find the electronic editions of the entire series online, as well as audiobooks. I'll see you over at my website, www.shelleyadina.com, where you can sign up for my newsletter and be the first to know of new releases and special promotions.

Don't miss Maggie's book, *A Lady of Spirit*, the next in the Magnificent Devices series!

ABOUT THE AUTHOR

RITA Award® winning author and Christy finalist Shelley Adina wrote her first novel when she was 13. The literary publisher to whom it was sent rejected it, but he did say she knew how to tell a story. That was enough to keep her going through the rest of her adolescence, a career, a move to another country, an MFA in Writing Popular Fiction, and countless manuscript pages.

Shelley is the author of twenty-four novels published by Harlequin, Time/Warner, and Hachette Book Group, and several more published by Moonshell Books, Inc., her own independent press. She writes romance, paranormals, and the Magnificent Devices steampunk adventure series, and under the name Adina Senft, also writes women's fiction set in faith communities.

Shelley is a world traveler who loves to imagine what might have been. Between books, she loves playing the piano and Celtic harp, making period costumes, quilting, and spoiling her flock of rescued chickens.

AVAILABLE NOW

The Magnificent Devices series:
Lady of Devices
Her Own Devices
Magnificent Devices
Brilliant Devices
A Lady of Resources
A Lady of Spirit
A Lady of Integrity
A Gentleman of Means
Devices Brightly Shining (Christmas novella)

Caught You Looking (Moonshell Bay #1)
Immortal Faith

The Glory Prep series
Glory Prep
The Fruit of My Lipstick
Be Strong and Curvaceous
Who Made You a Princess?
Tidings of Great Boys
The Chic Shall Inherit the Earth

COMING SOON

Fields of Air, Magnificent Devices #10
Fields of Iron, Magnificent Devices #11
Fields of Gold, Magnificent Devices #12

Caught You Listening, Moonshell Bay #2
Caught You Hiding, Moonshell Bay #3

Everlasting Chains, Immortal Faith #2
Twice Dead, Immortal Faith #3

CPSIA information can be obtained at www.ICGtesting.com
Printed in the USA
LVOW08s1630060516

487046LV00007B/512/P